I've travelled the world twice over,
Met the famous: saints and sinners,
Poets and artists, kings and queens,
Old stars and hopeful beginners,
I've been where no-one's been before,
Learned secrets from writers and cooks
All with one library ticket
To the wonderful world of books.

ATLANTIC CITY PROOF

A chance meeting brings together Garvey Leek, an innocent back-bay clam fisherman, and the irrepressible Minnie Creek, a quick-witted hard-swearing and lovely orphan who can dig more clams than Garvey ever dreamed of; thus began Garvey and Minnie's partnership in a clamming enterprise. But when Prohibition comes they expand the business to include bootlegging and soon gain a monopoly on the best bootleg of them all—a Canadian rye so much in demand that it has its own label "Atlantic City Proof".

CHRISTOPHER COOK GILMORE

ATLANTIC CITY PROOF

Complete and Unabridged

ULVERSCROFT
Leicester

OCT 27 1981

LARGE TYPE EDITION First Large Print Edition
published September 1981
by arrangement with
Victor Gollancz Ltd.
London
and
Simon & Schuster, a Division of
Gulf & Western
Corporation

British Library CIP Data

Gilmore, Christopher Cook
   Atlantic city proof.—Large print ed.
   (Ulverscroft large print series: general
   fiction).
   I. Title
   823'.9'1F

   ISBN 0-7089-0683-4

Published by
F. A. Thorpe (Publishing) Ltd.
Anstey, Leicestershire

Printed and Bound in Great Britain by
T. J. Press (Padstow) Ltd., Padstow, Cornwall

To Margot

1

I WAS born inside an old elephant during a three-day dry northeaster. My mamma was a little over fifty then, and she told me later it was no trouble at all. She said she woke up when the wind stopped blowing and there I was, tired and hungry. My father was away at the time, at sea; but he said that as he coasted a mile or two off the surf he could see the green light glowing in the elephant's eye where my older sister had placed it. A green light meant I was a boy, and that's what my father had wanted even if I was a little late coming along. He'd wanted a boy who could help him out in his old age, but by 1900 he was already sixty and it would be a while before I could earn a dollar.

My dad owned the elephant. He'd bought her from a fat man named McFee who was a real estate developer with big ideas. McFee wanted to develop and sell Margate to the swells from Philadelphia who could afford summer homes. He paid a shipwright to build an elephant that was so tall a prospective customer could stand on the howdah and see all the lots that McFee had marked out with posts and string. I guess it worked, because by the time I came along most of the properties had been sold and some had houses on them. Dad got the elephant for a song.

Sixty feet high she was; big, fat and gray all over except for a bright-red blanket somebody had painted on her back. The front door was in a hind leg, and we lived, mostly, in her belly. McFee hadn't paid enough to have her properly insulated, so the winters were cold and we spent a lot of time in the kitchen, which was in the head. From her left eye I could look up the beach to Atlantic City.

Atlantic City is on the fat end of a pork-chop-shaped island called Absecon Island. Next comes Ventnor, then Margate and Longport on the thin end. From the right eye of the elephant I could see Longport and the Great Egg Harbor Inlet, which runs hard between my island and the next one down. I used to watch boats running the shoals in that inlet, and when I was a little boy I thought that spot was the worst place in the world to be when the tide was running. When I was a

2

kid I had nightmares about the Great Egg Harbor Inlet.

I dreamed that Dad and I were working alone on an old mossbunker boat and we had to run the inlet to get to shelter. At low tide the white waves rolled right over the sandbars three miles or more at sea, and to come too close was always certain death. We'd lose control of the wheel, or something would happen, and the breakers would come closer and closer until we heard the mighty thump as the keel made contact with the sand. Then the waves would break us up, beat us to death while the lightning danced about our heads. It was an awful dream and it took me years to shake it. I shook it because I had to. The time came when I had to make those shoals a playground for me and some people I loved. But that time did not come for a while . . .

Dad was a loser, I guess. Years before I was born he'd bought a sandspit on the southern tip of the island at Longport, which he'd planned to farm. There were about twenty acres of decent land with good high dunes between them and the beach. On the other side was the peaceful bay, where ducks by the thousands rested on their way up and down the coast. A duck could fly over Dad's farm, from bay to ocean, in about ten seconds, so narrow was the island there. At the end, where the waters met, was what people called the Point. Dad called his farm Point Farm.

There came a hurricane one early September, five years before I came along, and the moon happened to be full. The tide was high when the hurricane hit, and when the ocean came up and over the dunes, the bay met it right in the middle of Point Farm. Dad and Mamma May made a run for it, rode out the storm in a mule stable in Margate. The next day the farm wasn't there. The tide had washed that whole end of the island away, and it never came back.

Today, Longport only runs down to 11th Street, and Point Farm is just an old map I can't throw away because there were too many dreams attached to it. Dad never gave up hope that we'd get another hurricane that would bring everything back. He used to stand me out on the end of the rockpile at 11th Street and point to where the barn was going to be, where we'd dig the well and where we'd plant whatever. I could see it too.

Meanwhile, Dad, Mamma May and my sister Pumpkin needed a place to live. The elephant was up for sale and so run-down that

4

the only people who wanted her was us Leeks. Dad said it took him a week to get the pigeons out of her. Then he went to work on the rats.

When I was old enough to know where I was, the elephant was pretty comfortable. We had glass in the windows and plenty of light from above—sunlight that came down through the inch-thick glass floor of the howdah. The elephant's trunk ran down to a big red barrel, and the barrel was the out-house. Dad and Mamma May had a bedroom in the back with one window that looked out under the tail. The white sandy beach came right up to the big elephant toes, and some-times we'd hear ghost crabs inside the walls.

I never cared if people laughed at us; the elephant was a great place for a boy to grow up in. I never cared that Dad was a crazy loser, that Mamma May went senile early, that my only sister was twenty years older than I and as fat as a drumfish. They were all good to me and let me grow up the way I wanted.

From the howdah I used to look over Mar-gate to the back bay and the salt marshes beyond. More than a mile in width, they too were a fearsome place. It was all boggy ground, underwater at high tide, and filled with crabs, snakes, muskrats and mosquitoes. Duckhunters used to go in there, and sometimes they'd get lost in the high tule weeds. The story was that a North Jersey man got too far in there once and couldn't find his way back to his boat. The weeds were only a foot over his head, but there was no point of high ground for him to get a look over them. He walked around in circles for days until they found him, out of his mind, about fifty feet from his boat. The mosquitoes had driven him crazy.

I never went to school. The nearest school was miles up the beach, and Dad knew I'd never make it on the windy winter days with the weather all out of the northeast, usually with a lot of rain in it. So, when I was five, I had to have a private teacher. That was my sister, Pumpkin.

Pumpkin was a real schoolteacher who had a state certificate. She'd taught the first and second grades in Atlantic City for two years before they fired her for being too fat. We never weighed her, but I'd guess she was well over four hundred pounds. Her saving grace was that she was tall, over six feet; so her great weight was spread out over a large frame and she never seemed out of proportion. But the people at the school let her go anyway, and by the time I was old enough to learn I had her all to myself.

Pumpkin's and my bedroom was in the left shoulder with a good north light coming in the window most of the day. She taught me to read early on, and I spent at least an hour every day reading aloud. By the roar of breaking waves I read Mark Twain, Bret Harte, Sarah Orne Jewett, Henry James and everybody else who was new and wrote the kind of stories we liked. After dinner she'd read poetry to me, always taking the time to explain difficult passages so that I could understand what was going on and share the beauty of the lines with her in a private world we had all to ourselves. We formed distinct literary opinions, I remember, with Pumpkin loving Emily Dickinson and Walt Whitman, while I leaned closer to the simpler Oliver Wendell Holmes and Sidney Lanier. We both hated Longfellow, and Whittier bored us no end. I grew up loving and memorizing poetry, and Pumpkin warned me once that at a public gathering, especially one held on Absecon Island, one should never recite poetry for more than one minute. It took me years to find out what she was talking about.

She taught me to write too, and to figure. I studied history and geography from great books she'd bring home from the library in Atlantic City. We studied all the great empires, especially the French empire, which held something for Pumpkin that captivated her spirit. We'd walk along the beach and she'd talk about the courts and palaces of the French kings, about the courtiers who were real men, men who were hard and soft, great warriors and great thinkers, at one and the same time.

The beach was a wonderful place for walks. In the winter we shared it only with the great brown gulls, who often objected to our presence with long, hysterical cries which only we could hear. In winter we'd set out with big sacks over our shoulders, and in them we'd carry all the wrack and jetsam left along the high-tide line from the day before. Left to dry a week or two, these bits of driftwood, parts of wrecked ships and things which had floated in from God knows where made excellent firewood which burned in rainbow colors in the kitchen stove.

In summer we'd go swimming. Pumpkin was an excellent swimmer who could move with real grace through the shorebreak to the deep swells beyond. We swam naked; not only because we never owned bathing costumes, but because we rarely encountered a soul on the wide white beaches so hot under the summer sun. I learned to ride the waves on my stomach, a thing which Pumpkin taught me but could never quite master herself, perhaps because of the way she was structured.

Pumpkin was more of a mother to me than my real mother, Mamma May. Mamma May rarely left the elephant and seldom spoke to anyone except to ask about the weather. But she was a great cook, especially with seafood, and we were always on time for a meal. She cooked the mussels we'd bring home from the bay, clams we'd dig from the surf at low tide, fish Dad caught with his long bamboo rod or his lead-weighted throw net which he'd cast from the Point at tide change when the snappers were running. Mamma May's great speciality was box-turtle chowder cooked with leeks and potatoes when they were in season. We ate no meat of any kind.

Once, when I was very young, my dad made me a model sailboat. She was blue, light-blue, and about two feet long. He put

9

lead on the keel and Pumpkin made the sails. On the day she was ready I took her back to Risley's Lagoon and sailed her attached to a ball of twine I'd bought from the store. In my ignorance I'd bought postage twine, which was made of paper. When it got wet it broke, and my boat sailed out of the lagoon and out of the bay on the tide. I lost sight of her in the bay behind Longport and was brokenhearted. The following day, believe it or not, I was swimming in the sea when I suddenly saw the blue hull, overturned and being battered by the waves. She was only a few feet from me and I quickly had her in my arms. Everything—mast, sails, rudder and rigging—was gone, but I had the handcarved hull, and soon she was sailing again, but now in duck ponds only. The sea can do things like that, and when they happen all you can do is shake your head.

My dad had a story. He said he was surfcasting once off Longport at high tide. He'd just cast his lure as far as he could throw it and was reeling in, jigging along the bottom for weakfish. Suddenly a wave came which went right up and over his waders, nearly knocking him down. The wave went far up the beach, then receded with a strength which was difficult for Dad to resist. But he stood up to it and the wave sucked itself out, so far out that his lure was left lying on the mud. The tide had gone all the way out with a single surge, and it never came back in until the next day. Explain that.

There is something about growing up by the sea which gives one a sense of the mystery in the universe, some unaccountable force which acts in ways which are not meant for us to understand. And there is also the feeling of adventure and freedom associated with the vast waters which roll on to other continents carrying homeless flotsam in its currents.

With a boat, I felt, one could go just anywhere. And any floating thing might be a boat, not only these fragile shells man made. A cork has a better chance of crossing the ocean than a cutter, and if I were small enough to cling to that cork I just might wind up in France. This was a dream I had, which could be sparked off by the merest splinter of driftwood, or by the rotted rib of some sunken sailing boat left in my backyard by the retreating surf.

As I grew a little older I dreamed of fashioning a raft, back in the bay, which I could use to float myself and my gear over to the meadowlands. There I would build a shack and live quite alone on the results of my hunting and fishing skills. I planned to bring with me rod, reel, knife and slingshot. I planned to bring big rubber boots and mosquito netting. Of course I never did it, as I was quite content and happy with my situation on the island.

There is another dream I had which haunts me still. In my sleeping dreams I would look out to sea, out to the horizon, and suddenly, emerging from the green sea mist, was an island! I never got to it, I just saw it; but in the morning I awoke convinced that it was there. I imagined that on this dream island were the same people and things which were on my island, only they were reversed as if in mirror image. Over there were all the members of my family, everyone I knew from town, but they were somehow our opposites. I cannot describe it, as it was more of an impression than anything else. But so often did I have this dream that if that island were discovered today I would not be very surprised. Perhaps it is there after all.

I loved to wander, to explore my water-boundaried world. As I grew older I'd purposely leave Pumpkin behind. I needed to be alone, to develop my imagination and drift off into it at every new turn of every new path. With my knife I'd fashion a spear, and with that I'd go loping through the underbrush which practically covered Margate at the time. My games were violent, manly ones, and I skewered an ever increasing number of enemies as I came to them. I gave no quarter to the Green Men I'd invented; tall, thin snakelike people who lived near the marshy bogs and in the sandy clearings. They lived on the flesh of young boys, and when I came upon them unexpectedly it was them or me. I was good, accurate with my spear, and while killing them like so many brown ants, I never suffered a scratch.

Ah, I was the prince of a sandy land, a warrior from across the water with only my good judgment, my unmatched strength, my instincts to guide me. For always was one of my ears tuned to the relentless shuffling of waves on beach, on a kind of harmonious whispering of natural phenomena which guided all my real or imagined pursuits. I was the son of some lost sea god, and I could do no wrong. The sea, I felt, was my real home, and if I ever had a goal in life it was to recall the art of breathing underwater. I'd still like that. I'd still like to crawl to the shoreline, porpoise through the gullies, pass over the silent sandbars and go all the way out there and live on the bottom for a while.

Once I came home with a bayonet, a real French bayonet I'd found in the outhouse of a home back in the high dunes of Sandy Hills. When I showed it to my sister Pumpkin she asked me how I'd come upon it. When I told her, she patiently explained that it was not mine, that the bayonet had an owner whose right to it was far stronger than mine. Once explained, I understood. I took it back, and on the way it dawned on me that I was no king after all, that there were many real people in this world, people as real as I, and that they had ideas too. I was very depressed.

I could not help my father in his work, because the nature of it demanded the strong back and arms of a man. Dad always thought of himself as a farmer, which, of course, was a ridiculous fantasy. The only garden we ever had was a radish patch I planted when I was five years old, and all the radishes were well trampled under long before harvest. I'd put them in the middle of the path to the outhouse, a bad mistake, and for some reason I never tried again. But Dad always talked

14

about what a killing we'd make when we got some land again. Well, it was his illusion, not mine, and it just seemed like a lot of hard work to me. But there were few jobs on the island as hard as Dad's.

Dad worked on bulkheads. All the island towns were trying to build up their beaches, to somehow trap the shifting sands and put a little more distance between the sea and the beachfront homes. To do this they built jetties of rock or wood, and my father was the island specialist at this. He was boss of the work gang that put in the long rockpile at Longport, the curving rock-and-piling jetty on Quincy Avenue in Margate, and all the wooden jetties in Ventnor and Atlantic City. He worked long hours with men half his age and insisted upon doing the hardest work. He carried heavy pilings, dug deep holes, sawed the thick, tarred timbers and bolted them up with iron rods as long as a man's leg. For some reason the biggest jobs were always done in winter, when the sand blowing down the barren beach would peel the paint off the work wagon and half the crew would go down with pneumonia. I never knew Dad to have a sick day in his life.

Off he'd go on a cold January morning,

walking down the beach with his great boots, his rain slicker, his tools over his shoulder. He was very tall and very thin; thin like wind-fence lath and just as strong. His face was red and he had an enormous nose, sad eyes and silver hair. Off he'd go on a three- or four-mile walk against the wind, and we wouldn't see him again until just after dark. He'd leave his muddy clothes, all of them, in the outhouse and come up the spiral stairs bare-foot. He'd put on his old brown bathrobe and stay that way all evening until he went to sleep.

The truth is my father was a drinking man. He drank a quart of whiskey every night I knew him. He'd get loud, then quiet, then he'd go to sleep. I liked him best just as he was getting loud.

"Garvey?" he'd say to me. "What was Polonius's advice to his son Laertes?"

"To thine own self be true," I'd pipe.

"Hot diggity!" he'd say, giving his knees a slap. "Will you listen to the boy?"

He looked at me over a span of sixty years, that man. He looked at me as if I were some new breed of animal Pumpkin had brought home with a piece of clothesline around its neck. And I'd stare back, ready to answer another question or run for the door.

Because when he got very loud, just before he'd get very quiet, he'd get blasphemous. I had a great fear of him when he was blasphemous, a fear instilled in me by my sister Pumpkin, who was a Moslem and very religious.

Pumpkin was a Moslem and had been ever since college. She had gone to Washington, D.C., to join up, and over her bed was a framed photograph of a huge mosque in Cairo. Around her neck she wore a silver hand with Arabic writing, and she could quote the Koran. The Koran was the only book that bored me more than the Bible.

Dad would get loud and blaspheme the Bible like no one could. He'd end up by saying it was all a pack of lies. He'd never read the Koran, but to him they were one and the same, a ten-foot pile of lies.

"Well, what's the truth then, Daddy?" Pumpkin would ask.

"When you're dead, you're dead."

Then I'd run for it. I'd run up to the howdah, look up to the stars if there were any, and ask God to forgive my silly old daddy. He always did.

17

Dad went fishing on his time off, all year round. He preferred casting off the beach, but when the stripers, croakers, weakies or whitefish were running you'd find him on a rockpile, a dock or a bridge somewhere. He was a great sportsman who always wanted to give the fish a decent chance. He invented a "fallaway sinker," a little device that released the lead weight when the fish hit the bait and began to fight. He didn't think it was fair for the fish to have to drag that extra weight around. I never shared his interest in fishing, though I've caught many a fish.

What I liked most were boats. I've never met anyone who loved boats as much as I. I guess it goes back to my early dreams along the sea when water and wind were the only forces of destiny I could comprehend. I owned my first boat when I was seven.

I found her in the bay, hard aground on a mudflat behind Margate. She was a skiff of fifteen feet with a hole in the bow I could crawl through. She lay on the mud regardless of the tide. In her stern I'd sit, pulling her imaginary tiller, yelling orders to a nonexistent crew. The tide would come in through the hole and I'd have to put my feet up on the thwarts to keep them dry. When the tide came all the way up I had to jump for the mudbank.

I decided to float her, to make a real voyage, or "passage" as Dad called it. I found some old gunny sacks and filled them with black bay mud, set them in the bows over the hole. I had no oars but was ready with a long pole and one of Dad's whiskey bottles filled with fresh water. Up came the tide, lapping the cedar strakes of the boat, laughing at the old hulk being born again.

She moved. I felt her keel break away from the mud suction, and I felt her stern shift on the current. And then we were sitting on top of the water as light as any feather. I knew at that moment it was the first time I'd ever really done anything.

The feeling passed quickly. We were afloat about three seconds before the sandbags blew out of the hole and the bay rushed in. She shuddered and sank in three feet of water, never to rise again. That was my first boat, and she never even had a name.

When I was ten I found a sneakbox washed ashore on the bay side of Longport. It was just after a big storm, and her parted painter was still attached to the bowring. I pulled her far up on the beach, dumped her and scraped all the mud from the hull. She was nine feet long and built to ride low in the water, as a good duck boat should. I waited seven days for someone to claim her, and when no one did I painted her deck bright yellow with one coat of house paint. She was mine.

Pumpkin had told and retold me a favorite story about a little mouse whose mother had given him a brand-new boat. He could go with it where he liked, she told him, but she warned that he was never to go in the ocean. The bay was fine for him, but the sea was another thing entirely. Of course the mouse soon got tired of the bay, and one day he took his boat through the inlet to the ocean, got caught in the current and soon was lost out of sight of land. He was sitting in the stern crying when a big slammer bluefish came along and bit off the end of his tail, making matters much worse. But it was a talking fish, and it came back to ask what was the matter. When the mouse told him the fish offered a deal: he would lead the mouse back to the safety of the bay and glue back the tip of his tail, if the mouse would forever keep his promise to his mother. The mouse went for it, and the story always ended happily at home. I called my first real boat *Mouse*.

Again, I had no oars. But with a long cedar pole I could bump along the marshbanks behind Margate and explore all the creeks. I couldn't cross the bay, as it was too deep for my pole.

I begged Pumpkin to come with me, and on a fine August day she did. I tied down the hatch cover so the boat couldn't sink and set her in the stern. For balance I sat on the tip of the bow, which was pointed nearly to the sky. I poled us that way for two miles whilePumpkin reflected aloud on the beauty of the meadowlands, the sweet serenity of the green tidal salt marshes. We finally sank off the city dump in Ventnor, and Pumpkin had to swim to shore, pulling me and the sneakbox behind. She didn't mind and never mentioned it to Dad.

Dad never went near the boat. He'd been a sailor, briefly, around the time I was born. He'd had a bad experience in a squall off Barnegat and never went to sea again. He said the sea was just waiting for another chance to get at him and he wasn't about to help. But he never tried to stop me, and it's a good thing he didn't, because my love for boats and the water was something born hard inside me, something that could never be suffocated or denied. And he knew that.

Dad knew that I, like everybody else in the family, was different; but he was certain that I was headed for something bigger than anything he could guess. He gave me free range and told the women, Mamma May and Pumpkin, to do the same. When I came home from the bay covered with black mud and soaking wet, no questions were asked. I had to volunteer all information, and if I didn't feel like it that was okay too.

"By God," he'd say, "I don't care what all you do for your living just so's there's a lot of money in it, a whole lot of money!"

"Money!" I'd yell back at him just to get him going.

"Money and all the things you can buy with it! Money and the way money makes you feel when you look a man in the eye!"

"Right in the eye!" I'd respond.

"Money and the things you can do with it when you're rich! When you can sail off to France at the drop of a hat!"

And Mamma May would be standing at the stove with her teeth out and the flies buzzing around her old head, and without looking away from the frying pan she'd say:

"Shirttail out, hat stove in. And all because of drinking gin."

Then Dad would pretend to throw an empty bottle at her, look at me and wink. He had the loudest whisper I ever heard, which was because he was partially deaf.

He'd wink at me and whisper in his gravelly growl, "Crazy as a June bug!" Then he'd fall back on the sofa laughing.

Well, I don't know who was crazier in that elephant, he or Mamma May, I or Pumpkin. I just know that we all got along and I always woke up in the morning glad to be there.

And all this was years before anyone ever heard of Atlantic City Proof.

2

APART from my family, I had few friends. Other Margate boys my age went to school, and that left me out. They lived in white clapboard houses or red brick ones, and that left me out too. They called me "the elephant kid" and made childish remarks about my family, looked upon us as if we were from a different world. But while they were wasting precious daylight hours in the public school I was learning everything there was to know about our beautiful island home. I wasn't alone; I was independent.

The people I got to know were the old men who knew my father, who passed the days on the rickety old docks back on the bay. One, a former sea captain who lived modestly in a cedar-shake shack in Sandy Hills, used to let me bait his hooks for him. His name was Pegleg. He was missing his left leg and walked on a crutch he'd carved himself. Dad said that years before he'd been a great swimmer who would walk daily to the beach in summer, unstrap his wooden leg, hobble into the surf and swim for hours. One day the tide came in while he was out swimming and carried away his leg. Pegleg said two left legs were enough to lose in one lifetime, and he never got another. But everyone called him Pegleg anyway.

Pegleg fished for flounder on the end of Mush McGaragil's dock before it caved in in 1916. I learned how to open bait clams by smashing them with my foot and digging out the insides with my fingers. Then I'd cut them up with my own knife and put pieces on his hook, doubled up so they wouldn't come off. I asked Pegleg once if they were good to eat and he winked at everybody on the dock and said to me, "I dunno; let's see."

He cracked one open and popped it in his toothless mouth, swallowed once and grinned.

"Not bad at all," he said.

Of course Pegleg and just about everyone else on the end of that dock had been eating bait clams all their lives, raw or otherwise, but I never knew it. Right then and there I lost my taste for clams of any kind.

Pancake Schmeisser was a crony of Pegleg's who had once been the chief chicken catcher of South Atlantic City, which was what they called our end of the island when he was young and able. Some darn fool summer people had brought in a lot of chickens one spring and left them there in the fall. The chickens, a particularly hardy breed, had gone wild and were nesting all over the dunes and the low bogs. They were there for the taking, and all that was required was a good set of legs to run them down. Pancake had been the fastest runner on the island before he got married, they said. He and others like him wiped out the wild chickens over a period of fifteen years, but he still talked about them as if they were there.

"The trouble is," he said, "that the chickens have had to get faster to keep alive. They're as fast now as any man, and you have to trap them to catch them." Huddled down with Pegleg once in the lee of an oar locker, he gave him a nudge and told me, "You can catch chickens with a crab trap, if you want to."

I told him I didn't eat chicken, but he said I could sell them to the butcher at twenty-five cents apiece. This interested me. There was a four-point star crab trap rusting away in our outhouse, and I retrieved it that day and set out looking for wild-chicken tracks. The thought occurred to me that I'd never seen any, but it didn't deter me. I set the trap under a big bayberry bush and waited behind a dune with the string in my hand, dreaming of what I'd do with my first quarter. It took me hours to decide that I'd buy another crab trap and have twice as much business. Dad said I had an early grasp of capitalism.

When I didn't catch any chickens I returned to McGaragil's dock at sunset. Pegleg was there waiting for me. He told me I was a darn fool for going out on my own without first speaking with him privately. He said there was absolutely nothing to this chicken business, as the only chickens left were all legs and no body, and no butcher would take them. He tied a fish head inside the trap and lowered it into the bay, saying we'd catch some shedder crabs instead. I stared down at the trap spread out on the bottom. The fish head stared back at me.

"There aren't any chickens," I said.

"No," replied Pegleg without looking away from the water, "but there used to be. More than you could count. There was more chickens than seagulls."

"But there aren't any now," I said.

"Nope. Not really."

"Cut your own bait."

He spun around on one foot, the way he could, and reached to take my shoulder, to show me we were still pals, I guess, but I was gone.

I was back in a few days and things were forgotten. But nobody on that dock ever made a fool of me again.

I fished with a handline that Dad gave me and caught flounder, sometimes big five-pound "doormats" as they called them, and this was when flounder sold for as much as twenty cents a pound. In the fall Dad and I went after stripers, fishing from the Longport Bridge. We used bucktail lures, and when a wily old striper hit one the first thing he'd usually do was swim around a piling a couple of times, fouling the line. If the line held until the fish was tired out it was a simple matter of getting him to the surface and lowering the special bridge gaff that Dad had made. It had four big hooks on it, and Dad would twist it around the line, let it fall under the fish, then gaff him with a quick jerk. The bridge gaff, with its strong line, was the only way to get a big fish up onto the bridge.

One October night, around midnight, I

hooked a monster striper that was so heavy it broke the bridge gaff. We could just about see it in the moonlight, and Dad, who had been drinking but was not drunk, got excited. He grabbed the hand gaff—one big hook on a short pole—and jumped off the bridge. It was a cold night and he was wearing two sweaters and an Army coat.

The other fishermen were shouting to him and running for help. I kept calm and watched the water as best I could. The tide was running at about five knots, straight out to sea.

Soon I heard him speak. With no sign of emotion he said to me, "Garvey, I got him and I'm headed for the bank."

"Which one?"

"The closest one, boy."

We were in the middle of the bridge as far as I knew. I waited, listening for the splash of his kick. When it didn't come I realized he had the gaff in one hand and would be sidestroking. I took a guess and ran for the end of the bridge that touched down on the island, figuring that the lights from the Coast Guard station would make that bank seem closer from the water. The truth is I never thought he would make it.

In the time I waited there a thousand things passed through my mind. I tried to imagine going home without him, telling the story to Pumpkin and Mamma May. I thought about how the other fishermen would spread the story around town. I started to laugh. Then I thought about living without him, going fishing without him, and I stopped laughing.

Then he was there, crawling up on the bank with all his clothes on, even his boots, dragging the biggest rock striper either of us had ever seen. I helped him up with it.

He wasn't even out of breath.

We were downstream, about a hundred yards from the base of the bridge. He'd arrived practically at my feet.

"How'd you know I'd land here?" he asked.

"I allowed for the current," I said.

The fish weighed forty-two pounds on the butcher's scale.

Dad seldom got drunk outside the elephant. When he did he went all the way. Once, a black man who lived in a cabin on Hospitality Creek came running up to the elephant, banging on the rear leg with his fist. I stuck my head out a window.

"Your dad's lyin' flat on his back in the middle of Atlantic Avenue," he said.

It was a cold February night and I wasn't worried about him getting run over, but I thought he might have had a heart attack or something. So I ran fast with the black man, whose name was Taffy, to the place where he had found him. He was lying on his back at the intersection of Atlantic and Rumson Avenues, which was marked with a stick. He was smoking a cigarette. I shined a hurricane lantern on him.

"You all right, Dad?"

"Sure I'm all right!" he said. "What's all the excitement about?"

"Well, it's not every day we find you lying in the middle of Atlantic Avenue," I said in defense.

"Hell no!" he laughed. "Every other day!"

Of course this wasn't true, but it was one of his finer off-the-cuff jokes, which we often repeated. It turned out that he'd been on his way home from Muldoon's Saloon in Atlantic City and had been overcome by fatigue.

Dad loved Muldoon's. It was just a waterfront tavern back on Gardner's Basin owned by a big man named Dutchy Muldoon. On summer Sunday afternoons, Dutchy's was the place to be. Often Dad would take Pumpkin and me along to keep him company and show us a good time. There was a band there on the weekends that played Irish songs like "McNamara's Band" and "Galway Bay." When it rained, Dutchy's was mobbed with people just off the beach and still sandy. Many of the ladies would wear their bathing costumes, and I can remember hordes of them doing the Mummer's Strut whenever "Golden Slippers" was played.

Dutchy, a man in his thirties, would sit at the dark end of the bar with a big cigar in his mouth and bash out the beat of the songs with his big fist. When someone got too drunk he'd nod to one of his bartenders and suddenly the drunk would go flying through the air, straight out the window and into the bay. If the objectionable party staggered back in, wet and muddy, he'd be served again as if nothing had happened. I used to wonder about those who didn't stagger back in.

Dutchy's was all the way at the end of the streetcar line, at the north end of the island by Gardner's Basin. If there was a place I thought was paradise on earth it was Gardner's Basin. Filled with boats, large and small, the narrow lagoon was the busiest spot in Atlantic City. The fishing fleet moored there, as did all the coasters down from New York. The rich men kept their yachts there, and the Coast Guard maintained a boathouse near the entrance. I made two good friends up there, people who were to help me then and later in life.

Captain Frye, of the U.S. Coast Guard, took an early liking to me. He lived in a cottage down in Margate and knew my family well. He and Dad had been friends for fifty years. He traveled to and from the boathouse by bicycle, summer and winter, refusing to have anything to do with the mule-drawn-trolley cars or any other form of land transportation. Wearing his white Coast Guard hat and his khaki Coast Guard uniform, he was a familiar sight pedaling along Atlantic Avenue rain or shine.

"Garvey," he said to me once, "when some people have problems they go to hell. When I have problems I go to sea."

In those days Captain Frye went to sea in a thirty-foot surf boat left over from a still earlier age. With two crew members to help him, he'd launch the old double-ender, start her motor and putter through the inlet to the big ocean beyond. He and his men were on call for any ship in distress, and they were great heroes around the time of shipwrecks. When there were no wrecks he'd go out there and hang a handline over the stern and fish for hours.

Captain Frye taught me how to navigate and to use a polaris, a sextant, dividers and chart. He taught me how to steer a course and find an inlet in a fog. In return I worshipped the man and ran any errand he asked.

On any given day, when every other boy my age was suffering in an overheated classroom run by some halfwitted teacher, I'd be in the Coast Guard boathouse fiddling with equipment or listening to stories told by Captain Frye.

Or else I'd be right next door in the Walter Eberding Boat Works. This was where they made the beautiful skiffs so much in demand on the Jersey coast. Originally designed up at Sea Bright, these boats could take anything the ocean could dish out and take it for years. They were clinker-built, or lapstrake if you like, and their lines varied little regardless of size. Long, narrow and round-bottomed, they cut through the water like a racer whether powered by motor, oars or sail. Their Jersey cedar planks were copper-riveted to their

Jersey white-oak ribs. Their gunwales, thwarts, breast hooks, stems, transoms and thole blocks were of the same white oak the British had planted a century before for use in great warships.

I learned how these boats were made and the names of every part of them from the boat works' master, Walter Eberding himself. Ebby, as he was called, was a boat-building genius and a hard-working man. He planed all the planks himself with an old drawknife, and when a boat was launched she was tight, with no caulking whatsoever. He had his own way of doing everything, and if I caught him in the right mood, he'd explain things to me.

He said when you draw a line on a plank never use a pencil; use a nail. The nail scratch was finer and gave a better fit in the end run. I always had trouble seeing it, but he didn't.

"Let the tool do the work," was what he always told me, and this was a difficult concept to grasp. A tool, he said, even a common hand tool like a hammer or saw, was a machine. Machines have a mechanical advantage that is built in to save labor. The hammer sinks the nail, the saw cuts the wood; not the arms. The arms are there to guide and power the tool, not to do the job. Though the rule is hard to understand, it is easy to follow. Just set up the job, hold the tool lightly, sight the work and say to yourself, "Let the tool do the work." It usually helps.

Ebby was of medium height and very stocky, a man who could handle himself in any situation. In addition to boat building, he could hunt, fish, clam and sail. He could build a house or a barn, do plumbing, roofing, painting, anything required on the island. But he had a short temper and could not swim.

I used to varnish for him. He'd sit up on a trestle with a bottle of beer in one hand, a nail in the other, and say, "Ya don't *paint* it on; ya *lay* it on." I'd nod and go on painting the varnish on the only way I knew. He'd watch for a while, get fed up and take the brush with a jerk. He'd dip the hog bristles halfway in the varnish can and brush varnish on oak in long, smooth strokes, saying, "See? Ya just have to *lay* it on!" Then he'd give me back the brush and I'd go on as before.

I never could figure out what he meant, but just to be sure, I'd always say to myself while varnishing, "Ya *lay* it on." But I can still see him up on the trestle shaking his head, swigging his beer, waving his nail in disgust at my feeble efforts.

By the time I was thirteen I had a very good knowledge of boats, how they were built and steered. I was only lacking in experience, and I knew that soon would come. Dad always said that the world will stand aside for the man who knows what he wants. He said if you know what you want you don't even have to go out and work for it. All you have to do is go to somebody who already has it and doesn't want it and ask for it. Keep this up and pretty soon somebody will give it to you, just to balance things out. What I really wanted now was a boat.

I wanted a real boat, a work boat that was all my own. The sneakbox was just a duck hunter's toy and no good for anything else, besides which she leaked at every seam. I wanted a wide, flat-bottomed, square-bowed bay boat that didn't leak, or not too badly. There were hundreds of these vessels on the back bay with many variations on the theme, but all known by the name of "garvey," just as Dad had named me!

Ebby would build any man a new cedar garvey for forty dollars, guaranteed to last forty years. Of course I didn't have that kind of money, or any other kind, so I set about asking people, just as Dad had suggested. I asked around.

I asked Pegleg, Pancake, Pumpkin, Captain Frye, Ebby, even Dutchy Muldoon. Nobody had one, but they were all on the lookout. I knew it wouldn't take long.

I was wrong and Dad was wrong; it took two years.

I was fifteen in 1915 when I finally came across the garvey that was meant to be mine. Dad and I were up at Dutchy's on a cool night in early spring. Dad was blotto and Dutchy was buying him boilermakers, a shot of whiskey and a small glass of beer to wash it down. I was passing the time playing shuffleboard all by myself on the long table by one wall. I'd slide all eight quoits from one end to the other, then run down and slide them back. Dutchy, Dad, a bartender named Bullets and I were the only ones in the place, it being well after midnight.

The door to the dock opened and a boy came in squinting in the dim light.

"Holy Mother," he yelled. "This place looks like a morgue!"

We all looked up. The boy was not much older than I, but a lot bigger. He was barefoot and wearing a very dirty raincoat over muddy pants and shirt. On his head was a scraggly old straw hat. His eyes were wild with drink. He was a clammer.

Dutchy was making up his mind which window to throw him out of when he approached the bar demanding whiskey. Bullets looked at Dutchy and Dutchy spat on the floor. The boy got his whiskey.

He downed it at a gulp, sat back and dropped his raincoat on the floor.

"Boys," he said, as if we had all been sitting there together for years, "the name's Bonney, William H. Bonney; I am a desperate man."

With this he laid a .44 smokeless on the bar and grinned.

Bullets, the bartender, took a step back. Dad knocked over a beer glass. Dutchy Muldoon lit a fresh cigar. I stood there with a quoit in my hand and my mouth hanging open like an idiot out of the wind.

"You're a desperado?" asked my dad.

"I have killed twenty-one men," he replied. "If I live long enough to kill Pat Garrett and Barney Mason, I'll be satisfied." He pushed his empty glass at Bullets, who filled it to the brim with a steady hand.

"Do they call you Billy?" asked Dad politely.

"They do."

"Billy the Kid?"

The boy drank his whiskey, nodding all the while.

"We've heard of you, son," said Dad with great sincerity.

"We've heard of you from Puerto de Luna to Santa Rosa, from the Honda to Seven Rivers. You're a hero from here to Pecos Valley, and I would like to stand you to a drink but have no money."

The Kid nodded to Bullets, who filled Dad's glass.

"Think of it, Dutchy," said Dad to Muldoon, "we're havin' a drink with Billy the Kid!"

"I am here to rob this saloon."

Dad whacked the bar with an empty glass.

"Think of that, Dutchy! We're bein' *robbed* by Billy the Kid! Billy? How's the war?"

"What war?"

"Why the Lincoln County war!"

"We lost."

"Is that a fact?"

"We was sold out by the Department of the Interior."

"Damn their eyes!" yelled Dad.

"I am an honest man," said the Kid, "but my misfortunes have taken me to desperate attitudes."

"I'll bet," said Dad.

"I am alone and without friends."

"Where's all the boys?" asked Dad. "Where's Jesse Evans and the Dedrick boys? Where's Hendry Brown and Fred Wayte?"

"Dead," said Billy, "all dead."

"Hey, is it true you killed Bob Ollinger?" Dad turned and winked at Dutchy. Dutchy was not smiling.

"Ollinger was the biggest rat who ever lived, and I hated him more than any man I ever met. It was the happiest moment of my life when I looked him down the barrel of my twelve-bore and pulled the trigger."

"He knew it was you that did for him?" asked my old dad.

"He knew all right. I spoke to him to let him know it was me."

"What'd you say?"

"I said, 'Hello, Bob.'"

"Hot diggity!" yelled Dad. "Just like that!"

"That was all I said."

"Where you headed now? After you rob Dutchy, here."

"Montana. It's my aim to join up with the vigilantes."

Dad's face sobered. He looked at us all.

"The vigilantes of Montana," he said, "never hung an innocent man."

"Nope, they didn't," said the Kid.

"They shot all the innocent men!" said Dad.

This drew a blank stare from the desperado and the rest of us. Sometimes it was hard to follow Dad.

Dutchy had had enough. Everybody knew the legend of Billy the Kid, but this clammer and my dad seemed to know it better than the book. Dutchy resented this superior knowledge, he disliked giving away booze, and he was annoyed at the sight of the six-shooter on his bar. He ducked under the bar and came up in front of the Kid.

"Get back in your boat," said Dutchy, nodding toward the door to the dock.

The clammer pointed the gun at Dutchy. Dutchy took it away from him and tossed it out the window to the bay. Bullets tapped the Kid on the head with a billy, and the Kid slumped down on the bar.

Dutchy called the police, who came right away. We heard later that they got him drunk again the next morning and took him around to the draft board, which sent him off to a real war.

Meanwhile, just after they dragged him out, I had a look out on the dock. It was high tide, and lashed to a piling by a worn painter was a big gray garvey.

It had a little cabin in the bow; the waist was filled with clam rakes and crab nets. On the transom was a small out-board motor.

I went around to Dutchy's the next day and asked him outright if I could have the boat. Dutchy said I could have it all right, if he could have twenty dollars. I went looking for Dad.

Dad was putting in a rockpile on Cedar Grove Avenue in Margate. Several hurricanes had carried away much of the sand there and the rockpile would bring it back. Steel tracks were laid out on the beach leading to the surf, and handtrucks were on them bearing small boulders. Dad was supervising a crane operator, telling him where to place each rock. They were nearly finished, and I watched until the job was through.

The rockpile extended a hundred feet into

the surf and was not high. The tide was nearly in, and most of the rocks were underwater. Dad pointed to a long, pointed rock in the last car and told the crane operator he wanted it placed on top of the pile, as close to the end as he could get it. Once in place, it jutted alone from the sea like a milepost on a sand dune.

"That's to show where the rocks is," explained Dad.

To this day that rock is known as Sharkfin Rock, and, I regret to say, it has torn the bottom out of many a boat. I mentioned this once to Dad, and he said, "Serves 'em right."

The job was over and I saw a chance to speak privately with Dad. I told him about the boat. I told him I'd asked Dutchy for it and that Dutchy had asked me for money.

"Why, it's not Dutchy's to sell," he said.

"It is," I said. "The police gave it to him."

"You mean they sold it to him," I didn't know that.

I put Dad's shovel over my shoulder and we started for home. Eyes on the sand, I waited for him to speak.

"What would you do with it?" he finally asked.

44

"Make money. It's all set to go clamming. I could pay you back in one week."

"What do you know about clamming?"

"I know it pays money."

When we got home, Dad went down through a trapdoor in the kitchen floor and found his money jar, which he kept hidden in a tusk. From it he gave me four five-dollar bills.

"Clams is free," he said. "They're like pennies lying all over the ground in a dream. All you gotta do is pick 'em up . . ."

". . . put 'em in the boat . . ." I chirped.

". . . put 'em in the boat, take 'em to the dealer, get the money," he said.

"And get more clams."

"All there is to it."

"I will cause the rich man to carry a great weight to a great height," said Pumpkin, reciting from the Koran.

"Aw, stow it," said Dad.

That afternoon I paid off Dutchy, took the garvey down Beach Thorofare and tied it to McGaragil's dock. Pegleg and Pancake were there.

They weren't much, but they were all the friends I had at that end of the island, and I wanted to share with them the great feelings

45

of joy and promise I was experiencing. They came aboard and looked her over well. Pegleg stuck his penknife into the wood in many places and pronounced her sound. Pancake came out of the cabin with half a dozen ripped and moldy Western magazines. On the front of one of them was William H. Bonney, alias Billy the Kid, and he was gunning down a deputy with a .44 smokeless. Pancake asked if he could have them, and I said to take them along.

"What you gonna call her?" they asked.

"*Desperado.*"

3

MY sister, Pumpkin, opened the Elephant Hot Dog Stand the same spring I got my garvey. She put up all her savings for the materials and Dad built the shack in two days. It stood on the beach just forward of the left foreleg so that we could keep an eye on it from our bedroom window. It was white with blue trim and a blue roof. Inside, the walls were white, the floor white sand.

She had to wake up before sunrise to receive the ice for the root-beer machine and to start the wood fire in the hot-dog steam-box. I woke up with her to go clamming.

Mamma May would make us breakfast, speaking to herself in a private language all the while. The seagulls would cry and dive for the scraps she threw out of the big round eyes that stared at the horizon with never a blink. We ate our cereal, scrambled eggs and toast while listening to the waves slap the beach. Then it was off to work.

Dad had a bicycle which he never used. He

had found it in the bay near the end of a dock and cleaned it up, but it would forever be rusty. The salt water was somehow trapped inside the frame and the decay was from within. The nice thing about the rust was that no one ever bothered to steal the bicycle no matter where I left it. I left it each morning at the foot of McGaragil's dock.

McGaragil was long dead and his dock had only a few seasons to go. There was no rent to pay for the slip I'd made for *Desperado*. She rode free on the tide, her lines kept taut by cast-iron sash weights lashed to their ends.

My first job was to bail her out. She had a leak up by the forefoot, one along the starboard chine, one at the transom, and one big one I never could locate. Every morning there was a foot or so of clear green water in her. I bailed with two tomato-juice cans that I'd found in her cabin.

On an oak rib inside the cabin I found the word KID dug in deeply with a penknife. There were two letters, just the envelopes, addressed to Oswald Flynn, care of the Beach Haven Fisheries at Long Beach Island, which was some twenty miles up the coast from us. Both the letters were from the state prison of

Rahway. I assumed Flynn and Billy the Kid were one and the same.

Long Beach Island clammers had a head start on the backbay gang from Atlantic City, and immediately apparent was the presence of the long-handled twelve-tooth clam rakes that took up the length of the hold. Atlantic City clammers used their toes. I decided to master the rakes. I cleaned them up, replaced the netting and painted the handles gray. There were two of them; I never knew why, since clammers always clam alone.

I'd bail her out, set the rakes over to one side and work on getting the motor started. It was an Evinrude of three horsepower, and it started with a rope.

Wind the rope around the flywheel, adjust the throttle and the choke, pull the rope. Do this ten or twenty times, then stop and dry off the sparkplug while waiting for the motor to unflood. Wind and pull even harder than before, and in half an hour or so, your motor will start. While she warms up, sit and regain your breath. All there is to it.

I'd cast off first the bowlines, then scamper back to the stern and free the boat from the dock. With my right hand on the motor's tiller, my left on the gunwale, I'd head out into the bay.

The sun rises from the sea. I'd catch my first sight of it peeping over the dunes, glaring its promise of a new and glorious day through the morning mist. The bay waters were calm, my boat slow. It was a dry ride to Scull Bay.

Scull Bay is about a mile behind Margate, well into the marshlands at the end of Risley's Channel. The water is always shallow there, and in 1915 it was a good place to find clams.

I'd find my last working spot by lining up landmarks, cut the motor and let my ears grow used to the silence. Marsh birds of many varieties would be bringing food to their nests, the baby heron and egrets squeaking for worms, bits of crab and such.

Standing on the cabin roof, I'd heft a long clam rake over the side and feel for clams. The mud was black and soft as sea foam, the water clear until I stirred up the bottom.

There I would stand, all the morning long, scratching for cherrystone clams to feed the summer people who crowded Atlantic City clam bars to eat them by the thousands. I always worked alone, and as I was the only downbeach clammer, I had Skull Bay all to myself.

I was the only downbeach clammer because the other Margate boys spent their winters in school and never had the time or inclination to go into business for themselves. In early spring when school let out they found jobs on the boardwalk, passed the hot summer sweating in hot kitchens for pennies. I knew better.

I knew that there could be no finer pleasure than standing alone in my own boat, thinking my own thoughts, gazing at the beauty of a secluded bay whose clam harvest was mine alone to reap.

When I got tired there was a straw mattress laid across some orange crates in the cabin. There I would lie reading one of Pumpkin's borrowed books until I felt like clamming again. I never pushed myself; when I grew tired I rested. I will admit I rested much more than I worked.

My only problem was that I caught very few clams. Sometimes it seemed like hours would pass between one clunk of a clam in my rake and the next. Sometimes I would return home in the afternoon with only a dozen or so clams. My record for the first two years was one hundred and twenty-six clams in one day.

I was paid a penny a dozen by a man named DiOrio who had a truck. DiOrio was a tight-fisted Philadelphia fishmonger who had struck it rich in the clam business off Atlantic City.

He received clams with his truck parked at the foot of Gardner's Basin. There were several Ventnor boys in the business at the time who worked the nearby Lakes Bay, and DiOrio would bring his truck down the island to a place called Parker's Landing to buy their catch. To save gas I'd pedal my clams all the way from McGaragil's on my rusty bicycle. When I had too many clams for the basket I'd put them in a wooden wagon that I could pull behind.

DiOrio refused clams which were too big, too small, or of any variety other than cherry-stones. And we had to scrub all the mud from them. He gave us our money as if it were charity. He insulted us, saying we were lazy bums content to earn a dime a day. Sometimes he didn't show up, which was worse.

So, my record earning for one day was ten and a half cents. After two years I had not paid off Dad even half the money and was in debt to Pegleg for gas. I'd clammed under scorching sun with mosquitoes buzzing in my ears; I'd clammed on freezing winter days when the snow would fall audibly on the water and the clams were dug so deep that it took all my weight to sink the rake through the mud to get to them. All this, and business was running at a loss.

It's a miserable, sunken feeling when a young man realizes he cannot quite fit reality to his dreams. He can mature and get used to being miserable and sunken, and not complain to himself or others. Or he can give up his dream entirely and start out on a new one.

One summer day in Scull Bay I was lying on my cabin roof reading a French novel some genius had translated into readable English. It was about a rich young man who had so satisfied his every lust and passion that he had to find new, artificial ones. The author had reversed every idea I had about the way one's life should be led, and I was beginning to wonder if perhaps I'd learned everything wrong. I was considering drastic measures to attune my destiny closer to the real world, like learning to dance, or getting really good at pool. Small clouds drifted from time to time over the sun, and the day was not hot.

My arms grew tired holding the book, and as I rolled over for a nap I saw another boat.

It was a vee-bowed rowboat without paint. There was a split along one side with rags stuffed in it, and a section of the gunwale was missing entirely. It was riding low in the water, loaded with clams.

There was a small mountain of clams in the middle of the boat. As I watched it grew taller. Someone on the other side was tossing clams from the water to the pile.

After two years on Scull Bay I considered its clam beds mine alone and resented the intrusion. I knew there was nothing I could do about it except wait to see who this infringer was and say something hostile when I had the chance. I looked at that pile of clams in the rowboat, and I looked at my pile in the garvey. I had less than a dozen.

The rowboat swung around, revealing the clammer, up to his hips in the water. He was bent over double, feeling around with his toes. Every other second, it seemed, he would bring up a clam, pass it to his hand, throw it on the pile without looking. Sometimes he threw it with his foot, just for the heck of it.

I let out some anchor line and drifted closer to my rival. His deeply tanned back was to me, but he knew I was there. He looked once over his shoulder, peeked at me from beneath the brim of a worn straw hat and went on clamming. He was shirtless and not very muscular. I guessed his age at around fourteen, and reasoned that getting rid of him would be no great difficulty.

"Excuse me," I said in my deepest clammer voice, "but I've been working this bay for two years, and I don't need any help getting these clams up." That's all I said.

He turned around and straightened up.

"How'd you like a number six Swanson oar down your number ten mouth, ya pug-ugly, flounder-faced goon?"

I turned away in total shock. I didn't have to look more than once to see the intruder was a girl.

"Put your shirt on, please," I said over my shoulder. My tone was that of sensibilities outraged.

"That's what I'm doin', bozo!" she hurled back.

I gave her another few seconds and turned around. She had a muddy flannel shirt on now, arms rolled up to her muddy elbows.

She hopped up into her boat and sat in the bow with her muddy knees pointed at me. She took off her hat and her yellow hair fell down across her breast. Her mouth was set straight, her eyes narrowed to dangerous slits.

"Look here," I said, "it's a big bay. Why don't you just go off somewhere else?"

"Ain't no law in Atlantic County can tell me where to clam and where not to clam, dope."

"There's decency and respect," I countered, doubting if she'd ever heard the words.

"Decency? Why, it's only decency that's keepin' me from runnin' you outa here under a hail of cherrystone clams!"

She picked an oversized clam from the huge pile behind her and flipped it over in her muddy hand.

I was not afraid.

"You'd better watch your mouth, you sassy little sister, because . . ." I didn't have time to finish. She launched the clam sidearm, and it came whizzing at my head as I dove for the cabin. Several more clams followed, smashing on the sides of my boat. Her accuracy was deadly.

I stuck my arm out a porthole and yelled, "Hold it!" The clams stopped.

"I give up!"

"You better! I ain't wastin' no more clams on you."

"I'm comin' out."

"Come on out."

"Don't throw no more clams."

". . ."

"Here I come," I said. "Comin' out slow!"

Out I came into the sunlight. She was sitting as before, flipping a clam in her right hand. I could have sworn I'd seen her throwing right and left. I stood and regained my dignity.

Apart from Pumpkin, I'd never known a girl. By that I mean I'd never had a conversation with a female who was around my age. Margate girls had nothing to do with me, and I'd never been very interested in their company anyway. If I was different from other Margate boys, I was worlds apart from Margate girls. But this one was different.

"Where you from?" I asked politely.

"Who wants to know?"

"Me. My name's Garvey Leek—"

"Well now, there's a dumb name, Garvey Leek, for Christ's sake." She spat in the bay.

"I only asked you where you were from."

"Atlantic City, where else?"

"I'm from Margate."

"Where's that?"

"Over there," I said, pointing to the dunes in the distance.

"I thought only mules and chickens lived down there."

"You be nice," I said. "I'm bein' nice."

"I'll be nice soon's I see your stern movin' for that creek over there."

"What's your name?" I asked.

"What's it to ya?"

"Well," I patiently explained, "you know my name, Garvey, and if I knew yours perhaps we could circumvent this antagonism that has risen between us."

She shook her head sadly and spat once more in the water.

"Minnie Creek," she said, staring at her toes.

"Minnie Creek? Now that's a heck of a name, Minnie Creek."

"Now that we know each other enough to say hello," she said, "I guess we can say goodbye. Goodbye, Garvey, I gotta get to work."

With that she hopped back into the bay and began searching with her toes. I came closer, smiling.

58

"Hey, would you like a clam rake?" I held up one of my rakes, thinking she might trade me her clams for it, and possibly some cash besides.

She looked at me and at the rake.

"Ha!" was all she said.

"What's the matter? It's practically new," I lied.

"Those doohickeys ain't worth the time or trouble to look at 'em." Saying this, she tossed two clams into the boat.

"They're not?"

"Course not, dummy. Only way to get clams is with your toes."

"Then why do they make clam rakes?"

"Same reason they make peaches in a can," she said. "So some shoeboxer like you can come along and waste money on nothin'."

"Really?" I asked, taking a new look at my rake.

She tossed several more clams into her boat. I'd never seen anyone bring up clams like that.

"Workin' one hour with that contraption is like workin' two hours with your toes, except you don't wind up with any clams."

I regarded the dozen or so clams in my boat and laid the rake carefully upon them.

"I got to admit that you sure are getting a lot of clams out of Skull Bay."

"This ain't nothin'. I get twice as many outa Lakes Bay without even tryin'."

"Well, how come you're here and not there?"

She set both elbows on the gunwale of her rowboat and said, "Because I got chased outa Lakes Bay."

"By whom?"

"*Whom?* Why, by about fifty-odd clammers, that's *whom*."

"Why?"

"For hittin' one of them upside the head with an oar."

"Why'd you do that?"

"He was takin' liberties," she said.

I bailed a few cans of water out of my boat while she went back to work.

"I'll go away if you like," I said.

"Makes no difference to me. Free bay."

"Maybe you'd be more comfortable if I was to leave."

"I don't mind workin' with a shirt on, if that's what you mean. And if I want to take it off, you bein' here won't stop me."

"Well, you just tell me if you're going to do that."

60

"I will."

I shook my head. I'd never talked to anyone like her, and certainly not as casually as I was now. And I was not at ease talking casually about delicate subjects.

"Minnie," I said, "you've got more clams there than I've found all summer."

"What do you expect? You don't get clams with a rake, and you don't get 'em sleeping on top of your boat."

"I was reading."

"Yup, I believe you was."

"Well, it's backbreaking work and I get tired."

"Poor baby."

"I'm not looking for sympathy," I said, "I'm trying to tell you how I feel."

"How do you feel comin' home with no clams?"

"I do not like it."

"Well then, get your fanny off that scow and find some."

"I don't like that either."

"What?"

"Wading around in the bay."

"Why not?"

"Crabs down there. And eels . . ."

"So what?"

"You could lose a toe!"

"They may bite you, buddy, but they don't chew nothin' off."

"One's as bad as the other," I said, "to me."

"Then you better find yourself a new profession," she said.

"How do you stand it?"

"What?"

"Pushing your toes around in that primordial slime?"

She looked around. "I don't see no primordial slime."

"I mean that black bay mud. Gives me the creeps to touch it."

"What you got against mud?"

"The way it oozes around my feet, is what."

She shook her head and went back to work.

In ten minutes her boat was full except for a small place in the stern. She looked a little weary as she climbed over the side. I thought the boat would sink.

"Where you going?" I asked.

"Parker's Landing. Got to see that bastard DiOrio."

"Would you please watch your language?"

"Excuse me," she said.

"What do you have against DiOrio?"

"He's a thief, a liar and a pervert. If there was another clam dealer around I wouldn't have nothin' to do with that skunk."

I agreed with her and told her I did. "Still, at a penny a dozen he's got to shell out some money for that load."

"Penny a dozen? That's what he gives you. Me he gives a penny for twenty."

"Why's that?"

"'Cause I'm a girl, is why."

"I get it."

"What do you get?"

"Well, here you are a girl infringing on a man's work."

"Why you dumb clod."

"Hold on now," I said. "I wasn't telling you how I thought about it; I was telling you how he probably thinks about it."

"Him and everybody else. You know how I feel about it? First, I get to feelin' really low-down, you know? Like a dog in a grocery store. Then, I begin to burn, see. I begin to get real mad. I wind up mad enough to kick the first man I see and the last one too. That's how I feel about it. How do you feel about it?"

"I think it's wrong."

"Good. I'll be goin' now. See you." She picked up an oar and began to pole herself out of Scull Bay.

"How you getting to Parker's Landing?"

"Down Whirlpool Channel with the tide."

"That's dangerous."

"I beg your pardon?"

"Look," I said, "how about a deal? I'll tow you up there and sell your clams for you at the regular rate and keep the difference."

"He'll know they're mine."

"Not if they're in my boat."

"It's a deal," she said.

We lashed our boats together and began to transfer clams. When her rowboat was empty I attempted to start my outboard motor. After thirty or so pulls on the rope she began to count out loud.

"Thirty-three, thirty-four, thirty-five . . ."

"Will you stop doin' that?" I said.

"Why don't you let it have some gas?"

"I'm givin' it gas." I showed her the throttle set on "start."

"Not gettin' no gas."

"No?"

"Nope. Your air screw's turned down."

"What air screw?"

She came back to me and showed me a small silver handscrew set in the middle of my gas-tank cap. She twisted it open and some air hissed through it. She wound the rope around the crank and started the motor on the first pull.

Her face was very close to mine, and suddenly I could see right through the mud and the grease. I could see that she was simply beautiful. Bright-blue eyes, freckles on her cheeks, a tiny nose and mouth. She looked like a baby sandpiper a little too close to the surf.

I was frantic.

Here was another loner, another desperado racing with me over the purple sage, blasting off silver bullets at civilized men.

And she was darned good-looking, for a girl.

Minnie's poor old rowboat sank on the way to Parker's Landing. It was my fault; I was showing off.

I wanted her to see how swiftly the little outboard pushed my boat through the water, even under a full load such as this one. I had her boat at the end of my anchor line, my throttle halfway over, and we moved smoothly down Whirlpool Channel with the tide, which was now entering the bay at full rip. Passing into Beach Thorofare, I set the throttle on full speed and waited to hear what she would say.

"You just pulled the stem outa my boat," she said.

I looked back and the remains of her rowboat were far astern. At the end of my anchor line was the stem of her boat; attached to it was about half of the keel. I turned back and found the rest of the boat in three large pieces. It was beyond repair, and I felt terrible.

"I should have gone a little easier," I said, referring to our top speed of three knots.

"She wasn't meant to go that fast," said Minnie. "Bottom hasn't been scraped in twelve years."

On the bottom of her overturned hull I saw vegetation resembling a triple-canopy rain forest with a tribe of shedder crabs thriving in the underbrush. Little barnacles were growing on top of old ones, and some seaweed strands were over three feet long.

"Well, let's get to Parker's Landing and deliver these clams. Then I'll figure out what we're going to do."

"Sure." She said that like she'd heard it all her life.

There were four garveys with their square bows pulled up on Parker's Landing. On the dirt road leading to Ventnor Heights was DiOrio's old Reo. DiOrio was stalking the beach in his big black rubber boots.

We beached my boat and set about cleaning the clams. DiOrio approached me with an eight-foot tule weed in his hand. He touched the pile.

"Garvey boy," he said, "looks like you've been working."

"Yessir!"

"You got little Minnie here to help you?"

"Yup."

"Well, it's a sweet thing to see. Sunset on the bay, day's work done, the two young comrades back to port." Saying this, he touched us both once with the tule weed.

"Hey," said Minnie. "It's like you're welcoming us to a new land."

"Ah, yes," said DiOrio. DiOrio had long black hair, long as a woman's, and it got in his mouth often when he spoke.

"A land filled with promise," said Minnie.

"Heh, heh," replied DiOrio, becoming annoyed.

Minnie eyed a clam, eyed it carefully and tossed it on the pile of clean ones. "A land conceived in liberty and dedicated to the proposition that all men . . ."

"That's enough, Minnie," he said.

". . . are created equal."

DiOrio started to walk away.

"It sure is nice to have you here waiting for us."

He spun around.

"I don't like you, girl. You're nothin' but trouble. Why ain't you in school?"

"None of your business."

"You're a ward. You could get in trouble not being in school."

"It's my problem."

I was working as hard as I could while things got worse. I was scrubbing away, pretending I could not hear what was going on. I was thinking only of the dollar or so we'd get out of this.

"You got a big mouth, little girl," he said.

"You got a big nose, DiOrio. Keep it outa my affairs."

I'd never heard anyone speak to an adult like that. I had always been taught to treat my elders with the greatest respect, no matter how little they deserved it. Now here was

Minnie, a clam in her hand, standing nose to nose with Mr. DiOrio, who looked like he was about to explode. He got control of himself.

"Garvey boy, you better keep this one outa my sight. Because if she bothers me again I'm gonna slap her bottom."

I straightened up. As nicely as I could I said, "Now you wouldn't want to do that, Mr. DiOrio."

"No?"

"No. Because then I'd have to slap your bottom." It was Minnie who had given me the courage.

DiOrio looked at me like I was mad.

"I don't want these here clams," he said. That was it; he'd exercised his only perogative. I could hear clammers in the others boats laughing.

"Then you don't get 'em," I said.

"So you better just go and put 'em back in Skull Bay, because otherwise they'll rot."

"No they won't."

"Who else is gonna buy 'em?"

While I was thinking of the perfect rejoinder, Minnie spoke up.

"Hey, DiOrio. Somebody's throwin' clams at your truck." We looked at the truck. As we

69

did, Minnie winged a cherrystone through the windshield.

Before either of us could say anything she'd splattered another one on his fender.

DiOrio went for Minnie and Minnie ran around the boat. I grabbed a clam rake and tossed it in front of DiOrio, who fell loudly on his face. By the time he was up we'd launched the boat and Minnie was loosing a barrage of clams. DiOrio ran for cover.

Minnie directed her fire at the Reo, and DiOrio ran to protect it. He started it with the hand crank while clams whizzed by his head. He dove for the cab as the other windshield shattered. He backed out of Parker's Landing at full speed. We poled back to shore.

All I wanted to do was get our clams back. I'd never had that many, and I knew there must be a way to get some profit from them. I set about transferring them to the boat.

We were quickly surrounded by hostile clammers. DiOrio was gone, and it was clearly our fault. Keeping my eyes on the pile, I tossed clean clams in the boat, one by one. Minnie stood by me with an oar.

The boys were furious and looking for a way to bring their anger to some sort of action, violent I thought. I got the last clam off the beach and stood up.

"Boys," I said, "we did you a favor. DiOrio's a crook and we all know it. He's been robbing us for years. Pays us a penny a dozen for doing all the work, and sells them for a penny apiece."

"Better than nothing, Leek," said a blond-haired boy.

"He may be a crook, but he pays cash,' said another.

"We need him," added his sidekick.

"The only reason we need DiOrio," I said, "is because he's got a truck. If we had a truck we could sell them up in Atlantic City in a minute."

"So, who's got a truck?"

"I do," I said. I said it because I was sure they were about to jump us. I said it because I knew if I had time I'd think of something. I said it because there was nothing else to say. It worked. They were quiet long enough for me to expound.

"Just leave your clams right here. Minnie and I'll take care of everything. We'll get the truck, pick up the clams, sell 'em tonight, pay you tomorrow."

71

"We sell you our clams from now on?" asked the blond boy.

"Let's see how things work out tonight. Don't worry, everything's going to be fine." I smiled.

Having nothing else to do with their catches, the boys left them on the beach and climbed in their boats. They departed with a few vague threats and the crisis was over. It was time for the next crisis.

Minnie and I looked at the little piles of clams. All together there were more than a thousand. I tried to picture how they'd look piled together. It would take a truck at least the size of DiOrio's Reo.

"That son of a bitch," said Minnie.

"Watch your mouth."

"Well, pat my ass and pardon my French."

"Minnie, will you stop saying things like that and let me think?"

"You don't have a no truck."

"Nope."

"Oh, boy."

"But I got an idea!"

We got back in my boat and I let Minnie start the motor, which she did on the second pull. We headed up the Inside Thorofare to

Gardner's Basin, arriving after dark. I ran the garvey up on the beach beside the Coast Guard boathouse. Before us was Captain Frye's old inboard surf boat, high and dry on the ways. The boathouse was dark.

"You're outa your mind," said Minnie.

"We could have it back by midnight. Captain Frye's home in bed in Margate. His boys will be at the big station, except for the lookout, and he's most likely asleep."

"This is the worst damn plan I ever heard of in my life," said Minnie.

I patted her knee and she pushed my hand away.

The skiff was on high wooden wheels so that it could be launched in a hurry. I took the bowline off the cleat and began to roll her to the bay. When she was afloat we jumped in.

"This here's a federal offense," said Minnie.

"My first one," I said.

"You know how to run this thing?"

"I've done it. I mean I've steered it for Captain Frye."

"Can you start it?"

I'd never thought of that! I didn't have the slightest idea how to turn that motor over. I admitted it.

"I'll get her goin'," said Minnie Creek.

She pulled back the engine box and made some adjustments. She spun the crank starter and the engine came to life. It was only twenty-horsepower and ran quietly. I eased her out of the basin and soon we were on our way back to Parker's Landing.

The tide had come up as I knew it would, and the clams were safely underwater. Some we had to dig up again, but it was only twenty minutes' work before the skiff was loaded. She was thirty feet and piled to the gunwales with clams.

"I still don't see no truck," said Minnie on our way back to Gardner's Basin.

"You'll see," I said.

It was a dark night, and having someone at my side was just lovely.

"Don't run into nothin' in the dark," she said.

"I've been out plenty of times at night."

"Not in a goddam Coast Guard whaleboat, you haven't."

And never with a pretty girl, I thought.

We made it back to the basin with no mishap. The first part of my plan had gone smoothly. Why not the rest?

The Coast Guard hauled their boats by

mule power, and I found the animal sleeping in the lee of the boathouse. With some difficulty I backed him down the ways and hitched him to the launching wagon, which was half underwater. We floated the skiff onto the carriage and lashed her down, and the mule did the rest. When we were out of the water I just kept on going, down the road that led along Gardner's Basin.

"You mean this is the truck?"

"Why not?"

I stood in the bow holding the reins to the mule. Minnie sat on the pile of clams. The dirt road snaked along docks and fisheries, all dark, quiet, closed for the summer night.

Something had taken hold of me, giving me courage I'd never known in myself. All I could think about was getting me and Minnie off the hook with the clammers. I thought I saw a way it could be done if only I kept cool and steady. I never considered what would happen if we failed.

Gardner's Basin is in the Inlet section of Atlantic City where clam bars were as common as black-and-white cats. But I was headed past them, over to the hotels by the beach, where I thought I could get the best price in town.

It was a summer Saturday night and Atlantic City was packed with weekenders down from Philadelphia, only an hour or so away by train. By the time we reached Captain Starn's restaurant we stood in the middle of a brightly lit street jammed with well-dressed revelers, most of them in various degrees of intoxication. The crowd found us quite a novelty.

Suddenly Minnie stood atop the pile, her blond hair glistening under the gaslights, her hands on her hips.

"Clams!" she yelled. "Ten cents a dozen!"

"Minnie, we've got to lay kind of low, don't you think?"

"Impossible," she said as the first customer approached.

He ordered a dozen clams, and Minnie began handing them to him two at a time.

"Where do I put 'em?" he asked.

"In your hat."

He held out his hat and it was filled. He gave Minnie a dime. Behind him a line had formed.

We were making money hand over fist up there in the Inlet when I spotted a familiar face. There, next in line, holding out his Coast Guard cap, was Captain Fyre.

Captain Frye, like my dad, was a drinking man. I'm sad to say it, but he drank maybe a little bit more than Dad. Of course he never drank on duty. He was off duty now, and a part of me wished he was blotto.

He wasn't. He held out his cap with steady hands and eyed me with a steady eye.

"Evenin', Garvey."

"Evenin', Captain Frye."

"I'll have a dozen clams."

"Yessir." I filled his hat.

He thanked me, handed over a dime, patted his boat on the sheer plank and turned away into the crowd.

Maybe he thought he was drunk and seeing things. Maybe the sight of us standing in his skiff selling clams hand over fist in the Inlet tickled his sense of humor. I quit wondering; I was too busy selling clams. If our situation seemed too droll to Captain Frye, it was certainly real to me. I'd never seen so much money.

We sold the last clam by midnight and headed back. Minnie announced from her seat in the stern that we had more than eight dollars. From this we would have to pay the Ventnor clammers just a small portion. We were rich!

The boathouse was as dark as before. I set the boat and its carriage back on the ways, tied up the mule. My garvey was waiting on the beach, ready to take me back home. I hopped in, thinking Minnie would follow. She stood fast on the sand.

"Where you goin'?" she asked.

"Why, home."

"You ain't forgettin' something?"

I hopped out of the boat. "I forgot you lived up here."

I felt my pocket full of dimes, trying to figure out her share. There was much to consider. She'd caught many of those clams. She'd helped me transport and sell them. She'd taken much of the risk, and she'd lost her boat. Still, she was just a girl.

"Minnie," I said, "I think you're entitled to ten percent. You did a great job; you—"

"Ten percent? Why you mangy old yellow dog! You must have a head like a piling and bolts for brains! Why, you mean sonofabitch, you're worse than old man DiOrio in midwinter—"

"If you will kindly quit your odious cursing we'll negotiate," I interrupted. "I am quite open to negotiation."

"You just go negotiate somewhere else,

78

pigeon brain, because nobody negotiates with Minnie Creek, hear?"

"Minnie, how much do you want?"

"Minimum, twenty percent!"

I counted out sixteen dimes and handed them over. She counted them again and slipped them into her back pocket. We stood there breathing hard, staring at each other. I couldn't think of a further thing to say.

Just then a tear rolled down her cheek. I was shocked. I put my hand on her shoulder and she brushed it off. I asked her what was the matter.

"I got a dollar sixty," she said, "and no boat." She didn't sob, but more tears rolled down.

"What do you mean?" I asked. "We got my boat!"

"How do you mean?"

"I mean we should team up and go into business. We're the tops!"

"You mean partners?"

"Well, not exactly partners. But you work for me and you'll make more money than you ever could out there by yourself."

"You think so?"

"Why, honey, I know it!"

"Don't honey me, ya big tunafish."

"First time I ever honeyed anybody," I said.

"Better be the last."

"Minnie, will you do it?"

She dug her toes in the sand and had a long thought. She'd stopped crying, and that was something. The crickets were chirping, and now and then a minnow would jump out of the water. I gave her time. Finally, she spoke.

"Okay," she said. "I'll take the job. I'll work for you at twenty percent. But Garvey, if I don't make more money than I been making, it's gonna be you and me."

"It's a deal, Minnie. Will you shake on it?"

I held out my hand and she took it. I felt like I was floating on a sea of maple syrup. It was the first time we'd touched. Her hand was smooth and small.

"Your boat's leavin' without ya, blockhead," she said.

The tide had changed and my garvey was headed out of the basin. I stood there, her hand in mine, and stared at my drifting craft. All I could think about was Minnie.

She gave me a shove and I swam for it. When I got aboard I looked back at her. She was sitting on the sand, staring at the moon.

4

WE had agreed to meet the next morning at Parker's Landing, and Minnie was there, ready for work, when I showed up. I was a little late owing to some worse than usual starting difficulties with my motor. I thought she would be angry with me, but she was not. She had good news.

"Good news, Floyd," she said, hopping aboard. "I got us an outlet for all the clams we can catch."

"Who?"

"Captain Starn. I talked to him this morning when his boat came in. Says he'll buy direct, six cents a dozen!"

"Six cents a dozen! Hey, that's swell."

"So, let's go get us some clams, bozo."

"What are we going to do about the other fellows?"

"Pay 'em off for last night, tell 'em to tell old man DiOrio we ain't coming back. That's all."

I had an idea.

"Hey, why don't we just buy them from

the boys? We could pay them a penny a dozen like DiOrio, only we'll clean them ourselves. They'd go for that."

"You got brains, buster."

"Would you please stop calling me names."

"Where we going?"

"We're going to find the other fellows and firm up the deal, up in Lakes Bay. You mind steering?"

Minnie did not mind. I went forward and sat on the cabin roof while she sat back by the tiller. When I was not looking at the good old bay I was peeking at Minnie Creek.

It was a long ride out to Lakes Bay, and on the way I got Minnie to tell me the story of her life, a sad one to say the least. To the best of my recollection, here it is.

Minnie's father, Ben Creek, was from Philadelphia, a bricklayer by trade, and a very religious man. He had certain convictions that gave him great peace of mind, a trait not often found in members of his profession.

Bricklaying, at the beginning of this century, was a trade attractive to a certain kind of man. When he had work he made good money, and the labor was not all that difficult. But because there were so many bricklayers at the time, no one had more than six months of work per year, on the average. The other six months were spent drinking beer and listening to the radio while the wife went out and worked.

The only real obligation a Philadelphia union bricklayer had during his period of unemployment was regular attendance at weekly union meetings. These were not peaceful affairs. The unemployed were usually faced off against the employed, and many barrels of beer were on hand to keep everyone happy during the long-winded speeches by ward politicians, union officials and the like. The beer usually maintained its mellowing effect until the evening wore on and intense boredom broke out in the ranks. Then it became a free-for-all that would be stopped only by the arrival of several squads of police.

Ben Creek was not a man of aggressive temperament, nor was he attracted to violence. But the trouble was that Ben, born a Methodist, had converted to the Church of the Fourteen Burning Kings for Christ, a Protestant sect whose advocates were disposed to preach on any occasion, but in a singularly peculiar manner. Drawing on some relatively obscure Biblical references, the church maintained that the only true way to spread the gospel was through music. It was music, inspired by the sacred words, that counted, and not the words themselves, since these had long been committed to memory. Ben was no musician, but, seeking some outlet for his evangelical urgings, he had come upon the jew's-harp, an instrument which he mastered with no difficulty. Thus it was that he was inclined to spend many hours of the day reciting the psalms silently while twanging the primitive metal instrument which, when held to the teeth in the pre-scribed manner and twanged, made a kind of repetitious buzzing sound that pleased him and the other members of this sect no end.

As a part of his effort to put his listeners at the highest level of receptivity, Ben preached while riding a unicycle, which he had made himself. It was not quite a true unicycle, as there was a second wheel just behind the first, but this wheel was very tiny and not seen easily at a distance. Ben had intended to cut it off when he'd perfected the art, but somehow he had developed a dependence on it and it stayed.

To Ben a weekly meeting of the Philadelphia Bricklayers' Union was a chance to preach, to fire the Word with music and showmanship at a band of sinners sorely in need of spiritual guidance.

As a meeting progressed with mounting ennui, Ben would choose the right moment to bring forth his unicycle from a cloth bag, straddle it, and ride in widening circles over the waxed wood floor while playing his jew's-harp. The membership didn't mind this so much at first, as the figure of Ben, a tall man, on a very small and unique machine had its humorous aspects, and no one likes to laugh more than a tipsy bricklayer from the City of Brotherly Love.

But after an hour or so of this, the trouble began. It usually began with someone throwing a brick at Ben's head and knocking him to the floor. Bricks were not allowed at union headquarters, an ironic but understandable rule. But someone would always smuggle in a brick or two with Ben Creek in mind.

Ben would lie on the floor and play as best he could while the mayhem developed. The fellow who threw the brick was usually soundly drubbed for his discourteous aggression, then the drubber would be

85

attacked by another, and the fracas would intensify until the wail of the sirens was heard through the open windows.

Ben, still twanging, would be carted off to the hospital with the other injured, and would not again be heard from until the following meeting.

It was worse when he was on the job. Ben could lay bricks at an alarming rate, at least twice as fast as the average bricklayer. Now there never was, in the history of his union, a policy for the amount of bricks to be laid in one shift. A man worked at his own pace, varying it to suit his mood, depending on the weather, his physical state or his frame of mind. Ben, however, was steady.

When the gang returned to work after a lunch of several gargantuan sandwiches and half a dozen bottles of beer each, the work slowed. There was a tendency to fondle each brick, get the feel and heft of it. They were apt to spend an extra moment or two sighting along its edges, fitting it mentally to the work in progress before the mortar was applied. Not so Ben Creek, who ate only one hard-boiled egg while sipping cold tea. Feeling as light as he had all morning, Ben would lay into his pile of bricks and soon be calling for more. His hands would fly faster than the eye could follow, while his fellow workers looked on with ill-concealed resentment. They could never figure out a professional way to tell him to slow down a bit, to fit his standards to those around him.

So they usually clipped him with a brick. Ben would revive himself after a short space of time and continue, but in a groggy state which matched his speed to the others.

But twelve years of sustained and regular concussions began to tell on him, until one day in May a brick was dropped on Ben's head from the floor above, and when he regained consciousness he was a changed man. He stood up with a wry smile on his face, looked about him while rubbing his head, and walked off the job.

He ditched his trowel on the walk home along Race Street, deciding never again to come in contact with bricks or those who dealt with them. He had an idea, one which would free him from the dull, day-to-day drudgery that had been his existence. He would enter show business!

At home he confronted his wife, Gisala, a hearty woman of German descent, with his inspiration. They would, with their daughter

Minnie, aged five, form a family act and go into vaudeville, where there was plenty of work and an honest wage to be drawn. Gisala played the rhythm sticks with some dexterity, while Minnie had for several years patiently practiced the headless single-jingle tambourine. Could they not form a rhythm band featuring him on unicycle? Gisala, who had often attended Philadelphia vaudeville theaters, asked if this were enough. After all, there were so many family bands, and all of them could play melodies. Perhaps some additional talents could be devised. Ben said he would think about it.

In the meantime Ben devoted all his efforts to preaching with the jew's-harp, riding the unicycle, and asking for information about the vaudeville circuit, especially that in nearby Atlantic City, the town where he had spent his honeymoon. The family lived on his small savings and trusted in the Lord to provide for an exciting and less violent future.

By some stroke of luck one of Ben's brothers in the Church of the Fourteen Burning Kings for Christ was a keeper in the Philadelphia zoo, and a veteran of the reptile pit, one of the largest in the country at that time. He happened to mention at the end of a long and vigorous church meeting a curious story which caught Ben's ear.

The keeper had in his charge a very old and senile crocodile named Roquefort, a beast some eighteen feet in length, who had been born in the zoo many years before when the reptile pit was only a bit of fenced-off bogland. Due to a lifetime of inactivity Roquefort had reached a stage of complacency which afforded very little movement of any sort except at feeding time, which lasted only a few seconds, as his five-pound portion of horsemeat was easily devoured in a single crunch. The rest of the time he spent lying on his back, an uncommon and unattractive position for a reptile. To zoo visitors he appeared dead, and there had been many complaints. The zoo's board of directors had decided the day before that the animal had lived too long and must be destroyed. The job was entrusted to the keeper.

He had not been successful. He was unable to bring himself to shoot Roquefort as he lay so trustingly on his back. Turning him over was a simple matter involving only a gentle twist of the tail, but each time he brought the double-barrel shotgun to bear on the crocodile's cranium, Roquefort would sigh, close his big yellow eyes and roll over. The keeper, unnerved after an hour or so of this, had given up, resolving to get someone else to do the cruel chore.

Ben's mind, freshened by a two-hour frenzy of jew's-harping and unicycling, was on show business. Might not this animal prove an attraction on the vaudeville stage? He could pretend to hypnotize him, an art which was steadily growing in popularity. There were family acts, animal acts and feats of mesmerism, but had all three ever been combined?

He offered to solve the zookeeper's dilemma. He would rescue the beast from an untimely death, flee with him from the city and reside at the seashore where he could perfect and find work for the act. The keeper, his heart gladdened, agreed to help in any way he could.

Ben, handy with tools, fashioned that afternoon a large box of pine which was in appearance similar to a coffin except that it was nearly twenty feet long. Hiring a dray for the job, he went that night with his friend to the reptile pit and with him passed several anxious moments getting Roquefort into the box and the box out of the pit and from the confinements of the Philadelphia zoo. The crocodile, it will be noted, suffered the removal in silence, offering not the slightest resistance.

The dray carried the crate to the train station, where Ben's wife and daughter had waited half the night, sitting on a single trunk which held all their possessions. In the early morning the family, with its cargo, was loaded aboard. The train left the station in a cloud of black smoke and cinders, bound for Atlantic City, sixty miles to the east.

Vaudeville was rife in Atlantic City at that time, and there were already many public houses and theaters, amusement piers and arcades which drew crowds eager to watch the assorted entertainers. Cook's Pier, which stretched half a mile into the sea, was the zenith of Atlantic City vaudeville and the goal of Ben Creek. He knew it would not be all that easy, that the act would have to be developed, practiced and polished, but trusting the Lord, he rode confidently on the train to the city of his hopes.

The weather had not been seasonable in Philadelphia, but in Atlantic City it was a true day in May. The sun was shining in a sea-blue sky as he rode proudly on the hard seat of a hired wagon, his family and the box loaded behind. Traveling slowly down Atlantic Avenue, he looked off to his right at the low undeveloped land there, where only a few shacks had been raised in an area called Ducktown, because of the many ponds of rainwater frequented by thousands of ducks and other fowl during the warmer months. Turning down muddy Mississippi Avenue, he found a crude shack, covered with tarpaper, with a for-rent sign nailed to the door. The owner was found and, in a short time, the Creek family had moved in, pot, pan, dish and crocodile.

There was a small, quiet pond at the rear of the shack, perfect for Roquefort once a fence had been erected to conceal him from view. Many of the other residents, he noted, kept ducks and rabbits and might fear for their safety if Roquefort's presence were known. That night he freed Roquefort from his box, but put a long chain to one hind leg, shackling this to a post driven deeply into the soft ground. With the wood from the box and many other planks found floating in the bogland, he built the fence.

Gisala found work the next day in a small taffy factory. Ben stayed at home with

Minnie and the crocodile. He determined to develop the act at once. He would attempt to hypnotize Roquefort by staring deeply into his eyes.

That afternoon, Minnie, after serving her father his midday meal, took a nap under a small bush by the side of the shack. When she woke all was still. Wondering at the quiet of the place, she searched for her father. In the middle of the duck pond was some high ground forming a small island about twenty feet in diameter. There, lying on his back, all four feet in the air, tail in the water, lay Roquefort, unchained, in his usual trancelike coma. But what was far from usual was the prostrate body of her father, lying quite close to the animal's nose. Ben lay on his back and, even at a distance, appeared cataleptic. Minnie was now more frightened than curious, but always a brave child, she waded toward the island as fast as her short legs would take her. When she reached her father's side she found him in a rigid state, his eyes closed as if in sleep. She tried to wake him, but could not.

With nothing else to do, she tried to wake the crocodile. The muscles in her arms were not strong enough, however, to produce even the slight tail twist which would overturn the crocodile. She tried pounding his stomach with her tiny fists, but they merely bounced off his scales. Finally, taking a long run, as long as the island would allow, she leaped into the air and landed with all her weight on Roquefort's stomach.

Roquefort's mouth was open; that is to say, his jaws, some three feet in length, were slightly spread, and the force of Minnie's body landing on his stomach pushed sharply upon his diaphragm. A column of air from his lungs burst through his vocal cords, and from his jaws came a loud honk, not unlike that of a baritone saxophone before it has been properly warmed up.

"Honk!"

This sound instantly awoke her father. Ben rolled over, blinking in the harsh sunlight reflected from the pond.

At first he was at a loss to say what had happened. The last thing he could remember was staring Roquefort in the eyes and lulling him slowly to sleep. It then occurred to him that the crocodile had returned the glance with an equal power, and that it was he who had fallen victim to a hypnotic stare, and a powerful one at that, as, by his reckoning, he had slept the better part of an hour. But what, he wondered aloud, had awakened him?

Minnie told him of her efforts, of the final plunge she had taken on the crocodile's belly, of the resulting sound which seemed to have done the trick. He asked her if she would do it again, and she readily agreed.

Taking a shorter run than before, and jumping not quite as high, she landed her soft little bottom on Roquefort's smooth stomach.

"Honk."

Ben dropped to his knees to see if the animal was actually mesmerized. It was not. Roquefort's eyes were opened wide. They produced in Ben a dull memory of two golden orbs boring into his soul just before he lost consciousness. At that moment he rejected all plans of further experiments with hypnotism, determining to concentrate on the unusual honking sound.

He asked Minnie to jump again, which she did. Landing a little harder this time, the sound was repeated, but louder and in a higher tone.

"Honk!"

Ben took a ladder from the side of the house and set it into the ground beside Roquefort. He asked Minnie to jump from a high rung, being careful to land bottom first on the crocodile's belly.

"Honk!"

Ben was sure they were on to something. The sounds were musical in nature and rather pleasing. He instructed Minnie to jump from all the rungs of the ladder, starting at the top and working down, to see if they might develop some sort of scale.

This was not to be. Volume, it seemed, could be regulated. But the pitch never varied from the original three tones.

It was the loud honking of the crocodile which attracted the attention of a passerby who would be instrumental in their future efforts.

The stranger was a colored man of middle age who sometimes earned his living playing the piano or banjo in the local saloons. His professional name was Razmataz, and he was in the neighborhood looking for a duck to buy for his grandmother, with whom he lived on occasion. Hearing the strange tonal sounds he looked over the fence.

Minnie jumped from the top rung of the ladder at that moment and Roquefort bellowed a mighty honk.

"B seventh," said Razmataz quietly.

Minnie scrambled halfway up the ladder and jumped again.

"A," said Razmataz.

Minnie was a little tired and simply sat down, hard, on the croc's belly.

"E!" yelled Razmataz.

Hearing this outburst, father and daughter looked up. Razmataz, wearing his most charming and affable smile, asked if he might come closer. He was invited in on the instant by Ben, who was prone to welcome the aid of all strangers.

Razmataz introduced himself, saying that he was a musician. Ben immediately explained his problem. The beast could play only the tones which he had heard. Razmataz clapped his hands and told him it was no problem; it was a miracle! What other explanation could there be? Locked deeply somewhere in the animal's subconscious were the three chords necessary, vitally necessary, to play the blues!

Ben asked what the blues were, and Razmataz tried to explain. Failing this, he launched into an unaccompanied blues riff, twelve bars of a tune which he had written, called "Pushin' Chair." Ben liked the song, finding the melody a catchy one. From his pocket he whipped out his jew's-harp. Razmataz sang, and they both laughed at Ben's accompaniment, which seemed to fit so well. In the summertime Razmataz had been pushing a rolling chair on the boardwalk when he needed extra money. The song was about him and how hard the work really was. He sang,

"I push them boardwalk dandies
With the girls they like the best.
Sometimes I push 'em east,
Sometimes I push 'em west.
I push 'em to a bathhouse
Or to a picture show.
I push them fancy flappers
Anywhere they want to go.

"Pushin' chair, pushin' chair,
Pourin' off sweat and blowin' out air,
Four miles of boardwalk and what do they
  care?
Hey, rich man, can't you hear?
That's me back there, pushin' your chair.

"My daddy was a barber,
My mamma was a shill.
If I don't push that rollin' chair,
I know my grandma will.
She's been workin' in a roomin' house.

Since nineteen hundred and two.
Ain't nobody in Atlantic City
Work as hard as that lady do.

"It only costs a quarter,
  That's the regular fare.
My pocket's full by midnight
And I'm breathin' free air.
If the people don't see me comin',
That's no sad affair.
They move aside when they hear me yell,
'Watcha chair, watcha chair, watcha chair,
    watcha chair!'

"Pushin' chair, pushin' chair,
  Pourin' off sweat and blowin' out air,
  Four miles of boardwalk and what do they
    care?
  Hey, rich man! Can't ya hear me puffin'
    back there?"

Razmataz asked Minnie to jump from the first rung, explaining that this was an E, and that all blues were played in that key. Razmataz then sang the first bar of his song one octave above Roquefort's. It worked. They arranged a series of hand signals so that Minnie would know when and from what rung to jump. With this they worked their way through all twelve bars of "Pushin' Chair", then tackled the bridge. It worked.

Razmataz explained in some excitement that he had to buy a duck for his grandmother, but that he would return that evening, if he might, with his banjo. Ben thanked him for his aid, saying he was a welcome guest who might pass by whenever he liked. At nine o'clock that night Razmataz was back.

Gisala was home and ready with her rhythm sticks. It was a warm evening and the little group sat out by the pond with Minnie, her ladder and the compliant crocodile on the island in the center. At first there was some difficulty tuning the banjo to the crocodile, but this was soon accomplished. Razmataz tapped his foot four times and they all played a slow blues number called "Green Tomatoes," then another, "Lost My Way." At the end of this Ben held up his hand.

He explained to Razmataz that as a member of the Church of the Fourteen Burning Kings for Christ, he was obliged to play songs only of a spiritual nature, and that his jew's-harp melodies were actually Holy Scripture paraphrases, or special wordless messages from his heart.

Razmataz countered with the argument that the blues could be and often were of a highly spiritual nature, drawn as they were from old gospel songs. He said that not all prayers were of thanksgiving, but that many of them asked things of the Lord, or simply complained about earthly struggles and misfortunes, such as parting from a loved one. Ben, a man who could easily grasp strong logic, then and there accepted the blues as a preaching medium. After all, they were all his crocodile could play.

Ben brought up the act, stating that this was the family's goal. Razmataz replied that he was out of steady work at the time and would be more than happy to join. He was enthusiastic and assured them that the act, once practiced, would surely be billed that summer on Cook's Pier, with which he had some connections.

They played all evening, stopping only when young Minnie no longer had the strength to mount the ladder. Razmataz bid the family farewell, saying he would return the following evening with the words of his songs written so that Minnie and Gisala might join in the singing.

Before sleeping, Ben gave thanks to his

Creator for bringing so much good fortune his way. He prayed, naturally, with his jew's-harp, and the soft steady buzzing intermingled with the sounds of cricket, frog and duck outside.

Razmataz was back the next night with handwritten lyrics, his banjo and an old Marine Band harmonica, which he thought Gisala might like to play. Minnie produced her tambourine, and in no time at all the Ducktown Squatters Blues Band was formed.

Ben packed the earth on the island so that he could ride his unicycle while playing. Minnie learned to sit on Roquefort's stomach and bounce up and down while ringing out the basic blues beat on her tambourine. Gisala picked up the harmonica with little effort and, over the following weeks, the little band learned a wide variety of numbers, all of them written and orchestrated by Razmataz.

An audition was held in the first week of June. The stage manager of Cook's Pier was delighted with the music and the unusual appearance of the musicians. In addition to accepting the act for immediate appearance, he offered the family a place to live, a homey cottage on the very end of the pier, where there was a small pool which had been built some years before for a seal act. Ben accepted on the spot.

That was a fabulous summer for the Creek family. Life became exciting. There were three shows every evening, with the Ducktown Squatters Blues Band appearing last. Roquefort, riding a low-wheeled dolly, was transported to the vaudeville theater each day at sundown and returned to his pool at night. Razmataz never missed a show, nor any of the rehearsals held during the day. Gisala decorated the little cottage, blessing the day they had left Philadelphia for good.

It is quite remarkable that the family could adjust so quickly to living some twenty feet over the broad swells of the Atlantic Ocean, half a mile at sea. They were not alone, as several other entertainers and members of the pier's staff lived in similar cottages, though much closer to land. Over three hundred people worked on the pier during the summer months and there formed a little world unto themselves. The good Creek family was readily accepted into that world. Minnie became the darling of the pier and quickly learned every nook and corner of the vast wooden structure, every man and woman, old or young, who drew his wages there. She had never been so happy.

The act became a sensation and was advertised all over the Eastern Seaboard as the only one of its kind. Though the audience was not familiar with the blues medium, it certainly took the musicians to its heart. Ben had decided at the onset that costumes were necessary, suggesting that they dress as ducks. Gisala and Minnie loved the idea, though Razmataz was not so sure. But in the end he complied and dutifully donned his outfit, which consisted of large yellow cardboard feet, an outsized set of long underwear with a pillow stuffed at the stomach, and many white duck feathers glued on. White wings were suspended from the shoulders and white skullcaps were worn. Roquefort who needed no such visual enhancement, wore only a red bow on his tail.

The summer ended with many offers to appear on the vaudeville circuit in other American cities, but these were rejected. Ben had become enamored of the beautiful place he lived in, with birds above and fish below. He looked forward to the coming winter, its peace and tranquility. In September, the day after Labor Day, he accepted the position of winter watchman for the pier. The wages were small, but room and board were provided free of charge. Razmataz went back to bar work, but dropped by often to rehearse new material.

Winter came, bringing with it the usual high seas and storms, but snug in their cottage the Creeks lived, worked and made music. Roquefort lay on his back in his pool, comfortable in the heated shack which had been hastily built over it.

Minnie was lonely. The transition from the summer life of endless friends to the barren winter days when no one came to the pier was a strain. She was still too young for school and there was little, at first, for her to do. She helped her father on his rounds, helped him feed the other animals on the pier, but this was not enough. She tried fishing, but this only made her more lonely. She ached for a companion, or in lieu of that, something meaningful to do.

She found it one day in January when a party of workmen, mechanics, came aboard the pier to make repairs on the roller coaster and other amusement machines. She watched the workmen's hands with fascination as they overhauled steam and gasoline engines, made adjustments on chain hauls, undercarriages and suspension systems. Her bright mind prompted questions, and these were answered with great patience and understanding. Minnie longed for tools of her own. She dreamed of working with grease-smeared hands over the oily surfaces of machines. For her birthday, in February, she asked for a set of wrenches, which were given her by her father, who wished to promote this new enthusiasm that so delighted his daughter. Soon she was often found tinkering with an old discarded engine used to pump water to the porpoise pool, now empty. At the age of six, when other girls were playing with dolls, Minnie often appeared for dinner with skinned knuckles and grease beneath her little fingernails.

And so the winter passed into spring and the pier became busy again. Signs were changed, billing the Ducktown Squatters Blues Band as the highest permanent attraction on Cook's Pier. It was vaudeville time again, and the band never played better. Minnie was given wages, which Ben kept for her, but she begged him for a part of them and Ben acquiesced. She wanted the money to buy more tools.

That summer, and the others that followed, flew by. The seasonal routine was established, the family prospered, the act grew in expertise, and Minnie became a mechanic, working at small wages by the time she was twelve. All went well until the fateful hurricane of 1914.

No one who lives in Absecon Island will ever forget the hurricane of '14, the worst since the monster in '95 that had washed Point Farm away. Each of us has his own vivid recollection of the events immediately preceding the storm, the little things we were doing or were about to do just before disaster struck. Minnie, only twelve at the time, was on the boardwalk hard at work on a crack-the-whip car coupling. Her parents were still in bed in their cottage on the end of the pier. It was late in September and the pier was closed for the long winter. A cold dry wind began to numb her little fingers as she struggled with the heavy castings. She decided to return home for her woolen gloves, which she had put away the previous spring. She put down her tools and entered the pier.

She could feel the pilings beneath her trembling under the onslaught of the waves. It was midday, but a mushroom-like cloud obscured the sun entirely and there was no light. The wind, which had blown hard for three days out of the south, suddenly died. Her ears ached as the atmospheric pressure changed abruptly. Walking, she tried to keep her mind off the furious and hostile elements.

Suddenly the pier shook as if slammed by an invisible roller coaster. Two or three shocks followed. Then the wind reappeared, but now from the north. Minnie knew something awful had happened. She began to run. Fear gripped her as she sped across the polished floor of the empty ballroom, raced through the damp and barren vaudeville theater, where an unfamiliar sound reached her ears. In the dim light from small windows high above she saw that a portion of the floor had given way, that a huge hole had appeared in the pier's deck, just before the stage. Looking down, she saw waves thrashing among barnacle-encrusted pilings just a little lower than where she stood.

Dodging the hole, she sped for the Game Room tunnel, which led to the Sea Circus at the end. The tunnel, long and gloomy, looked like the cargo hold of a ship thrown up on a reef. Coin-operated games lay smashed on the floor. Old Grandma the Fortuneteller stared at the ceiling, her turban askew, her hand moving across the cards.

Minnie reached the end, threw open the double doors and stopped abruptly. She was staring at the vague horizon.

Nothing was left. The entire end of the pier was gone, swept away by a freak series of waves. Her parents, their home, the croc house and the crocodile were somewhere in the boiling sea.

That is all Minnie remembers. Days later she recovered from the shock of the catastrophe and realized that she was an orphan, that life, as she knew it, had altered drastically. She was left with the clothes she wore and a small box of tools.

That was four years before we sat in my boat headed for Lakes Bay. In those four years she had seen many changes. Cook's Pier had kept her on. The entertainment manager had accepted responsibility for her upbringing. But, bitter over the cruel turn of events, she had drifted away. At the moment she was living under the boardwalk in a little hidden chamber Razmataz had helped her to build. She had found a boat, the little one I had destroyed, and was trying to get into clamming, to get into the bay and forget the fickle ocean for a while.

I felt an intense grief for little Minnie as she sat there, her hand on the tiller of my old outboard, telling me her tale in an offhand way. But I could see that she was strong, a tough little Atlantic City beach girl, as tough as they come.

"Minnie," I said, when she had finished and was staring at the shoreline, "some people get all the bad breaks when they get old, and some people get them when they are young. I think you've had yours. I think the rest of your life is going to be smooth and easy."

"Don't bet on it, bugsy," she said.

And I'm glad I didn't.

5

WE had no trouble convincing the Lakes Bay clammers that we were offering a better deal than DiOrio. We paid the same, but took over the cleaning end of it and, what was more important, we would pick up the clams right out there on the water. In one day we had lined up fifteen clammers who would work for us and us only.

We picked up and cleaned and delivered three thousand clams to Captain Starn that night. He paid cash and said to keep 'em coming. Of the fifteen dollars I gave Minnie three and pocketed the rest.

"What you gonna do with that twelve dollars?" she asked at our parting.

"Why, I'm going to *re-invest* it," I said. "That's the only way to get rich. You sink your profits back in the business. That's capitalism!"

"What end of this business you gonna sink it in?"

"*Desperado*. She's too small and she's too

111

slow. First thing I'm going to get is a new outboard motor, a ten-horsepower."

"You're gonna burn more gas."

"I'm going to get more clams."

Minnie grinned, then handed me back her three dollars.

"I'm proud of you, Minnie girl," I said. "You're part of the business."

"It's a loan, jerk. Twenty percent. See ya tomorrow morning." Saying that, she turned and walked away.

The next day Minnie and I ripped the cabin off my garvey so that she could hold more clams. I put in a culling rack at the bow so that Minnie could clean clams while I steered the way to Captain Starn's. We enlisted three more clammers that afternoon and had a full boat, a mountain of clams that I had to look over in order to see her.

Minnie could clean clams faster than anyone I had ever seen. She must have inherited her dexterity from her father, Ben Creek, who had laid bricks so fast, too fast. But she couldn't clean clams too fast for me. If there were any muddy ones left by the time we got to Starn's I had to help her with them, a job I disliked.

My end of it, as I viewed the situation, was

steering the boat. I was darn good at it. There is an art to keeping a loaded-down garvey on a straight course, to keep her level and running at maximum speed. I was beginning to put in hours of this every day and got better and better at it as I liked it more and more. I was saving all the profits, dreaming of that ten-horsepower.

In two weeks we had it, a bright new Evinrude right out of the crate. It started on the third pull. I had to run it slowly for a week, to break it in, but I could feel that reserve power just waiting for me to release it. But Minnie would glare at me if I took it just a hair above midspeed, and that was that. When that anxious week was over I cautiously opened her up.

We were empty, on our way to Lakes Bay. There was no wind and the water was flat, like oil on glass. It seemed like we were flying. Minnie sat in the bow to hold her down and we almost planed off. The wake behind looked chiseled, so perfect were the chine waves, so smooth the fluffy white water, like an ice-cream soda. Steering was different, and I had to learn anew the control that I thought I had mastered.

Minnie made a sign for me to cut the

motor. When I did she came aft with a screw-driver between her teeth. I went up to the bow to give her room. In a minute she had the cover off and was adjusting the two needle valves on the carburetor. She started the motor, idled it and listened. She took it up to midspeed and made an adjustment. She opened it up and made another. She frowned throughout, her lips set in concentration, her ear toward the exhaust. The motor was running beautifully when she returned it to my care. I thanked her kindly.

"Big deal," was what she said.

We were cleaning up out there on Lakes Bay. With the garvey's new speed we could make two runs a day, necessary now that we had more than twenty boats working for us. And I began to yearn for a bigger boat.

I went up to the Eberding Boat Works one night and cornered my old friend Ebby, who was carving a duck decoy. I noticed a funny thing about the model he was making. The head was turned to the side. I had never seen a duck decoy with its head turned that way. I asked him why he had done it.

"Well, just take a look at ducks," he said. "They ain't always lookin' straight ahead. Sometimes they're lookin' all over the place."

"Maybe so," I said.

"The only ducks always lookin' straight on is the ducks in your head, the *ideal* ducks. But they ain't *real* ducks. Real ducks don't measure up to the ideal ones, but they taste a whole lot better."

"Where did you get an idea like that?" I asked.

"Plato."

"Plato who?"

"Yer Uncle Plato, boy. Now what's on your mind?"

I told him I wanted a garvey, a bigger, lighter garvey than *Desperado*, which was tethered to his dock. He went outside with me to have a look.

"I want one longer and wider and deeper," I said.

"*Sure* you do! You want to get more *clams*, is what you want."

"I want to get more clams."

"Oh, I heard all about you and Minnie out there on Lakes Bay. You're makin' it hand over fist!"

"Yup."

"Let me ask you something. What you gonna do when the summer's over? You

115

thought about that? What you gonna do when Captain Starn closes down?"

"I hadn't thought about that."

"Nope."

"What am I gonna do?"

"You're gonna have to find a new market, and you know where that is? Philadelphia!"

"How would I get them to Philadelphia? On the train?"

"Train don't run but once a week in the winter."

"Truck."

"Yup. You're gonna need a truck like old man DiOrio's got. You're gonna need a Reo."

"I haven't got the money," I said.

"You still want the boat?"

"Yes, sir."

"Well, I could build you what you want. Make her twenty foot by five, half-inch cedar."

"Half-inch seems awfully thin."

"She'll live half as long, but she'll go twice as fast."

"Build her," I said.

I talked to Minnie the next morning about the truck, about Philadelphia.

116

"I don't want to have nothin' to do with Philadelphia," she said.

"Neither do I."

"Maybe we can get someone to come down here and pick 'em up."

"I doubt it."

"So do I."

"We have a lot to learn, Minnie. We have to learn to distinguish between the real and the ideal."

"Plato," she said.

You just never could figure out what that girl was going to say next. I knew she was very intelligent, for a girl.

Ebby had the garvey ready by early August. Sixty dollars she cost me, about five days of clamming. I was not worried about the winter as I sat at the stern and took her out for her first shakedown cruise. Right away I was disappointed. She went slower than *Desperado*. I had planned to go a whole lot faster.

"I need a new motor," I said.

"Well, what did ya expect, fathead? You're pushin' a whole lot more through the water."

The largest outboard motor made at the time was a twenty-five-horsepower. They were expensive and I'd only seen one of them in my life. But I knew old Larry Englehard,

117

down in Longport, could get me one if I had the money.

"Nobody's ever put a twenty-five on a garvey," said Minnie.

"Nope. It's never been done."

"Pound the bottom out."

"Maybe."

We had to put that motor off for a while. Running slow, we worked twice as hard as before. But our big hold held twice as many clams, and the money was pouring in. We had more clams than we could clean, and Minnie suggested that we employ someone to help us. She didn't suggest it, she said I damn well better get somebody or she was quitting. Minnie threatened to quit at least once a day, but now I knew she meant it. I told her to find someone, and the next day she turned up with Razmataz.

Raz, as we called him, was the first colored man I ever got to know. Atlantic City was about twenty-five percent colored at the time, which was more than New York or Philadelphia, but I lived down in Margate, where there was none. I liked him the minute I met him. He said he had never been in a boat, nor had he cleaned a clam, but he was willing to try. We shoved off with him riding up on the bow.

He and Minnie loaded clams all day, cleaned them all afternoon on the trips up the the Inlet. They worked fast and they sang as they worked:

"I saw you on the boardwalk, baby," sang Razmataz.

"You were with another man," sang Minnie.

"You were wearin' the dress I bought you."

"He was holdin' your little hand."

"Well, I almost fell off the railin'."

"I almost jumped into the sea."

"I never saw you strut that way."

"When all you had was me."

I'd never heard words to a song like that. Minnie said it was the blues, and I thought sadly about the Ducktown Squatters Blues Band. I imagined Roquefort honking out, right on key, which was difficult.

Raz never missed a day, and business was booming. Summer was going to last forever and clams would always be on demand. In mid-August I got my twenty-five. It was a monster. It took the two of us, Razmataz and I, to lift it and set it in place on the transom.

Two motors and a new boat all in one summer! I amazed myself.

I suffered through the second running-in period, but it passed quickly. At halfspeed we were doing better than we had in old *Desperado* with the ten. When Minnie had tuned the twenty-five I opened it up.

We planed! That is to say, the boat leaped right out of the water and instead of pushing through it she rode right on the surface. It pounded like heck, but I was confident that she would take it. Steering was hard. She turned in big circles, skimming sideways across the bay, just missing docks and channel markers. But in a little while I had it down. With a full load of clams we must have been making fifteen knots or better. This was an astounding speed for those days, and the clammers stopped their work as we flew by. They shook their heads, and some of them, the older ones, called us daredevils and cowboys. Among themselves they agreed that a boat just wasn't meant to go that fast, that I was destroying a fine Walt Eberding garvey by overpowering her. Of course they never said any of that to my face, not right out. They were too busy selling me clams.

There was one thing about high speed over

the water that took some getting used to. That was the infernal pounding that went right through the bottom into our bones, our teeth and our brains. If the bay was flat it was not so bad. But if there was a chop it was Hades, to be sure, at wide-open throttle. Raz and Minnie used to beg me to hold her down, but I never could.

I was into speed! It may have been partially the business end of it, the fact that I had to make two and sometimes three long-distance runs every day, through a bay that twisted and turned along sandbars and marsh banks, through narrow channels and under bridges. But the pure challenge of keeping her on a true course, of taking her through hairpin turns with ease, excited me no end. Also, back where I was sitting just a few inches forward of the transom, there was little pounding, as that part of the boat was always in the water. Minnie and Raz had to stay well forward to keep the bow down, to keep air from getting under us, or there was the danger of flipping over backward. This nearly happened once.

We were tearing out of Great Bay behind Brigantine, the next island to the north of us. We were all in the stern for some reason, unloaded. The wind was against us, and blew a cold spray in our faces every time we hit a chop. I had her opened up. The tide was low, and the wind had kicked up the water somewhat. Suddenly the bow went up, straight up, and pointed at the sky. I killed the motor and she slapped back down the right way. I never forgot it, and from then on we kept weight in the bow.

I taught Minnie and Raz how to stand rather than sit, to take the shock of the pounding in their legs, which they kept slightly bent. This helped a lot and I stopped getting so many complaints. But there were always complaints, especially from Minnie.

Minnie could really complain. Nothing was ever perfect for her, as if anything was *ever* perfect. Most of the time she had that frown on her face, particularly when speaking with me. Speaking, or having a nice conversation with me, was nearly impossible for her. Mostly she preferred to argue. But it really didn't mean anything, it was just words. She liked what she was doing, or else she wouldn't be doing it. She liked me well enough, or else she wouldn't be in my boat. I would catch her smiling sometimes as we roared along with a boatload of clams, and I would smile back, try to make her laugh. Then she would frown and turn away, shrug her shoulders like I was just a fool. But I knew.

Minnie had suffered a great tragedy at a tender age. She felt that God and man were against her. She felt that there was no one she could really talk to about these things because no one else had experienced them, or so she thought. I always had Pumpkin or Dad to talk to, and I could converse with them at length on any subject and feel better when I had. Minnie had nobody, not even me. Our relationship seemed to be stabilized at skipper-crew, and that was the way it worked best. But there was always that distance between us. Sometimes she would laugh and cut up with Razmataz, but seldom with me. Well, my mind was on other things. Usually.

Like everybody else's, my mind was on me, mostly. I was having my first taste of success and prosperity. I could see no end to it. I dreamed of a clam empire, one that would take me right to the top. But where was the top?

The tallest hotel in Atlantic City was a place called the Union. At the top was a kind of balcony they used to call a widow's walk, a place for the wives of lost sea captains to maintain a vigil, though the one on the Union was purely decorative. Pumpkin had taken me up there once when I was very young. She had wanted me to gain perspective, to see how the world I was growing into went on and on. One evening I went up there again, alone.

Six stories high she was, a man-made promontory on an island as flat as a desert. The Union was the closest thing we had to a mountain, and a mountain is what I needed. I was dressed up like a paying guest and walked right up to the top by the main stairs. A few tourist couples, honeymooners I guess, were up there, but they left me alone. I was a little dizzy from the height, but when that passed I took a good look around. To the south was my end of the island. I could see the elephant, the Point, the Great Egg Harbor Inlet and Peck Beach, the next island down. I could see the bay, pastel by sunset, languidly twisting toward me, shooting off hundreds of channels and creeks into the marshes. My eyes followed it up the coast and north, to the Absecon inlet, to Brigantine, where a sailing ship of that type had gone aground some years before. The bay, the ocean, those waterways to the unknown, went on forever. But Atlantic City did not. This island all around me; this was the world I meant to conquer. How hard could it be?

Below me was Pennsylvannia Avenue, where the richest of the rich had built stately summer cottages, some of them with more than twenty rooms. It ended at the boardwalk, crowded that summer evening with strollers, boys and girls on bicycles, people being pushed along in rolling chairs. Amusement piers jutted from the boardwalk into the sea, the beaches between them empty now that night was approaching. What did it all mean?

It meant money. To the man who was lining his pockets with tourist greenbacks, it meant a lot of money, more and more of it every summer. I reckoned that I'd sold enough clams in the last two months to give a hatful to every man, woman and child that I could see. And I had been clearing about three cents on the hatful. If there was a king of Atlantic City, was I not already a prince?

I tried to imagine who that king might be, where he lived in the city below me. It was beyond my scope. I had never met a rich man, had never been inside a rich man's house. But he was down there, I was sure. Maybe it had been he who had built the boardwalk. God made the ocean, the island and the bay; but *somebody* had nailed down a forest of planks. Penny a nail, dime a plank? What was he doing with all that money?

Then it dawned on me that *I* was the king of Atlantic City. There I was, up higher than anybody in town, money in my pocket and a boat in the bay. Young and fresh as a racehorse in the middle of his first race. I had never been so healthy, so glad to be alive. I could have anything I wanted, anything I could see down there. But what did I want?

The answer was not there below me. I did not want a pier or a hotel. I did not want to live on Pennsylvania Avenue, or spend my time walking the boardwalk and saying silly things to blushing girls. No, there was something else I wanted, something more than money could buy. But for the life of me I could not say what that thing was.

The stars appeared above me, one by one. Their light was reflected on the darkening sea like diamonds tossed carelessly onto a black beach. A steam calliope from some dizzy carousel whistled a ragtime tune while I watched my honky-tonk world put on evening dress and step out for a night of seaside carnival.

I walked down with more questions than when I had walked up.

I strolled south on the boardwalk, my hands in my back pockets. I bought a hot dog and an ice-cream cone, sat on the railing and looked around. People dress well for the boardwalk, and the ladies, many of them, looked elegant. Their hats and dresses were from Philadelphia and New York, their accents strange. The men who escorted them looked happy and prosperous, each with a long cigar and straw hat. No one looked my way. Talking and laughing, they looked at things in shop windows, fed the pigeons, hailed their friends as they passed. I sat there for over an hour wondering how and if I would ever fit into all that. I left when a policeman told me to move along.

Summer was quickly drawing to a close, and I had still to reckon with the problems the winter would surely present. We were working harder than ever in order to build up some capital. One evening, as I drew up to the dock at Captain Starn's, there were two men waiting for me, a policeman and Mr. DiOrio.

DiOrio pointed to the small mountain of clams in my boat, and the policeman made a note in his notebook. He looked at me with his pencil in his hand.

"Garvey Leek?"

"Yes, sir."

"Let's see your license."

"I don't have one. I didn't know you had to have one."

DiOrio laughed loudly at this, saying I'd been cheating him and the city all summer. The policeman explained nicely that I was required to have a mercantile license, which was applied for at City Hall. In the meantime I could not sell my clams to Captain Starn or anyone else who did not have a license. That left DiOrio, who was a wholesaler. It turned out that his end of the business was closely controlled and taxed. I was given a summons to appear in court the next day.

DiOrio bought my load of clams for the old penny a dozen and we had to sort through them for ones too big or too small, but at least we broke even. He chuckled the whole time we were going through the clams, and I tried not to hate the man. Minnie kept her mouth shut. The two of them ignored each other.

The next morning I was at City Hall with Dad. I was charged with operating a business without a license and ordered to disclose how much money I had made. The only way I could figure it was by how much I had, a hundred and twenty dollars cash, a new boat and motor. I had to pay the city the hundred and twenty for taxes. I had to give over my boat and motor to DiOrio for damages. Dad and I were real quiet the whole time. He had warned me: Never open your mouth in a court of law; it just makes things worse.

Dad was looking for DiOrio after the trial, but I pulled him out and walked him over to Dutchy Muldoon's. At the bar was my old friend from the Coast Guard, Captain Frye. He was drinking boilermakers and he bought Dad a beer, me a glass of milk as that was all I wanted. He listened to our story, shaking his head.

"It's all sewn up, you see?" he said when we had finished. "DiOrio's got the only license on the island. He paid for it."

"Well," I said, "I'll pay for mine."

"You don't understand. He *paid* for it. He paid them off."

It sunk in. It was a fix. I was up against DiOrio and City Hall, an unbeatable combination.

I felt awful. I left Dad to get drunk with Captain Frye and Dutchy, found Minnie by the railroad bridge where I had told her to wait. Razmataz had disappeared the day before, at the first sight of the policeman, and was not there. She got in my boat and sat in the bow facing me as we moved smoothly into Beach Thorofare. I told her what had happened.

She sat there leaning back on the coaming, her legs spread, her hands thrust in the pockets of her jeans. She kept nodding her head as if it had all happened the way she knew it would.

"So where we goin' now, Clyde?" she asked.

I told her that DiOrio had demanded delivery of the boat at the old Causeway Boat Works, where he planned to pull her out of the water and caulk and paint her.

It was our last cruise, and I wanted to go slowly, but I could not. I took her all the way up and danced that boat from one side of the bay to the other. Darn it, I was proud of myself; proud and ashamed at the same time.

In one summer I had built my way up to this boat, the fastest garvey on the bay. And only to lose it to a snake like DiOrio.

I ran over the wake of a passing sportfisherman and my boat leaped out of the water. Spray flew and Minnie laughed. I laughed too. It was all like such an old joke. We could not look in each other's eyes.

That low-down skunk DiOrio was sitting in his truck when we arrived at the abandoned and defunct Causeway Boat Works. At one time they had built big pound boats there but it had not worked and they were gone, up the coast, to Sea Bright. Now this old bandit was going to haul my boat on her old railway and use the dock space to do his work.

I could not think what to say to a man who had played me such a dirty, miserable trick as he had. DiOrio had let me go on all summer long, knowing that in the end he would get everything. I tied up my boat and started to leave, my back to the rat.

"Hey, give me a hand, Garvey boy," he said.

I kept my back to him, shook my head.

"Might wreck it if I do it alone," he said.

Minnie looked at me with disgust as I turned back to help him. I could not have

131

stood it if he had hurt that boat. I knew he would sell it as soon as he got it caulked and painted. He would sell it to somebody who knew boats, who would take care of her. I had to help him.

There was a long wooden ramp, half rotted away, that led down from the dock to the water. On it were rusted-out railroad tracks and the remnants of the winch. DiOrio backed his truck down the ramp, set the brake and got out with a heavy rope over his shoulder. He could hardly keep from laughing. He tied one end of the rope to his rear axle and the other to the bowring in the garvey. I put an old rotted roller under her bow to make it easier.

"This ought to teach you a lesson, boy," he said.

"What's that—what lesson's that, Mr. DiOrio?"

"Not to get too big for your britches."

"I'll remember that," I said. "I'll remember you said that."

"Another thing. Teach you not to fool around with that girl, Minnie. Brought you nothin' but trouble, she did."

I did not know where Minnie was, but I was glad she had not heard that. Rage boiled

132

within me, but I kept it under control. I was not afraid of him. He was just an old man with hair growing out of his nose and ears. I was afraid of myself, what I might do or say that I would regret. You have to show a certain amount of respect for old people, no matter what they are like. I held my tongue.

It worked. He got back in his truck and put it in gear. I watched my beautiful new boat hauled up the ramp. I could have cried.

Halfway he stopped so that I could put the roller back under the bow. While I was struggling with it he did not lose the chance to further taunt me. He got out again, came back to me and looked under the boat.

"Caulkin's pounded right out of her," he said.

"This here's the fastest garvey on the bay," I replied.

"Yeah," he said. "I ought to get a good price for her. Wrong time of the year, though. Maybe I'll wait for the spring."

Just then we heard an unfamiliar sound, a clunk coming from the direction of DiOrio's truck. We looked up and the Reo was moving. The boat was moving too, back down the ramp toward the bay.

The old man made a dive for the cab,

climbed in. I watched boat and truck moving steadily toward the water. DiOrio put it in gear, eased out the clutch. But it was too late. His rear wheels were on the bottom end of the ramp, which was covered with slippery bay weed. The wheels spun, but the truck kept moving backward. DiOrio got out at the last moment.

My boat, refloated, was just missed by the end of the truck as it rolled off the ramp into about eight feet of water. Nothing, not even the top of the cab, showed. Little bubbles came up for a while, and then nothing.

DiOrio, his wits addled by this unfortunate turn of events, seemed to think it was my fault. Shaking his fists, he came for me. But when his boots hit the bay grass he lost his balance and slid off the ramp. I figured this was a good time to leave and wasted no time scurrying up to the dock.

Minnie was up there laughing her head off. I tried to get her going, but she made me turn around and have another look. DiOrio had just hauled himself out of the water and was trying to crawl up the ramp. But he kept sliding back, all the way back into the bay. Finally, after trying two or three more times, he swam around to a ladder. Minnie and I got going.

We were jogging down the dirt road that led from the boat works to the causeway, laughing like mad angels. I kept looking back, but the old man never appeared. We stopped to catch our breath when we got to the main road.

Minnie stuck our her hand.

"Garv," she said, "it's been a pleasure doing business with you. We didn't make much money, but we sure did have a lot of fun."

I looked at her hand. It was greasy.

"Obsolete machine," she said, blinking her big blue eyes. "Chain-drive Reo."

"I always preferred the Ford," I said.

6

ISTILL had *Desperado*. She was on the mud and full of water when Minnie and I came by McGaragil's dock a few days later. I bailed her out and clamped the old three-horsepower to her transom, laughed aloud when it started on the first pull. I sat up in the bow with Minnie and played a little game with that old outboard as it warmed up.

"Great motor," I said. With that the engine stopped whistling. I threw it a kiss.

"Never let me down," I said. It stopped coughing.

"Runs like a Singer sewing-machine," I added. The outboard revved, all on its own.

"Smoothest-running motor on the bay." It began to purr.

"See that, Minnie? Motors are like dogs. They love praise. If ever I get trouble from this one I just have to tell it what a wonderful and noble machine it is. Then it fixes itself. From pride."

"Bull roar," said Minnie Creek.

We tried our hand at eeling that fall, but

our hearts were not into it. I could only raise enough money for three eel pots, and we never caught enough eels to make it worthwhile. We did not like eels and nobody we knew liked eels, but there was a local eel industry made up of out-of-season clammers like us. Once a week a man came down from New York with a truck full of empty barrels and left with his barrels full of eels. What he did with them we did not know, but the rumor was they were shipped to France and sold at high prices.

Minnie got a job in a garage in Atlantic City, and I only saw her from time to time. She would turn up at McGaragil's early in the morning and we would go for a ride on the bay. But boats and cold water are not much fun. Our meetings became less frequent as the weather grew colder.

It was a hard winter for me. I had no job, nor did I want one. I had resolved to work only for myself, but none of the ideas I came up with paid off. I would put in a day or two with Dad, sinking jetties, but it was too much for me. I was not made the way Dad was and tired easily. Mostly I stayed home in the elephant, reading books Pumpkin brought from the library. Pumpkin's hot-dog stand had been a success. She had money right up until the trouble that came in March.

In March my sister, Pumpkin, was tried as a witch in Ventnor. I would say that hers was the last witch trial in the United States, though there may have been others. Her trial was certainly a circus.

It is odd that this travesty of justice had an immediate effect on all of our future lives. Fate works in strange ways, and it was Pumpkin's trial which marked the beginning of a career I had never dreamed of.

Pumpkin was on her way home from the Atlantic City Public Library with a bag of books over her shoulder. She was on the beach and it was low tide, cold and barren. It was about noon when she reached Little Rock Avenue in Ventnor, and she sat down there to rest.

Behind her, living in a brick house a few yards from the bulkhead, was an old woman, sick, lonely and rich. She had never married, but the word was she had lived in sin with her chauffeur for twelve years before he took off for Florida with her car and some of her jewelry. Her new chauffeur was a woman. The two of them were sitting on the sunporch regarding the beach, which they considered their private domain, especially in the winter. If ever there was anything to complain about on the beach in front of the brick house, they wasted no time in calling the police. The police had to be very nice with them, as they paid the city a lot of money in taxes. That day Pumpkin gave them something to get upset about.

As I have said, Pumpkin was a great dancer in spite of her bulky proportions. She walked heavily, but when she danced she might have been a trim little girl. Dancing freed her mind from her body. She was like another person, one totally absorbed with wild and reckless liberty, dancing unseen on a windy beach, wailing, screaming with the gulls overhead. But that day she was being watched carefully.

A mossbunker boat was working the shoreline, quite close in. Pumpkin, who had dropped her heavy coat and big housedress, was dancing naked and did not see it. But the captain on the boat saw Pumpkin with his binoculars and steered the boat in for a closer look.

The old ladies were already dialing for the police to tell them a big fat girl was desecrating their beach when a curious thing happened.

The sun came out from behind a gray cloud for the first time that day, a hot sun that burned with noontime intensity and lit the sand silver all around her. The wind stopped howling and even the sea seemed to settle slightly. Pumpkin danced with her eyes closed, feeling the heat of the sun like a summer day suddenly dropped down in March. Swinging her arms and spinning gaily across the hard low tide sand, she danced for the rare beauty of all natural phenomenae such as this. She did not question the weather, as it had often played kind tricks on her and she was used to the unexpected.

But at sea the bunker boat was having trouble. Her Gardner engine suddenly quit, leaving her only a little way outside the breakers. The captain quickly ordered an anchor thrown over, but it would not hold in the fine sand bottom. The swells pushed her toward the shore at the place where Pumpkin danced.

The old ladies paused in disbelief, watching the girl, the naughty naked girl, lure the boat onto the beach. They watched her part the clouds with her hands, chase the pesky gulls with her kicking legs. They heard the boat strike the sandbar with a deadly crunch. Then they made the call.

When the policeman arrived, nothing had changed. Pumpkin, oblivious to all, was dancing by the water's edge. Forty feet away, four fisherman and their captain were wading through the surf shouting curses at her. Their boat was just beginning to break up. The wheelhouse had already fallen into the sea. The same eerie light lit the scene, the same quiet air lay heavy and hot over all.

The old ladies came running from the house declaring they had seen a witch act, that Pumpkin had been trifling with the devil down there, that she was a demon, a Circe, a Siren, and had caused disaster to honest fisherfolk. The police had only to look for themselves to see the witch in her frenzy.

Hating the fine white sand that filled their shiny black shoes, the Ventnor policemen trudged across the beach, hands on their guns. The fishermen met them, told them a story similar to the one they had just heard. They had been at sea, fishing, when suddenly came an abrupt change in the weather. Looking in at the beach, they thought they saw a beautiful naked woman dancing, with sea-gulls flying around her head. With that, their boat began to make its way over the water toward the figure on the beach. There was nothing they could do to halt or alter its progress. The girl had pointed their way, and as she did, their engine stopped. When they were beached and close enough for a good look they discovered it was not a beautiful sea nymph at all. It was just an extremely fat woman dancing, wearing nothing but a green turban. Her metaphysical powers were undeniable.

Pumpkin continued to dance close by. The men, showing caution, stood back and called to her. But my sister's eyes were closed, her mind was sealed to anything but its own song. She did not stop even when one of the policemen discharged his revolver in the air.

Finally, one of the fishermen waded out to the wreck and returned with a bucket of cold seawater. Waiting until she whirled by, he threw the water.

Pumpkin stopped, opened her eyes. The boat was groaning on the bar. The fishermen and policemen were gawking, standing in a circle around her. The two old ladies were on the bulkhead waving their fists.

Calmly she found her housedress and pulled it on. She rewound her turban, which had come loose, and pinned it in front with a silver star and crescent moon. She put on her coat, hefted her bag of books and began to walk toward Longport.

The policemen stopped her, told her she was under arrest. The fishermen, very superstitious, stood to one side, chanting, "Witch, witch!"

Pumpkin could have saved herself, and she tried. She argued with the policemen and answered the fishermen. But she was unnerved by the suddenness with which she had found herself surrounded, and her words came out in classical Arabic, a language she spoke with studied fluency. This only caused more confusion. She was wet now and cold; the sun had retreated permanently and the wind had returned. Suffering a chill, she began to shiver, and this further affected the peculiarity of her speech. The men backed away from her.

She moved south down the beach, and the men moved with her, keeping the circle. The old ladies called the dogcatcher.

The dogcatcher arrived in his mule-drawn wagon, bearing a large wire cage and two hoop nets. He ran to the scene, holding one of the nets. The men on the beach welcomed his arrival.

When Pumpkin saw the net the fight went out of her. She sank to her knees in the sand and cried. The dogcatcher threw the hoop over her and the men came closer. The policemen ordered her to stand and follow them. She obeyed.

Pumpkin walked up to the bulkhead with the net over her, the metal hoop banging her knees. She walked to the police car among the silent men, the staring old women. They made her get inside the car, hoop and all.

The police chief in Ventnor City Hall tried to interrogate her, but in her utter despair she was unable to answer his questions coherently. They locked her up in a foul cell in the basement.

Dad began to worry about her when she missed dinner, a rarity. After eating he set out on the rusty old bicycle to find her. It took him most of the evening to track her down. She was released into his custody, and they walked home together, nearly freezing to death. Pumpkin was ordered to appear in court the following Tuesday night, trial night in Ventnor.

On Monday night Dad came home from an evening at Dutchy Muldoon's in an excited state. He was at his loudest and most overbearing stage of intoxication and spoke to us with a sense of infallibility.

"Pumpkin, my dear," he said, "your problems are over."

Pumpkin's only problem at that moment was a decision between the cherry cheesecake and the banana cake which Mamma May had made for her. She put a bite of each on her fork and eyed Dad.

"All of our problems, all of our petty anxieties, are illusions, Daddy. We are shadows living in a world of shadows."

"Well, I just wish your shadow wasn't going on trial in Ventnor tomorrow night," said Dad. "It's just a good thing your old daddy has rallied around you, is all. Because this particular illusion just vanished, so to speak."

Dad held up a thick finger, winked, grinned, coughed for half a minute straight, found his breath and whispered, "The fix is in!"

Pumpkin's eyebrows met in a suspicious frown. She gave me a look that said we might just have a whole set of new illusions to deal with.

"The fix is in, daughter, and that's that. I have had dealings with the judge."

"You paid him off?" I asked.

"We made a deal. Now listen. The guns of Ventnor are loaded for Pumpkin. And this is straight from the judge himself, who allowed me to buy for him more than one boilermaker at Dutchy's on this very day. Right now Pumpkin stands charged with disturbing the peace, a very small misdemeanor, five-dollar fine, which I have just paid in full, or almost."

"You paid off a judge for five dollars?"

"I paid him three-fifty and he gets the rest next week."

"Daddy," said Pumpkin, sighting him with her fork, "I am mildly curious about a five-dollar payoff. I can't help wondering what kind of justice five dollars can buy."

"Darn right you are! But you got to hear something else first. See, those people—the two old bags and the mossbunkers—are going to change the charge!"

Dad now dropped his voice to his very loud whisper.

"They got themselves a lawyer! When the

facts are in, when the testimony has been made, that lawyer is going to request a change of charges . . ."

"Change to what?"

"Thaumaturgy!"

"What's thaumaturgy?" I demanded.

"Magic," said Pumpkin. "Miracles."

"There is no law against magic," I said.

"There is in Ventnor!" said Dad. "It's an old law, but it's still in the books. Those people mean to brand Pumpkin here as a necromancer! When they do that they'll turn around and instigate a civil suit. If she's found guilty of thaumaturgy she's liable for damages to that damned boat! Thousands of dollars. But I put a stop to them. I fixed it all."

Pumpkin waved her finger in a circle above her head, a signal to Mamma May to bring coffee, which she did.

"It's all set, Pumpkin," he said. "You're going to plead guilty to disturbing the peace! You're going to do it before they can change the charges! Soon as you say the word, down comes the gavel, guilty as charged, and it's all over. You can never be charged for it again. Double jeopardy! You're off the hook!"

147

Pumpkin shook her head and sipped her coffee.

"What's the matter?" asked Dad.

"I won't do it," said Pumpkin. "I am not guilty. I was not disturbing the peace. I was alone on a public beach in the winter. I was dancing and I was a lot more peaceful than those old biddies by the bulkhead or those men out there murdering fish! They disturbed my peace."

"You don't want to stand trial for thaumaturgy, do you?"

"I'd rather be found guilty of magic than plead guilty to a lie."

"But think of the cost! There'll have to be a new trial. Then a civil suit. And you'll be judged guilty by the people even if you win. You'll be guilty of being charged with witchcraft! You think you could ever live that down?"

Pumpkin sighed, shifted her weight. A pigeon flew into the living room, and we all looked at it for a moment. Dad sat there breathing hard and clicking his false teeth. At last my sister spoke.

"That's not very much justice for five dollars."

"Three-fifty down," Dad reminded her.

"That's just about the worst fix I ever heard of. You just paid my judge to find me guilty."

"Well, you don't think of it like that, daughter. I fixed it so you're not guilty of something worse."

"Well, I won't have it. I'm innocent and that's what I'll tell them. I'll tell them what real peace is. I'll tell them how to find true peace with a pure heart and a heavenly mind. I'll tell them what those people did to my peace. I'll countercharge them! I'm not going to accept this, Daddy. I'm sorry you're out your three-fifty and all that booze."

This gave me an idea. Dad gave up and went to bed, but I tossed my idea around inside my head half the night. I could see Dad's point. If Pumpkin were actually accused of witchcraft she would lose no matter how the trial came out. And there was a very real chance that she would be found guilty, because the truth of it was that Pumpkin was a bit of a magician. Many of the things she believed in were highly suspicious at the time. If they got her to talk in front of all those people she would convict herself. I had to do something, and I thought I knew what that something was. In the morning I made a visit to Ventnor which I told no one about. We all went to court that night.

Everyone was there. Me, Dad, Mamma May, the fishermen, the old ladies, the dog-catcher, the entire twelve-man Ventnor Beach Patrol and half the population of the city. It was a witch hunt and no doubt about it.

When Pumpkin pled innocent the judge stole a look at Dad. Dad shrugged and the judge sighed. He could have ended it right there had she gone along with the fix, but now there had to be testimony. The captain was called to the chair.

The captain had lost his boat in the worst way he could have, running aground. His reputation and license were at stake, and he was determined to place all the responsibility on Pumpkin. The way he told it, she had drawn him, his boat and its crew onto the bar with her evil and unseen powers, which could be felt but not seen. He described her dervish dance and the guttural curses she had hurled at him and his men. He spoke at length about the unexplainable sudden change in the weather, the light and the atmosphere.

No one laughed during his speech. The crowd became somewhat unruly when the old ladies, the dogcatcher and the policemen took the stand, one after the other, to back up the captain's story. Then all the witnesses had been called and it was time for the accused, my poor sister, Pumpkin, to be sworn in.

Dad and I knew that as soon as she had completed her testimony there would be a formal request for a change in charges. Then that awful word would be spoken and her life would be changed for good. I hoped my timing would be right.

The judge very politely asked Pumpkin to explain her actions on that day. Pumpkin held up a book. It was bound in green leather and there were words in gold on the cover. The words were in Arabic symbols and the book was the Koran. The crowd grew silent.

"This is peace," said Pumpkin. "This is the only peace there is. From this book I obtain the ability to endure. Allow me to read, if you will—"

At that moment several things happened. First, up jumped some spectators who did not want to be read to from Pumpkin's book, which looked very different from those that could be found in the Ventnor Public Library. To begin with, it opened backward. Arabic is read from right to left, but only Pumpkin and I knew that. Up jumped some spectators with raised fists and stamping feet. The judge banged his gavel and Pumpkin raised her voice. I could only hear snatches of her reading, and they were all about hell. The Koran, I always thought, dealt unnecessarily hard on the subject of hell, even more so than the Bible. The Koran is also very repetitious in parts, and Pumpkin had chosen one of those parts.

"And the Prophet has said that those who do not believe shall suffer the unmentionable agonies . . ."

More people were on their feet, and there was danger of an outright riot. The judge was standing, the policemen were fondling their bullets. Pumpkin, in a high-pitched voice that began to sound like a cackle, made some sounds which had never been heard in Ventnor. Mothers covered their children's ears. Men drowned her out with their voices. Just then the big double doors in the back of the courtroom flew open.

In trooped the full force of the Ventnor Ladies' Patrol for a Dry America. Eighteen of the city's most influential women, all of them over seventy, marched down the center aisle carrying hand-lettered placards reading "Down with Drink," "No More Booze," and

"Ethel (Alcohol) Is Not a Lady." In their shrill and fervent voices they chanted their slogans while advancing on the judge. Their leader, Mrs. Fitzsimmons, addressed the judge, her son-in-law.

"We're here to present new evidence, Jerry, so just sit down."

The judge, Pumpkin and everybody else sat down to listen to the new evidence.

"The Ventnor Ladies' Patrol for a Dry America has uncovered the true and piteous story behind these sordid affairs. The poor girl is not to be held responsible for her actions the other day, and here's why."

Mrs. Fitzsimmons lowered her voice after a dramatic pause. "We have it from a private and reliable source that on the day of these events that poor child was given drink in Dutchy Muldoon's Saloon. Against her will. She was thirsty from the long walk from her home to the bar. She'd gone there to collect her father. Some masher put gin in her orange juice."

There came a gasp from the crowd, especially the women. Mrs. Fitzsimmons continued.

"It was booze that drove her to the beach where she could hide her shame. It was booze that made her dance. And as sure as that man is a fisherman it was booze that sent his ship upon the shore!"

One of the ladies shook an empty amber whiskey bottle at the captain, yelling, "Save yourself from the bottle!"

"The only devil in this room is that old demon rum!" shouted another.

"She's a child of drink, Jerry," said Mrs. Fitzsimmons. "She's more to be pitied than censured."

The crowd began to murmur, the people began to think. Ventnor people are not fools. It dawned on them that they had heard some very strange testimony. It was one thing to call someone a witch. It was another to believe in witchcraft. It was a lot easier to accept the fact that Pumpkin and probably the captain were drunk. At last someone began to laugh.

People grinned and shook their heads knowingly. The judge threw up his hands. The Ventnor Ladies' Patrol formed a circle around my sister and sang a wordy song called "Please Don't Sell My Daddy No More Wine." Some of the people joined in. I nudged Dad and he nudged me back.

Mamma May, who thought she was in church, got down on her knees.

And there stood Pumpkin with her book. She wanted to go on, to tell the truth, but they would not let her. The Ventnor Ladies' Patrol for a Dry America yelled and shook their signs. The judge slammed his gavel, missed the wooden block and smashed his water pitcher. But he too was laughing.

He found her guilty of disturbing the peace, a common charge brought for drunkenness. He did it with a smile and a knowing wink to the court, Dad and me. Only Pumpkin was furious. During the only pause in the yelling she approached the judge with an extended forefinger. Her eyes were wide.

"You know," she said, "I can make a wart grow on the end of your nose."

The hilarity was complete when the judge ducked away from her finger, laughed and called for the next case. The trial was over.

I never told Pumpkin that it was I who had called in the Prohibition ladies. It might very well have been someone else. But I knew that if she had known the truth she would have classed me right along with Dad. Her father, after all, had paid off a judge to find her guilty. And her brother had set her up as a drunk. But as it was, things turned out for the best. The people forgave her and no one ever thought about magic in Ventnor again.

Pumpkin took it all well, and we were laughing on the way home. When we got to the elephant she grew serious.

"The beach," she said, "is a free place. You should be able to do anything you want on the beach. Even get drunk."

"Nope," said Dad, "not anymore."

It was true. The island had grown in the past decade. Beachfront homes lined the bulkhead in Ventnor and were appearing now in Margate. Lifeguards patrolled the surf in the summer, and there were restrictions against dogs and other animals. Most of the dunes had been leveled, and there was a wooden jetty every block or so, all the way to Longport. It was no longer our private world, and Pumpkin had paid a high price for not realizing this. She was well into her forties by then and had no friends. She had grown to love the privacies of winter Margate, but they were deceptive. Ready and waiting to pounce were new people, rich people who wanted everything to be fashionable and respectable. They planted bushes in straight lines and tended lawns of soft green grass sown in turf that had to be brought from offshore. They painted their houses white and kept their shades drawn at night. They walked their dogs, small yapping dogs, to the market. They washed their automobiles and voted regularly for the things that people should vote for. And when they were not doing anything else they were sitting ready for someone like Pumpkin to come along dancing. Then they called the police.

I made my sister a treat that night, one that she had always loved. It was a large bowl of bananas, pudding, cake, ice cream and jam. I brought it to her in bed, but she was not feeling well and could only nibble at it. So I ate it while she read poetry aloud. It was the *Rubaiyat,* and it set us thinking the long thoughts of winter nights.

"Garvey," she said, "one of us has got to get rich."

"I'm for that," I responded.

"It won't be me because it's against my religion."

"Right."

"So, it's got to be you."

"Fair enough," I said.

"You showed a natural talent for the clam business. You had class."

"That's true."

"But they beat you down. They did it with paper."

"Yup."

"Paper and deceit."

". . ."

"Garvey, it won't be like that next time."

"No."

"Next time paper won't touch you. You will be of a higher order of things, invisible."

"I'd like to be invisible."

"You're learning."

"I am?"

"I was down at McGaragil's on your birthday last August . . ."

"You were?"

"I had a little cake for you. Banana cake. You were gone so early I missed you. I sat on the dock and shared it with Pegleg and Pancake. We were just sitting in the sun, eating cake with our fingers, when you flew by in your boat. You were invisible."

"I was?"

"Just a blur."

"I see what you mean."

"You had stepped out of our matrix. Everybody goes so slowly, like the man walking up the mountain. You were like the boy running down the mountain, going so fast you couldn't communicate."

"Hey, that's neat."

"As long as you keep going so fast they'll never see you. They'll never pin that paper on you."

"Speed!"

"Brother dear, I'm going to give you some advice. You know I read a lot and I know what's going on."

I was not sure about this, because I had never seen her reading a book about America in the present day. But I said nothing. Pumpkin surprised me.

"The country's changing. We just won a big old war and we're on the top. The rest of the world is watching us and we're very conscious of it. We're taking on a new role. We're not cowboys anymore. We're the cavalry. We're up on our high horses looking down. We're airmen in airplanes looking down at the earth deciding what's right and what's wrong. We land on the good places and we bomb the bad places. Nobody cares.

"Do you know what I've been thinking about? Those old ladies. The Ventnor

Ladies' Patrol. They are the people who are running America right now. Everybody always thought they were a joke. But they weren't today. Today they marched right into a courtroom and brought a trial to a standstill. Garvey, they had their way with us. And they are having their way with America.

"Do you know what's going to happen when the Wartime Prohibition Law goes into effect? The war's over, but the law's just beginning. They ratified the Eighteenth Amendment!"

"Suits me," I said. "I never take a drink, and maybe it will stop Dad."

"Don't be absurd. Dad would never take the pledge."

"No, I guess not."

"Neither will anybody else who drinks."

"Maybe not."

"Moslems are not supposed to drink, but they do."

"They do?"

"Sure they do. The men, mostly. And that's a law that's been ratified by Allah. It doesn't stop them."

"I never could see the appeal," I said.

"Whiskey helps people get along together. They need it just to get along with themselves. It makes them forget how little they think of themselves. There's a lot of guilt."

"Dad doesn't feel guilt."

"How do you know?"

I saw her point.

"Garvey, this law is going to make a lot of changes very quickly, especially in Atlantic City, which is right out the back door."

"You think people will stop coming?"

"Just the opposite! They'll come in droves. Atlantic City was built as a place to have fun in, and that means whiskey and sex. There are plenty of laws in this country against sex, but do they touch Atlantic City? Why, the cathouses are going strong, even now in the winter. There's laws against gambling, and I know four gambling rooms in town that have been there over ten years. Atlantic City's a place where you go to get away from laws. You watch. In a year or so there will be twice as many saloons as there are now and they'll all be full from morning to night."

"Heck," I said. "That's no good."

"It could be good for you, Garvey. It could be very good for you. It could make you rich."

"Me? Open a bar?"

"I'm vegetarian and I have a hot-dog stand."

"I can't see myself running a saloon."

"No, and that's not what I'm suggesting. You didn't run a clam bar, did you?"

"Nope."

"And you didn't dig clams, did you?"

"Not after things got going."

"You got yourself in another end of the business, a big end that nobody had thought much about. You used your head, not your feet."

"Not my toes."

"You went fast, Garvey, faster than anybody on the bay."

"I was invisible."

"Brave, Garvey."

"Not so brave."

"Sure you were! You know what old Pancake said? He said he would never get in that boat with you. He said boats weren't meant to go that fast, that it would end in your destruction."

"He's an old man."

"The world's full of old men. Right now this country's run by old ladies. It was two old ladies that got me into a big mess and eighteen old ladies who got me out of it. You,

you're like an infant raised by wolves. There's nothing old about you, nothing that doesn't come from within. You don't feel guilt and you never get scared."

"Cut it out."

"I'm serious. America's in trouble when the old people start telling the young people what to do. And if you don't think that's what's happening, just look at the facts. It's a country full of boozers. Not drunks, but people who like to drink. They like it because it makes them forget about business. Business is not natural, never was. A man spends his day worrying about the wholesale price of potatoes. At night he can't even eat a potato, much less digest one. That's not normal. He takes a drink and he begins to feel normal. Can you deny him that? Would you tell Dad to stop drinking? Would you force him to stop? Heck no! The talks he has at Dutchy's are the best conversation he gets all week. Now these straitlaced puritans want to close down Dutchy's, they want to close down anybody who's not like them. It's bigger than booze. It's war."

"Well, maybe it is. But I can't see how it can make me rich."

"You've got to fight. You've got to get rich

163

by winning. Money will make you win, and winning will bring you more money. Prohibition might be dealing this country a dreadful blow, but it just might put you on top."

"What's at the top?"

"Freedom. If we had the biggest house in Margate instead of this old elephant, do you think I could dance on the beach?"

"You could dance on the mayor's desk."

"Right! Now look here, brother of mine, I want you to spend a long time thinking about this Prohibition business. It's got to be fought and you've got to fight it. Not for booze, but for freedom. I want you to lie down in your bed and think about how you can fit into it, how you can turn the whole thing to your advantage. You're going to fight the kind of thing that went on in Ventnor today and you're going to do it with what you have, what you know that nobody else knows."

"I know boats," I said.

"Boats and bays."

"Boats and bays and beaches."

"Now you've got to think about booze!"

Mamma May came running into the room waving a wet dishrag and yelling, "Booze!"

Pumpkin and I, brother and sister who had

164

never had a drink, jumped up and down on the bed, yelling, "Booze!"

Dad, alone on the howdah above us, shook a bottle of gin at the stars and yelled, "Booze, booze, *booze!*"

7

DAD woke me up one sunny morning that May to tell me I had a visitor.

"It's a girl," he said and winked. I got dressed quickly, knowing that it could only be Minnie Creek, whom I had not seen in a month.

She was in the living room, the belly, looking up at the curving rafters high overhead. She was dressed like a cowgirl; boots, jeans, leather jacket, black Stetson.

"Weird," she said, looking around.

Mamma May came in from the kitchen with a frying pan in one hand, a spatula in the other. I knocked my knuckles twice on the top of my head, which meant "two eggs," pointed to Minnie and knocked again. Mamma May yawned with her whole body and went back to the kitchen.

"Weird," said Minnie.

"I just got you some eggs."

"Ya didn't ask me how I want 'em."

"Scrambled," I said, "is all she does."

Over breakfast Minnie got down to business. She had a job and there was an opening for me. We would ride horses on the beach, in charge of greenhorn tourists who rented them by the hour. We would also tend to the horses' needs—feed them, clean them, bring them from their stables in the morning and take them back at night. Pay was a dollar a day plus tips. I agreed immediately.

She said I had to look like a cowboy. We had a look through my clothes box, which I kept under my bed, and I came up with my old cowboy belt with the horseshoe buckle, my jeans, sneakers and a flannel shirt with clowns on it. Dad lent me a gray felt fedora, and Pumpkin tied a pretty silk scarf around my neck. Suddenly my whole family plus Minnie were in my bedroom anxiously dressing me. No one had seen me do a day's work in the past few months. They were as eager as I. Nobody bothered to ask who Minnie was. All that mattered was that she had brought me work, a rare commodity in 1919. Of no concern to anyone was the fact that I had never been very near a horse.

We walked up the beach to Atlantic City. Minnie filled me in on what she had been doing; keeping warm mostly, and serving drinks in Dutchy Muldoon's. I did not like that, but I knew better than to say anything. She was glad to be leaving Dutchy's for some outdoor work.

We took the horses from their stable on New York Avenue and led them to the beach in four trips, four horses each time.

"Don't let 'em see you're scared," said Minnie.

"Who's scared?"

We had five tourists for the first ride of the day, a family. The father and mother rode alone, but Minnie and I had to hold the bridles of their children's mounts. At first Minnie had to hold mine, too, as I had only a vague idea of how to steer.

We went along slowly, the horses old and gentle, the day calm and truly spring. In the cool shadows beneath the piers we stopped to look seaward through the pilings where the surf thrashed wildly among the barnacles, a scene I have found in my dreams since childhood. Piers had always been something special to me, something magical about the way they stood so solidly against the waves. At the base of Cook's Pier I saw Minnie look out to the end, which had been lengthened. She shook her head sadly, looked at me. I wanted to hold her then, to comfort her, but my hands were full and she would have been shocked, I guess.

We were on our way back from the Inlet when I noticed a string of boats on the horizon. Minnie was just beside me and I asked her what they were.

"That's Rum Row, Nigel."

"What's Rum Row?"

"Those boats are loaded down with whiskey, waitin' for it to be picked up! The government can't touch 'em because they're three miles out, in international waters."

"How is it picked up?"

"In boats, dumbo. At night."

"Who does it?"

"I dunno. Dutchy, maybe. He just got himself a boat."

My mind went back to the discussion I'd had with my sister about booze. In March there had been no Rum Row, and for the life of me I had not been able to make the connection between me and alcohol, between alcohol and boats. Now it was shown to me with such simplicity that I dropped my hat and one of the kids had to get down and fetch it for me.

"Minnie," I said, "those boats out there . . . they're waiting for *us*!" I dropped the bridles

I had been holding and my horse waded into the surf. I forgot about the tourists, my job, the beach, and the piers. I wanted to swim out to those boats and make a deal. Then it occurred to me that I was up against many factors I had not considered. First and foremost was *Desperado*. There was no way in the world that I could take that beaten-up garvey into the ocean. Especially at night. At that moment the Coast Guard cutter, a new one, charged through the inlet and over the bar. Captain Frye was out there having a good look at Rum Row in the daylight. But he was only one of the obstacles. How would I pay for the whiskey and to whom would I sell it?

I wanted to get back to shore, but the horse would not budge. Seeing that I was helpless, Minnie rode out and got me. I was whispering to her all my thoughts, but her mind was on the job and I could not get her to listen. All that day I thought alone. In the evening, after we had fed and cleaned the nags, I told her I was quitting.

"I'm no cowboy," I said with finality. "I'm a sailor. Those boats out there . . . they're going to make me rich. It's too good to be true."

Minnie looked at me with that hard frown she always wore when weighing the facts. It took her about a minute to make up her mind. She asked if she should quit too. I told her to stay on and earn us some capital while I was lining up a boat. In a week or so, I said, we would be in business.

"Well, we sure as hell don't need a license," she said.

Then we laughed and I kissed her.

It was only a kiss on the cheek and I hadn't meant it, but she took offense.

"Lay off, buster," she said, wiping her cheek. "I ain't your baby doll."

"I never said you were! Boy, one darn kiss on the cheek and you think I think you're my baby doll."

"I'm nobody's baby doll. Keep your germs to yourself."

I assured her I would. I did not need to kiss Minnie Creek, or to have her as my baby doll. But I sure as heck wanted her around when I was out on the ocean, her and her big box of tools. I told her I would see her again in a few days, got paid my dollar and walked home with it against a freshening wind from the southwest.

The next day I went around to every dock

on the bay in Margate, asking for work. I went to the rich owners of private fishing boats, telling them I was an experienced bait boy who knew a lot about boats, the bay and fishing. I had never been deep-sea fishing, but I did not let on. In the afternoon, just as I was getting discouraged, I found my job.

Employing me was a certain Pennsylvania state senator named Stone, John Stone, who was old and fat but very energetic. He said he drove down to the seashore every week-end to fish marlin and bonito, and that I would go with him on these trips. During the week I would look after the boat, seeing that it stayed afloat and clean, ready and provisioned for early Saturday mornings. The boat was kept in a boathouse on Risley's Lagoon, not far from where I lived. It was just what I had in mind.

The boat, called *Stuffy*, was a beamy pound boat of twenty-five feet, powered by a four-cylinder Atomic inboard. She was not very new, but had been well maintained, kept indoors in the winter. Her bows were high, good for taking waves, and she looked seaworthy. There was no cabin, only a wheel mounted on the gunwale and a fishing chair bolted to the deck in the stern. There were two bamboo outriggers for trolling and many rods and reels clamped to her ribs.

The senator's wife, he said, had accompanied him on fishing excursions for the past five years but now was unwell and in her bed in Scranton. He knew few people on the island and was very interested in my background. He asked me many questions, which I answered honestly and without hesitation. I bragged a bit about my clam empire of the previous summer, and he laughed when I explained how it had all come to naught.

"You must go about things in the right way, my boy. You ignored the legal aspects of your endeavors and paid the price."

I did not tell him that over the winter I had become an avid outlaw. Two trials had shown me that without money, without respectability, the law would never give me an even break. I nodded my head like a boy just coming upon the beauty of truth, and asked him for a dollar a day.

"On the weekends, son. During the week it's fifty cents a day."

We shook on it, the senator and I, and that was that. I hurried home to tell my folks the good news. They had been quiet the night before when I told them I was no longer a cowboy. Only Pumpkin had seemed to approve.

The senator turned out to be quite a sailor. It was still dark when we set out that Saturday morning, but he knew that part of the bay well and we charged at full speed, five knots, toward the Great Egg Harbor Inlet. While he steered standing up I sat in the fishing chair watching our wake fall behind, watching house lights blink on in Margate and Longport. We passed under the rickety old Longport Bridge as dawn began to break. There was little wind, but I could see a swell mounting in the inlet where the tide was dead low, just beginning its mad rush into the bay. We hit the chop as we rounded the rock jetty, the one my father had built.

The waves were much higher than I had thought. The skiff took them well, but it was a wet ride. Though I was wearing an oilskin coat lent me by the senator, much cold water found its way inside, and I began to shiver. To keep warm I found an old galvanized bilge pump and went to work pumping out the water, which was coming in wave by wave. When the senator yelled over his shoulder to man the pump I yelled back that I was already on it. He turned and gave me a great smile, one that had won many votes I was sure.

The engine was not powerful, and it took a lot of skill to meet the breakers head-on each time as one must. On both sides of us huge swells were crashing on the unseen sandbars that would spell our ruin should we be cast upon them. But the course was steady, and soon we had cleared the inlet. The sun came up, warming us, and Senator Stone eased back the throttle so that we could change positions. In a minute he was strapped into the fishing chair with a rod as thick as Dad's thumb and the biggest reel I'd ever seen. On the end was a chain leader, and to that was shackled a lure he called the silver spoon. We were after big slammer bluefish, just beginning to appear at this time of the year.

I had some trouble getting used to the way she steered, but after a while I had it down. Without asking him I ran us up north to where I had seen the boats of Rum Row. After half an hour of steady going he appeared at my side, asked what course I was running. When I told him I had never used a compass he gave me careful instructions, and some of what Captain Frye had told me so many years before began to come back. I realized that in turning from the ocean to the bay I had given up many of the arts of seamanship which I would need now, and I listened carefully. It dawned on me that if I mastered navigation I could find my way anywhere in the dark. In the dark I was invisible.

When we reached the end of Atlantic City I headed her offshore toward the string of boats I had seen from the beach earlier that week. When we drew near I was amazed at what I saw. Of the seven boats which made up Rum Row at that time, there was not one of them younger than forty years. Five of them were old Nova Scotia schooners with their paint peeling off, one was a steam trawler and the last a packet boat with no paint to cover her rot. Rum Row looked like a ship's graveyard.

"The devil's fleet," said the senator.

"Yes sir."

"You know what those scoundrels are up to?"

"I believe I do, senator."

"Give 'em a wide berth, Garvey. They corrupt the very water that buoys them up."

"It's a bad business, sir."

"I'll say. This country's going dry, boy, dry."

"I can hardly wait," I said.

176

We caught nothing all day, but the senator did not seem to care. What he liked was being out on the water, and this pleased me. I steered all day except for a short break for lunch, which was a huge tunafish sandwich he had prepared for me.

Late in the afternoon I saw him take a silver flask from his vest pocket and drink from it. Dad had one like it, and I knew what was inside. I pretended not to see, but caught him sipping several times on the way in. He let me take the boat back through the inlet, which was a little smoother by now. I looked back once and saw a huge wave about to crush us. I closed my eyes, waiting for it to hit, but nothing happened. When I looked again it was still there, still rushing at us, but we were keeping a few yards ahead of the foam, and my confidence returned.

"Never look astern in a following sea," said the senator, and I could see what he meant. The next time I looked he had the flask to his lips, the old rogue.

We went fishing again the following day, and he hooked a big drumfish that fought for half an hour before the line snapped. While playing the fish he gave me orders, and I realized that boating the fish was a two-man

177

effort. Often I had to run down on the fish in reverse, sending a wall of spray off the transom and making the small motor groan. When the fish ran toward us I had to keep the boat underway so as not to foul the line in the propeller. I was disappointed when the drum got away, and so was the senator. Without bothering to hide it, he took a long draw from his flask. He saw me looking but said nothing. I winked, but he did not wink back. Well, that was all right. After all, he was a politician, a Pennsylvania politician, and could do as he liked.

When I tied her up that night he paid me two dollars and told me what he wanted done that week. I was to check the bilge every day and pump her out if needed. I was to clean everything in sight and wash down the rods and reels. He wanted the dock painted and the ladder replaced, promising to pay me extra for these jobs. He wanted me to start and idle the motor every morning. Under no condition was I to take the boat away from the boathouse. He made that clear. We shook hands, agreeing to meet again the following Saturday morning. There was whiskey on his breath and he was blotto.

Following my plans, I went to see Dutchy

Muldoon the next day at noon. Dutchy was sitting at the end of his bar talking to his dog. Dutchy had a little dog that liked to stay on the bar because there were so many fleas on the floor. If the customers did not like it when he came walking along, nearly stepping in their beers, they said nothing. Dutchy's was a dive, and there the customer was always wrong. If he did not like something he could leave. If he did not leave, but stayed to quarrel, Bullets, the bartender would throw him out the window into the bay, or else Dutchy would do it himself.

There was no one else in the saloon except for Bullets, who was washing glasses at the other end. I sat down next to Dutchy and let his dog lick my nose.

"Garvey, lad," he said, "it's been a long winter. How'd you get through it, then?"

"I slept a lot."

"Good lad, good lad."

"How's business?"

"Ah, the weekend the place was packed with shoeboxers."

"Then the summer's begun."

"That it has."

"Look here, Dutchy," I said lowering my voice, "do you need some booze?"

Muldoon looked straight ahead. Bullets, noting that his boss's glass was empty, came down and drew him a beer, then went back to his glasses, which he was polishing one by one. Dutchy drained half the glass and turned to me.

"Got some?"

"I'm getting some. Tonight."

"I got plenty of booze, Garvey. But I could always use a little more."

"If I were to get you some, where would I bring it?"

"Well, you'd bring it right here," he said, nodding toward the dock outside.

"What would be a good time?"

"Oh, about four in the morning."

"Cash," I said.

"Naturally."

"See you later, Dutchy."

"Good luck, kiddo."

I went down to the beach to find Minnie, but she was out with a group. I followed their tracks southward and saw them when I had cleared Heinz Pier. When Minnie rode up, looking pretty as a picture, I had a few private words with her.

"Do you have any money?" I asked her.

"Yeah."

"How much?"

"Who wants to know?"

"Come on, Minnie," I said, "I need every dime I can raise. Tonight's the night."

"Do I get to go?"

"Minnie, I would not go without you."

"Forty dollars."

I told her where to meet me.

I found Dad that afternoon fishing in the surf on Washington Avenue in Margate.

"Dad, I need some money."

"Well, you've come to the right man, son. As you can see it's practically falling out of my pockets. See that old oak back there? The greenbacks are just starting to bloom. Go on back and help yourself. Me, I'll stay right here. There is a fish out there, Garvey, and it has my number on it."

"I'll pay you back tomorrow. With interest."

"What kinda interest?"

"A quart of gin."

"How much money you need?"

"Half of what you have on hand."

"That could come out to be about thirty dollars."

"All of what you have on hand."

"Two bottles."

181

"One bottle."

"High-grade."

"High-grade."

We walked back to the elephant, and Dad crawled down into the left tusk. He handed me the sixty dollars as if it were nothing. I went to the boathouse to meet Minnie.

I had the key and let us in. It was very dark, as the quarter-moon had not yet risen. Minnie jumped into the boat, removed the engine cover and felt the motor with her hands. Quietly I cast off the lines and pushed us out into the lagoon with the boathook. Minnie started the motor with the crank, and we were going.

I was doing a wild and desperate thing, I knew, but I had resigned myself to it. It was a desperate business I was entering, it was above and beyond the law. But with a calm determination I eased the throttle open and headed for Longport.

Suddenly I found myself in the land of my dreams. The dark waves rose all around me and I could hear them breaking. I steered for the light buoy in the middle of the inlet and told Minnie to bail. It seemed to me that I could hear the wail of drowned men trapped below the surface, trying to drag me down with them. I wished Dad were there, or Captain Frye, but I knew I had to do this alone.

When we had cleared the inlet we were both soaking wet. The oilskins were in the lazarette, locked, and I did not have the key. I asked Minnie how she was doing.

"Freezin' my butt off."

"Watch your mouth."

"Go to blazes."

"Drop that pump and come on up here."

She moved to my side and I put my arm around her. She tried to squirm away, but I held her fast. Then she put her arm around me and we got a little warmer. I was very conscious of her touch, and I think she was too, but we said nothing, only stared ahead with exaggerated concentration.

In an hour or so I could see the red lights of Rum Row and took a compass heading. It was a good thing I did, because shortly afterward the fog began to roll in and I could see nothing. I kept her on course at half-speed, waiting to get a look through the fog. I knew I had three miles to go and figured it would take me about half an hour.

About that much time had passed when I saw a red running light to starboard, peering through the fog. I headed for it, figuring one rum boat is as good as another at this stage of the game.

Going very slowly, I positioned Minnie in the bow with the bowline, ready to throw it to the boat as we drew alongside. Then Minnie yelled back for me to cut the engine, which I did.

"Hey, I'm throwin' you a line," she called out to the darkness.

"Heave away," came a deep voice.

Minnie threw the line in the direction of the voice, and it was taken. I could feel us being drawn through the water, and heard the thump as we made contact. Suddenly it was daylight.

Someone on the other boat had turned on a big Half Mile Ray searchlight, and it shined in our boat, nearly blinding us.

"Evenin', Garvey," came a familiar voice. It was Captain Frye, standing on the roof of his new Coast Guard cutter, his hand on the searchlight. In the bow stood an ensign by the breech of a long deck cannon aimed our way. In the cockpit was a seaman with a sub-machine gun.

"Evening, Captain Frye."

"Foggy night," he said.

"It certainly is, sir."

The searchlight swept my empty boat in the silence that followed. Minnie, sitting hunched up in the bow, put on a big smile when the light fell on her.

"Evening, Minnie."

"Hi there, captain!"

"Just out for a spin?"

"Just for a spin, sir."

"Guess you want to get going."

"Yes, sir."

The bowline was released and we began to drift away. Captain Frye cut the searchlight, but I could hear him very clearly say, "At night all cats are gray, Garvey."

Minnie got the motor started and we headed away as fast as we could, feeling like fools.

"What'd he mean by that?" asked Minnie.

"A warning."

"What do we do?"

"Just what we set out to do."

"But he knows!"

"Yup."

"He'll be waitin' for us on the way in."

"It's a big ocean."

"Fish hooks."

"Watch your lip."

"See them guns?"

"I did."

"Scary."

"Yup."

"Think he'd use 'em? On us?"

"I think he would use them on the boat."

"We're in the boat."

"Yup."

"Maybe we need a gun!"

"No guns. We don't need them. We're invisible."

"Not in that searchlight."

"I'll never let him get that close again. I promise."

Our hearts were beating fast, our hands unsteady. Minnie paced the deck, frowning. Then she slapped her knee and laughed.

"That story's gonna be all over town tomorrow! We just did the dumbest thing ever done off the Jersey coast."

I agreed, but could only force a laugh. I was trying to see through the fog.

The moon had just cleared the horizon as the weather cleared, and before me I saw our intended destination. Not one light, but many peeked at us through the mist. I took the throttle up full and in a few minutes was abreast of Rum Row.

8

I CHOSE the second schooner in the line, because, despite her battered and aged condition, she had sweet lines. As I moved alongside, her cabin lights came up and I heard voices. Minnie threw the bowline to a crouched form which appeared on deck, and I watched the man lunge for it and miss. He tried again with the same result. We were drifting toward her stern. At the last moment Minnie jumped up to the schooner's deck and secured the line herself. I shut off my motor and came aboard.

The man in the shadows was trying to light a kerosene lantern but could not. He reeked of whiskey. Stepping over him, I made my way to the lit companionway, where Minnie was waiting. I knocked on the coaming and a deep voice from inside said. "Alphonse?"

The man with the lantern, still unlit, staggered past us, stepped into the companionway and fell headlong down the ladder into the cabin. There followed some loud exclamations in French. Then a face appeared in the light.

"Come in, my friends! Come, come! Watch your step on the ladder, eh?"

It was a big fat face, well in need of a shave. Black stringy hair hung down over a dark forehead, black eyes and reddened cheeks. Under a large nose drooped a huge mustache which had never been trimmed. His lips, thick and sensual, smiled widely, exposing white and even teeth. Red eyes blinked as if just aroused from a deep sleep. I told Minnie to stay where she was. Then I went down the ladder.

The man, whose name turned out to be Big Frenchy, was captain of the ship, and Alphonse was the only crew member. He was a large man, as tall as I and much heavier. He slapped me on the back and led me to a table with one thick arm around my shoulder. We sat down and I had a look around.

There were bottles everywhere. Wooden crates lined the walls, hung suspended from the ceiling. Bottles were stuffed in shelves, portholes, drawers and under bunks. On the table stood three amber bottles, all empty. Big Frenchy was as drunk as his mate, but could hold his liquor better. Alphonse sat in a stupor while we spoke.

"Look at him, the cow," said Big Frenchy, gesturing toward Alphonse. "Drunk from morning to night. Worthless when we're not sailing. Ah, but then he is good. He is like the monkey, so good is he under sail."

I told the captain that the Coast Guard was not far off.

"They are there every night! But only one, eh? What can one do? *Rien*! Ha!"

"They can't touch me here, right?"

"You're half a mile into international waters!" he roared. "They can do nothing."

"Until I come in."

"You go *out* first. Then run north or south. Then turn in. How do they know where you are, eh? Ha!"

I asked him if he was Canadian.

"I am French! Alphonse is from stinking Canada."

I told him my name and where I was from. I said I was just beginning in the business, but if all went well I would be a regular customer. I asked him how his end of the trade was going.

"Not so good. We are not visited frequently. Many nights there is no one, and few buy in quantity. Everyone on the Row is drunk, and a bad storm would wipe us out, so unprepared we are. Still, it is better than New York, as the competition there is so high. Too many boats off New York and four cutters. Shootings and some sinkings. They are ruthless, the New York Coast Guard. The man here, he plays by the book. That's all we ask."

I assured him business would improve.

"You bet! When the reserves are gone. Then we are here, waiting. It should begin this summer. If it does not I go back to fishing. I hate fishing. Alphonse hates fishing. We have been eating beans for more than one month because neither of us will put the hook in the sea. But it is our fate to fish if we make no business soon. It is the same with all of us out here. We know that if we can hang on we will make it. But one bad storm, *Garvay*, and we're all on the bottom."

I told him I would like to lighten his load. He asked what I wanted.

"Gin."

"Ha! Gin I got."

"High-grade."

"High-grade, low-grade, I got it. England gin. What marque?"

For the life of me I could not think of a single brand of gin. I had seen Dad with bottles of the clear liquid on many occasions, but the words on their labels escaped me. While I was thinking there came a knock on the roof and Minnie's face appeared upside down in a porthole.

"Dutchy don't want no high-grade," she said.

Big Frenchy shrugged, looked at me.

"That's my engineer. What are you saying, Minnie?"

"I said Dutchy don't want no high-grade gin, dumbhead. He wants High and Dry."

"High and Dry I got," said Big Frenchy with indifference.

I told Minnie to check the line to our boat and come on down. I had forgotten that much of her winter had been spent working in Muldoon's. I reckoned that she would know his taste and could help me on the deal. She came down the ladder, frowning. Big Frenchy tried to stand, bumped his head on a wooden whiskey crate and slumped back into his seat. I introduced them. Minnie held out her hand, which the captain shook while mur-

muring apologies. I supposed that Minnie was the first girl he had seen in some time.

"Let's see some High and Dry," she said.

Big Frenchy nodded to Alphonse, who crawled through a low doorway and reappeared a moment later dragging a squat case of square-shaped bottles that jingled. He got his shoulder under it and hefted it to the table, where we sat, tore a plank off with a rusty knife and pulled out a bottle.

Minnie took it from him and examined the label. She twisted off the cork and smelled it. She raised the bottle to her lips and swallowed a mouthful. I was shocked.

"Minnie!"

"Aw, stow it, Smedley," she said. To Big Frenchy she added, "That's the stuff." Big Frenchy smiled.

"How much?" I asked.

"Five dollars the case."

"Ha!" said Minnie. We both looked at her. "No wonder business is bad. You're a pirate."

Big Frenchy assured her he was not, that he was making an honest profit.

"Tell ya what, capitano," she said. "We'll just go on down the line and see if we can't do better. If we can't we'll come back."

"Four dollars the case, last price," said the captain.

Minnie looked at me and nodded. As she did so she took another swig from the bottle. I took it away from her and replaced the cork.

"I'll take twenty-five cases," I said.

Big Frenchy's eyes lit up. "Let's see your money, *Garvay*!"

I produced a roll of ones, fives and tens, with a ten-dollar bill on top, green side up. He stood up abruptly, banging his head once more but shrugging it off. Alphonse followed him through the low doorway to the hold. Soon the cases were coming up. Minnie and I began carrying them to the deck, transferring them to *Stuffy*.

I checked each case for water damage or broken bottles. They were all in new condition, all stamped with Canadian and British customs marks. When they had all been carefully stacked on Senator Stone's sportfisherman, I stepped back aboard the schooner. Captain and mate were both sitting on deck breathing heavily. I passed Big Frenchy the roll, telling him to count it.

Then I remembered Dad.

"I need one bottle of high-grade gin," I said. "For my dad."

"Gilbey's," said Minnie.

"Gilbey's I got," said Big Frenchy. He nodded to Alphonse, who crawled off and returned with the bottle I wanted. I searched my pockets for money, but remembered that the hundred dollars was all that I had. Big Frenchy waved me away.

"A present, *Garvay*," he said. "Come back."

I told him that if things worked out I would be back the following night. He smiled and slapped Alphonse across the back, causing the mate to convulse in a coughing fit.

As Minnie slipped the line I heard Big Frenchy say, "Watch yourself, *mon ami*."

We headed out to sea. The fog had all but dissipated and the quarter-moon was up. It was brighter than I had supposed it would be, but I was not worried. I remembered my compass headings and soon spotted the light of the six-mile buoy. Fetching it, I turned north and ran up the coast until I knew I was off Brigantine. Then I turned in.

A hot flash passed through my body when I realized I was inside the three-mile limit and, if caught there, would be in the worst spot of my life. I channeled all my fears into steering the boat, a difficult job with the load we were carrying. Minnie stood in the stern pumping out the water, which was splashing in each time a wave struck us on the port bow. We said nothing to each other for over an hour.

I crept in until I could hear the waves breaking on Brigantine beach, then turned south toward Atlantic City and the Absecon Inlet, which would take us inside. That spot, I knew, would be the tightest. The Absecon Inlet is not wide and therefore was easily patroled.

But as we approached I could tell it was empty. I took the throttle all the way up and we surged forward at about four knots. The engine seemed far too loud, the night too bright. But what could I do?

This, I realized, was the real test. Sooner or later, I must do this on every run. There were many ways into the bay behind Atlantic City, but each of them had a narrow entrance. The cutter could more than match my speed. If Captain Frye happened to outguess me, he could run me down at will. I thought about that searchlight, that cannon and those guns. Then I stopped thinking.

We charged in unnoticed by a soul. In a short time we had entered Gardner's Basin and were tying up at Dutchy's dock.

Dutchy stood above me on the rotted pier, his hands on his hips. On either side of him stood a man. He spoke quietly.

"Ah, Garvey lad, I see you're as good as your word. Right then. Get me them cases, boys, while I have a talk with Garvey here."

I left Minnie to help with the off-loading and entered the dark saloon. Dutchy carried a case of High and Dry under his arm.

"Where'd you get the boat, then?" he asked.

"I borrowed it."

"Well, we can't have that, can we?"

"I have plans, Dutchy."

"Look here, now. I've got a boat! Bigger and better than that tub outside. But I've no one to run her. We could set things up on a regular basis."

"No thanks, sir," I replied. "I mean to get my own boat. You'll find another captain, but in the meantime I can bring in all the stuff you can handle."

"I'd rather have you workin' for me, lad."

"I'm sorry. I don't work for anybody but myself."

Dutchy said we would see about that. He offered me eight dollars a case, two hundred dollars for the load. I took it. Dutchy said he would be there again the next night.

I noticed on the way out that the cases were loaded into a truck which had been backed into the alley beside his saloon. I did not ask him where it was going. He had not asked where I had come from. That was the way things must be.

It was a long ride through Beach Thorofare back to Margate. Minnie was as tired as I and said little other than a few complaints about the sound of the motor, the work she had been required to do and the chill of the night.

Silently we berthed *Stuffy* in the boathouse and cleaned her up as best we could in the dark. Minnie wanted to go home to her boardinghouse in Atlantic City but I told her to sleep in the boat, that I would be back early in the morning to help her do the work which must be done.

She held out her hand.

I counted out the forty dollars she had lent me and put a five-dollar bill on top.

"Five bucks? That's all?"

"Minnie, you're going to make five dollars *every night*! Plus fifty cents a day for work around here. If we make five runs a week that's almost thirty dollars a week! Take it or leave it."

"I'll take it, fish face," she said.

"Watch your mouth!"

"Keep your voice down, dippy."

I was too tired to argue. I squeezed her shoulder and thanked her. I showed her where some boat cushions were and found a tarpaulin to pull over her. She would not lie down until I had left. I knew she had not meant to sound ungrateful; it was her manner to question all transactions from a negative point of view. I felt pretty good in paying her more money than she would have made in nearly a week of horseback riding.

In the morning I paid Dad what I owed him and gave him the bottle of Gilbey's, which he hid with his money in the tusk. In my bedroom I counted out what I had left: ninety-five dollars—more money than I had seen all winter.

I could hardly wait for night to come, so eager was I to get on with this new enterprise. It was not greed which compelled me so; it was pure business sense. What I had seen for myself out there on the Row had confirmed all my precognitions about the industy. It was spanking-new, infantile, and if I was to rise in it to the top, the only spot I wanted, I had to grow with it from the bare beginning. At the moment, I knew, I was gambling. The odds were not against me, but they were at best even. I always had those inlets to chug through. As my adversary I had an expert with a faster boat. Money and time would alter those odds in my favor, as they must. With money and experience I would reduce the odds to a more American-businesslike ratio. For now, all I needed was luck.

That day was the first of a long heat wave that burst over Margate like an exploding star. I woke up Minnie in the boathouse and we set to work scrubbing down *Stuffy* and painting the dock. I wanted to get the senator's chores done, and I wanted passersby to get used to our appearance there.

Old Ben Risley sold the only fuel around, but I knew better than to pick it up with the senator's boat. Risley and Senator Stone were fast friends, and anything I did in daylight would be mentioned. So I brought old *Desperado* around that day and filled her tank plus an extra five-gallon can meant for *Stuffy*. Minnie had paint in her hair and on her arms and legs when I returned, but was in a good mood. I thanked the heat wave for that.

I only had to mention that I would be needing another small loan for that night. She handed me her little roll and went on painting. I could not help liking her for things like that. She had a great attitude, for a girl.

We set out that night well after dark. The sea was calmer, and getting to the Row was a dream. I found the skipper and crew of the old schooner as I had left them. They were surprised to see me, but tried not to show it. Big Frenchy had the same outlook as I. In this germinal period of our transactions the most important factor was that all went smoothly. And it nearly did.

Alphonse dropped a case of High and Dry over the side. Big Frenchy kicked Alphonse over the side, where he nearly drowned. Minnie had to get him. Then he was unable to work, and the three of us had to load thirty cases ourselves, the Frenchman acting like it was a big joke.

Now and then the searchlight from the Coast Guard cutter would pass over the Row. But we were on the sea side and unseen. I would not have liked Captain Frye to see me and Minnie struggling with cases like that. I had determined early on never to appear shoddy in the glare of that man's Half Mile Ray.

I loved it out there on Rum Row and was in no hurry to depart. It seemed to me that I was among a kind of brotherhood of outlaws, even though I was the only one taking real legal risks. Big Frenchy told me the name of his ship, *Queen Anne's Revenge,* and the names of the others, though I cannot remember them. Fate had led me to Frenchy, and I saw no reason to change destiny. He knew the other skippers and said that, of them all, he was the only honest man out there. The others, he said, would cheat me in the end, implying that his integrity would be true forever. He was cultivating me, just as I was cultivating him. At my request he made hot tea for me and Minnie, which we drank sprawled out on his gently swaying deck while the warm moist winds rolled in over us. Dimly on the horizon shore the lights of Atlantic City, a town just awakening after a winter's sleep. From time to time music would drift across the calm sea from the piers, and I could imagine fancy people dancing, spinning across waxed floors or dragging themselves through the first of that summer's dance marathons. I could see the roof lights of the Union Hotel and thought about the king of Atlantic City, whoever and wherever he really was, and at that moment I knew what I would do with my money if I were rich: I would be right where I was, buying all the booze on Rum Row!

I ran south, eight miles out, and turned for the Great Egg Harbor Inlet, which was unpatrolled. Now I had the long ride ahead of me to Dutchy's, with the current against me for half the trip. He was there, yawning, when I showed up. He bought the thirty cases without checking a bottle. But moored at his dock was a black bunker boat, and he showed me aboard.

He showed me her spacious wheelhouse, her large hold which could carry hundreds of cases. She was in bad shape, but repairs were underway. Again, he offered me the job as captain. Again I refused. I kept my reasons to myself, as they were good reasons and I could see no sense in telling them.

First, as his employee, I knew I would be paid by the run. This made a lot of sense to him, as he would be getting his booze at Rum Row prices, but what did it mean to me? A warm dry wheelhouse? A deck crane for loading? These in return for a few dollars. It angered me to know that Dutchy thought I was that dumb.

Second, I had different ideas about boats. Dutchy's moss-bunker was big and slow. *Stuffy*, even loaded to the gunwales, went faster. But what I was aiming for was something bigger than what I was using and faster than Captain Frye! I had no intention of spending the future sneaking by him. I wanted to fly by him, invisible with speed. I wanted to outrun him when I had to.

I did not want to step on Dutchy's toes, nor did I want him to think me a fool. But of the two I chose the latter. Let him think whatever he liked. Let him think that I was only stubborn. I told him what a swell boat it was, thanked him for his offer and left with his cash bulging in my pocket.

We made a run every night that week. The last one, Thursday night, gave me a surprise. At four in the morning when I appeared at Dutchy's he was not there.

I had no idea what to do with the eighty cases of gin I had aboard. The load represented the extent of my capital, and no place I thought of was safe enough for its storage. The senator was due back on Saturday morning, and I knew I had until then to find a safe cache. This was my first snag, and I faced up to it with calm. We ran down the bay to Margate and moored the heavily laden pound boat in the boathouse. The sky was growing light, and those cases, the boat, Minnie and I had to get under cover. We decided to sleep until we were rested, then I would go uptown and find out what had gone wrong.

At noon I was in Muldoon's waiting for Dutchy to finish a game of baseball darts he was playing with Captain Frye.

"Afternoon, Garvey," said the captain. "How's clamming?"

"Little early in the season, sir," I replied.

"Got to stick with it," he said, launching a dart.

"Ah," said Dutchy, "the lad's all industry."

Both of them were drunk, but Dutchy signaled for me to step outside when the game was over. The captain shrugged when I left, but loud enough for me to hear ordered a glass of High and Dry, which Bullets poured from a bottle whose shape I knew quite well. I had nine hundred and sixty of those bottles back in Margate.

"Garvey lad," said Dutchy when we had

204

gone to the dock, "I'm truly sorry about last night. It was unavoidable. I was at sea myself."

"You were?"

"I was. I had a big order to fill, two hundred and fifty cases, and I thought I'd go it alone, me and the boys. The night was so dark, you see . . ."

"What happened?"

"Well, we got the booze all right, but we were spotted comin' in! By the captain in there with his cat's eyes."

"That's bad, Dutchy."

"Aye. We had to dump it all."

"Dump it?"

"In the channel. We barely got the last case over before they was on us with their lamp! Then it was the captain, all sociable, asking me if I was having any trouble and did I require assistance. I had barely the breath to answer. And today the man's as you see him, like nothing happened."

"It's his way," I said.

"All's I can do is play along."

"Yup."

"You got some gin for me then, lad? Ya didn't sell it elsewhere?"

"I've got it. I'll bring it up tonight. Eighty cases."

"Not here, not anymore."

"Why not?"

"Well, the man's *on* to me! It's too risky."

"How about the old Causeway Boat Works?"

"At midnight."

"I'll be there."

I took the trolley back to Margate and thought about things on the smooth ride. Dutchy had been a fool. He knew practically nothing about boats, but there he had been, at night, running brazenly through the inlet with a thousand dollars' worth of booze aboard. And when he knew I was coming! Muldoon, I decided, was a greedy man. There was simply no room for greed in this business. Every risk had to be calculated. He had been lucky. If Frye had been on him still loaded, or with even a single case of contraband hooch aboard, he would have lost his boat and his liberty as well. I made up my mind to find a better man than Dutchy Muldoon.

My heart sank when I reached the boathouse. On the muddy street outside was parked the senator's Cadillac.

9

MY first impulse was to flee. But, in turning away, I knew mine was the kind of mind that could not run from anything. I would face the senator with my every thought and dream. I would be drawn back to that boathouse sooner or later to face the man. I turned back, let myself in quietly. It was the lowest moment of my life.

At an old table on the dock sat Senator John Stone. Looking at me. Nodding his head, his jaws working over the words he was about to speak. I did not give him the chance.

"Hi, senator," I said. "You're back early."

"Well, I sure am," he replied. On the table before him was an unopened bottle of High and Dry. Beside it stood his silver flask.

"They say the weakies are biting at the eight-mile wreck," I said.

"Garvey, explain yourself."

"That's my booze in your boat, sir."

"I gathered."

"I bought it out on Rum Row last night."

"You've got a lot of pluck."

"Yes, sir," I said. "I am a rumrunner."

The senator sat and stared at me like a judge. He probably had been a judge, I thought. He had probably stared this way at many a guilty man. I was again at the mercy of the court.

He picked up the bottle of gin, held it to the light.

"What did you pay for this, son?"

"Four dollars the case."

"And what do you get for it?"

"Eight dollars."

"From whom?"

"I cannot say, sir."

"Would his name be Muldoon?"

To this I made no reply. I tried to hide the surprise I felt at the mention of Dutchy's name. Somewhere I recalled that he had connections with the Philadelphia swells.

"Right, then," he said. "You were running it to Dutchy Muldoon. Who was not there to pick it up. Because he was out there himself, making a goddamn fool of himself."

"Maybe so."

"Yes, and maybe it was I who sent him."

"Sir?"

"I sent him. He assured me his boat was sound and that he knew the way."

"It's a tub, a sitting duck."

"Apparently. But no slower than *Stuffy*, here. No slower and a lot safer in high seas. But you've had luck on your side, haven't you?"

"I call it know-how, sir."

"Yes."

"You're in the business, sir?"

"I am."

I smiled. "Well, what am I standing here like a darned idiot for? There are eighty cases in that boat!"

"I'll take 'em."

Then he smiled.

I sat down on the dock while he took a swig from his flask and passed it to me. I politely refused.

"I want you to know the difference between real gin and this low-grade bilge-water."

"I'll take your word for it, senator."

"No more High and Dry, Garvey. No more low-grade. The best costs not much more. The profit is greater. Standards must be set and kept. No more cheap gin."

"And no more *Stuffy*, sir," I said.

"Too slow?"

"Too slow and too small."

"And too close to me," he said.

"That's true too."

"Well, we'll have to get you another boat. In your own name."

"That's it, sir. That's what I need. Something faster than the Coast Guard."

"The Coast Guard, Garvey, is your largest problem. There is also the Department of Customs and Immigration. There is also the Internal Revenue Service, the FBI and a few other federal offices who will be very interested in catching you in the time to come."

"Nothing you can do to help me there?"

"Not with the federals. They'd hang us both from the same tree."

"In a manner of speaking, sir."

"You're not going to get caught, Garvey."

"No, sir. Never."

"The Coast Guard, as I have said, is your most immediate problem. I understand they have a new cutter."

"The one that ran down Dutchy last night."

"How good are they?"

"Well, the captain, Captain Frye, knows the sea, sir. He's very good. But with just the one boat there's not much he can do."

"Except if your luck runs out."

"Then he has me."

"Can the man be bought?"

"No, sir."

"How do you know?"

"I have known him all my life. He will do his duty."

Suddenly I thought of Minnie. I had left her there, sleeping. But the pallet in the corner was bare.

"Senator, was there someone here when you came?"

"I heard a splash as I entered."

I got up quickly and looked around. In the shadows beneath the dock I saw her, clinging sound asleep to a piling. The senator, on his knees, was looking as well.

"Now who the hell would that be?"

"It's a girl, sir. Helper."

Minnie woke up when I shouted her name. Dazed and fully clothed, she swam for the ladder. The senator was amazed.

I introduced them and they shook hands. I told Minnie of our new understanding. She accepted it as a matter of fact.

"You've been making runs with Garvey?" he asked her.

"Yup."

"You're not afraid?"

"Hell no."

The senator had a twinkle in his eye, and so did Minnie Creek. Gosh, I was proud of her.

"Well, we've a lot to do if we're to go fishing tomorrow, Garvey. A lot to do. You're free the rest of the day?"

"Absolutely."

We left Minnie to dry her clothes in the sun and guard the boathouse while we drove uptown. In the Cadillac. Boy, what a ride. The senator did not say where we were going. Things were happening so fast that I did not bother to ask.

We cruised up Illinois Avenue to the boardwalk. Leaving the car at the curb, we walked down a small dark alley to a doorway under a sign reading "Penny Arcade—Service." The senator produced a key.

It was a small storeroom, filled to the ceiling with wooden crates. There was another door at the back. The senator knocked, standing back so that we both could be seen through a small peephole. In a moment the door swung open.

A thin and bowed clerk, pencil behind his ear, greeted the senator with a melancholy smile. For me his face was blank. Senator

Stone asked for Dixie, and the clerk nodded for us to follow.

i was quite unprepared for what I saw. I thought at first that the place was a saloon or brothel or both. But I was wrong. It was a gambling house! There were rows of shiny silver machines for the gambling of coins. There were green baize tables with wheels set in them and strange markings, large tables for playing with dice and smaller ones for cards. It looked like a summer palace of some French king, so elaborate were the decorations, the cut-glass chandeliers, the flocked wallpaper, the cushioned gold carpets with narrow red ones laid over. I felt a little shabby in my old jeans and bare feet. Luckily the place was closed until that evening.

The clerk tapped on a small door and we were admitted to the office, where a very attractive woman of about forty years sat behind a desk. She had long chestnut hair drawn up in a bun and wore a pretty frock, very tight and revealing. She was smoking a cigarette. The senator introduced me to Dixie.

"My God," she said in an accent that was very English, "you look like a great big candy cane!"

I was not sure what she meant by that, but took it as a compliment, as in her eyes I could read approval. I was nervous and kept looking at that wicked cigarette.

"Garvey," said Senator Stone, "has joined the company. He's our link with the Row."

"Fantastic," said Dixie. "I must go for a boat ride."

"It would be a pleasure," I replied with dash.

"Dixie controls distribution to Atlantic City. The casino is a front. It's as safe as City Hall. She will take all deliveries, paying incash. At this very early stage of the business one must tread carefully. There is no hurry."

"Except," said Dixie, "that we have a back-order of ten thousand cases."

"Yes. We're a little valve, as it were, on the pipeline to Philadelphia. The market is unlimited. The present rush is born of panic. Every saloon on the Eastern Seaboard is staring at the bottom of the well. Prices are up and climbing. Right now the opposition is concentrated on the Ambrose Bight, off of New York. Our little Rum Row is an enigma, barely kept alive in this its first spring by our efforts and those of a few other local adventurers. Naturally we want a monopoly. For

214

this reason we must have the utmost of cooperation at this end, the vital end, the source."

"We need you, Garvey," said Dixie. "And you need us."

"I need a boat, ma'am," I said, amazed at my pluck.

Dixie looked at the senator, who smiled fondly, like a patient father.

"Would you pay the captain for eighty cases of High and Dry at eight dollars the case? We can take delivery as soon as it's dark," he said, giving my shoulder a squeeze.

In a moment I had my money.

Dixie closed her little safe and raised an eyebrow.

"Cheap gin," she said, "is not a priority."

"He understands. All future orders will be high-grade."

I had a question. "Sir, ma'am, just how are we going to be a monopoly? What's to stop anybody from doing what I'm doing? Pretty soon everybody on this island who has a boat is going to be making a dash for Rum Row. We can't stop them."

"John has a plan," said Dixie with a wink.

"I don't want to talk about it just now," he said. "There's been too much talk already.

Just let me say that with the proper organization, given some time and hard work, the competition in our field will be minimal. We are going to regulate the market."

My head was spinning as we left. A truck followed us down Illinois Avenue and back to Margate, where Minnie and the driver loaded the cases from *Stuffy*. Minnie was used to the work by now and hefted the cases at a good clip. I paid her for the run, but she did not thank me. The senator asked her where she lived.

"Right now, in a boardinghouse," she said.

"Well, stick with Garvey here and you will presently find more comfortable quarters."

"I'm stickin'," she said. "The grass may not be very green, but it's on my side of the fence."

"Garvey says you know something about motors."

"Well, I know your old Atomic needs the valves ground. Needs rings and a rebore."

"Can you do it?"

"I can get it done. Up in Atlantic City."

"What about Ben Risley, right here?"

"Can't handle it. I seen his shop."

"You're a machinist, then. How nice."

"Mechanic."

"Yes, mechanic. You have other skills?"

"I used to be a clammer. Before that I was a handyman, Cook's Pier. Before that I was a musician."

"Really? What did you play?"

"I played a crocodile named Roquefort in the Ducktown Squatters Blues Band."

The senator took a large swallow from his flask and changed the subject.

"Right, then. It's time to talk about a boat. Have you any idea where you might find one?"

I told him I had one. I said I would like to have a boat built for me. By Walter Eberding of Atlantic City.

"He's good?"

"He built the Coast Guard cutter, sir. Government contract."

The senator beamed. He asked me about my finances. He was prepared to advance me some money. I told him I thought I had enough to get started, if I could continue to use *Stuffy* during the time a new boat was a-building. He said that I might, but if caught he could assume no responsibility and would have to say that it was stolen. I said that was fair enough.

The moon was full that night, so rumrunning was out for the next few days. I promised to be there the following morning for a day of fishing. When he left, Minnie and I had a talk. I told her about Dixie, about the senator's plans for monopoly, about my plans for a new boat.

"Politician," she said.

"Yes, but he's on our side."

"Don't be a dope. He's on the only side there is, his side. The thing he likes about you is you're honest. He's not used to it. He's used to crooks with class, not some back-bay clammer who won't cheat him."

Gosh, she was a hard girl. But I had to admit that what she said had some sense.

Minnie came along fishing, to look after the motor, she said. We caught nothing, probably because there was a girl in the boat. Pegleg, who had warned me all my life about this, would not even fish off a dock if there was a woman around. He said fish and women were akin, and I believed him. They communicate, he said.

On Sunday night, with the senator on his way back to Pennyslvania, Minnie and I took *Stuffy* up Gardner's Basin to a marina which would overhaul the Atomic four in a few days at a low rate. Minnie stayed around to help pull the engine. I walked over to the Eberding Boat Works.

Ebby was making a sneakbox. He had worked all day, I knew, and here he was, Sunday night, building a sneakbox. He had a bench plane in his rough hands and the floor was covered with shavings. Beside him, on a shelf, was a gallon jug filled with beer.

He looked at me, sighed, put down the plane and picked up the jug.

"Heard about you, boy," he said.

I looked innocent.

"Heard you was *smuggling*, har har."

"Just making ends meet, sir," I replied.

"Yeah. *This* end and *that* end."

"Yup. Looks like you're building a sneakbox!" He sighed again and picked up his plane. Why did I always have the straight lines? I was forever setting myself up for ridicule. But I knew what I was doing. I was being me, Garvey Leek, babe in the woods.

"Sneakbox?" he roared. "Why, don't you know a gun skiff when you see one? Sneakbox, my eye. *Anybody* can build a sneakbox, take it away for thirty dollars. This here's an Ebby special! Last a hundred years. Fifty bucks and she's yours."

I told him I had no need for a gun skiff, and he spat on the floor.

"Can't load no *gin* in a gun skiff, now can you?"

"No, sir. That's why I want you to build me a boat."

He put down the plane and picked up the beer.

"How big?"

"Thirty feet. Deep."

"A sea skiff."

"A sea skiff."

"You're talkin' to the right boondocker," he said.

He drew some lines on a pine plank.

"You want your overhang stern, you want your outboard rudder."

"Why?"

"'Cause you might have to draw her up on a beach, is why. You never know, do you?"

"You never know."

"You want her fast as she can go."

"I want her faster than the cutter. Loaded."

"I put a Gardner, forty-horse, in the cutter."

"Do they make a bigger one?"

"Nope. But if we can spend a little money

we could do us a marine conversion. We could put in a Pierce-Arrow."

"Is that big?"

"Sixty horses. She'd do fifteen knots full speed ahead."

"How much?"

"I can build her for five hundred even. The motor would run about two hundred more."

I peeled three hundred dollars from my roll and put it on the plank. He looked at it and then he looked at me.

"Take me three weeks."

"Build her," I said.

I know of no finer pleasure in the world than having a boat built especially for me. A boat is like a work of art, and the owner is like a patron. He has an idea which the builder reduces to numbers, then makes them into reality. Somewhere in the process a soul goes into her.

Minnie and I came by every day to watch the progress. Ebby had helpers, and the job went quickly. The keel was laid on Monday, with the stem and transom cut and joined. Her ribs were steamed that night and bent over the mold the next day. As they dried, Ebby cut out the planks, garboard and tuck. Each plank had to be hand-fit, and this took

221

time. But day by day the boat grew up from the floor. She was built upside down, and on the tenth day we turned her over with the help of some Gardner's Basin boat men.

As I have said, the Coast Guard boathouse was right next door to Ebby. Often the men on watch came by to look at the new skiff. The word must have been passed to Captain Frye, because he came by one morning as the big Pierce-Arrow was going in.

The night before he had chased me thirty miles up north and given up when I crossed the bar at Holgate's at low tide. He looked tired and a little tipsy.

"Morning, Garvey," he said as he entered.

"Morning, Captain Frye. Nice day."

"Spring, boy! Smooth sailing ahead."

"Yes, sir."

"What we got here?" he asked, giving my gunwale a pat.

"Skiff, sir."

"Nice lines, Ebby."

Ebby looked up with a twinkle in his eye.

"Special order, captain. Garvey here wants to go a little faster."

Everybody laughed. Even the captain cracked a grin.

"Yeah," he said, "they all do. It's youth.

Never content. Buncha cowboys. What you gonna do with her, Garv?"

"Clam the bay," I said.

"Well now, she ought to hold a good lot of clams."

More laughter. Old Captain Frye was enjoying himself at my expense. But I was watching my new boat built, at his.

"Yes, sir," he said, "a fine boat. And will you take a look at that engine? Why it's the biggest thing I ever saw."

"Just came out," said Ebby, feeling a little guilty. "Pierce-Arrow."

I wished Ebby could have been a little more discreet. But what could he do? Everything was out in the open, and that's the way it had to be. Still, I resented my secrets being known so clearly to the opposition. And that was what we were, the captain and I. We were looking at each other over a lot of deep-blue water.

"A Pierce-Arrow," said Captain Frye. "Who'da thunk it? Thought they was for automobiles."

"It's a conversion."

"Six cylinders," piped up Minnie, who was leaning over the motor with a wrench between her teeth. "Water cooled."

"Think of it!" said the captain. "And me with only forty horsepower."

We all thought about that.

"Can you get another one?" he asked Ebby.

"Why sure!"

"I'll send in for the contract, then. I believe in progress. I believe in keeping up with youth."

"Just keepin' up?" cracked one of the workmen.

"Well, that's all I gotta do," he said. "It's a matter of *range*."

Nobody laughed but Captain Frye.

Minnie spoke up. "Hey, me and Ebby here are tryin' to get a good seat on this motor while all you clowns sit around and gab. Why don't ya all go on outside and jump off the dock?"

On the way out one of the Coast Guardsmen, a boy my age from Ventnor who had gone to the Academy, asked me what color I was going to paint her.

"Paint her gray," said Captain Frye.

And that's just what we did. Minnie, Ebby and I painted her dark gray, top and bottom, inside and out.

"Whatcha gonna call her?" asked Ebby.

"She don't need no name," said Minnie. "She's got Rumrunner written all over her."

And that she did. She was big and fat and wide-open. In her stern was a huge gas tank with a platform over it for the helmsman, me. There was no wheel, just a tiller. Forward was the engine, under the platform. Forward of that was all open. We launched her and she floated at her waterline, looking like a sinister winter seagull hunched down on a windy beach. Minnie started the motor with a hand crank. It was quiet, too quiet.

"Look back here, barnacle brain," she said to me while lifting a hatch. "You got a cutout."

She showed me four exhaust pipes leading to holes cut in the stern. Two of them were big and square. Two were round, and straight and slim. She shoved a brass lever over and the engine roared.

"Split manifold, baffles for quiet running, straight pipes for speed!" she yelled over the sound of the mighty Pierce-Arrow.

I engaged the motor and we went surging forward. I took her out of Gardner's Basin and into Beach Thorofare for a shakedown cruise. Ebby was up in the bow, Minnie by my side. I eased up the throttle on a straight-away. I took her all the way up.

True, the big garvey had gone faster; she had planed. But speed is relative, and this was a much bigger boat. To feel her suddenly charge through the water at twice the speed of most skiffs, nearly three times that of *Stuffy*, was a real thrill. The big rudder that hung over her stern took the strength of both arms to hold steady, but I knew I would get used to it. What I liked about her was the way she could turn.

That boat could turn three hundred and sixty degrees in a space no more than twice her length. She rolled over on her side so that we had to hang on, but she turned right around and went the other way. Ebby said to watch it empty, but loaded she could not flip.

Then I took her down real slow while Minnie cut in the baffles. We ran up a short creek through the meadows, very quietly. A flock of wading marshbirds, egret they were, hardly looked at us as we crept by. This was sweet.

For the past three weeks we had been delivering cargo to Dixie atthree different points, all in the back bay. The creeks and ditches, I realized, were ready-made for the trade. I anticipated many clandestine rendez-vous on these waters, and it was a good idea to be as quiet about it as possible, change the meeting places frequently. We had a big choice, as many dirt roads were cut through from the pines to the bay behind our part of the coast. Any road that a truck could crawl over was good enough.

I ran up to Lakes Bay for a good look at our old clamming grounds. The clam fleet was out and working. In the biggest garvey of them all, my old one, sat DiOrio with a bottle of wine. He had two boys up on the bow with rakes and two over the side. He would have a new truck before long, no worry. I went by him at full speed.

I paid Ebby what I owed him and gave Minnie an extra nine dollars for her part in the work. Then I asked about Captain Frye's cutter. Would he really put a Pierce-Arrow like mine into it?"

"Well, I got to, Garvey," he said. "That's my job!"

"It's not going to make my job any easier," I said.

"Ya got nothin' to worry about. See, it takes him about three months to get up a con-tract, right?"

"Right."

"So, for the next three months or so you'll be faster."

"Yes, but what then?"

"Well, when I'm finished putting in a Pierce-Arrow in the cutter, then I'll go to work on this here smuggler."

"What will you do?"

"I'll put in another engine, Garvey. You'll have *two*!"

10

I WAS nineteen in 1919, the year I turned Rum Row into a trolley shop. Spring had turned to summer, and Minnie and I were out every night the moon was not. Each run became a little smoother as our confidence grew. Each time I brought in another load I laughed aloud at the ease with which I was thwarting the law of the land. But as I had foreseen, I was not the only desperado on the Jersey coast. I was, however, the fastest.

A fellow from Sea Bright named Redman Stickle had come down to Atlantic City with two skiffs of considerable size. He drove one and his brother, Crosley, handled the other. They glutted some of my best customers with cheap whiskey and offered higher prices at the Row than I. They were out to beat me, and they might have done it if Captain Frye had not found them one night while they were transferring fuel. Redman had run low and his brother had held back to help him out. When the captain appeared they all jumped into the boat that could run, but it was no good. The cutter was faster, and Frye almost blew them out of the water at close range. The brothers went to jail, the boats to auction. In a few days the same skiffs were back at the Row loading up.

Natty Bolingame, who had been a bartender all his life, thought he could make it as a rumrunner. He had rare luck in finding an old but sound sloop going cheap at Gardner's Basin. His plan was subterfuge, not speed.

Natty picked up his hooch in barrels which he chained end to end and suspended beneath his keel. Then he would sail slowly up the inlet in broad daylight as if booze were the last thing on his mind. He had a big sign, an advertisement for a local clam bar, painted on his sail, and he dressed his crew like day passengers. This worked exactly two times. The third run in he was boarded by the Ocean City Coast Guard, who knew a bit about sailboats. They wanted to know why he was making only three knots in a fifteen-knot wind. Natty could give no explanation. The ensign set her on a broad reach to see for himself. The sloop got going and the barrels underneath began to beat against the hull. Five planks were bashed in and she began to fill. Natty lost his boat and almost drowned, but the evidence was left below.

A lot of my competition came from the rich owners of the local sportfishing fleet. They had boats that cost thousands, boats with built-in bars and nickel-plated fish-fighting chairs, warm comfortable bunks below and decks laid down in teak. The urge to pick up a couple of cases at the row was irresistible, and some of them took it further than that. Boswel Clofine was doing big business in Irish whiskey, fifty or so cases at a time, when the law got onto him. This man had a mansion on the bayside of Margate and enough servants to make up a baseball team. He would get drunk in the early evenings, order his valet, his butler and his steward onto the boat and set out for the Row. The poor devils knew nothing of the sea and less about smuggling, but they did their best. One night he slipped into his private dock with two hundred gallons of McConnel Mist and the lights went on. Captain Frye was docked in the next slip waiting for him.

"Why Mr. Clofine," said the captain, "what have we here?"

Boswel pointed to his valet, who was groaning under the weight of a full case. "Do your duty, captain," he said. "Arrest that man."

Clofine paid a fine and his servants went to jail, all of them except the maids, who were just polishing bottles on land. The newspapers said his boat cost more than ten thousand cases of booze, and the whole mess was blamed on his butler, who admitted masterminding the operation, which was a bold-faced lie but a good one. When he got out of jail Boswell bought him a gas station to keep him quiet. For the duration the rich man left the trade to the rest of us, who were doing it for money and not out of pure greed.

There were nights out there when we had to hang a lantern in the bow as a running light for fear we would be run down by some madman in a motor launch who might panic at the sound of another engine in the darkness. There were nights when five to ten rumrunners were tied up at the Row waiting for orders to be filled. Gin, scotch, rye whiskey filled my boat until there was no room to walk. Fate and the sea have never been kinder to me.

Coming in was simple routine. I would set a course straight for the nearest inlet, usually the Absecon. I would take it easy, looking and listening for Captain Frye. At approach to land I would take her up to full speed and roar through with my exhausts wide open. Half the time the Coast Guard were far off somewhere chasing some amateur they had a chance of catching. When they were there waiting for me I would throw the tiller over and run down to the next inlet, knowing I had put miles between us.

Only once that summer did Captain Frye get us in range of his deck cannon. We were ripping up the Shark River with a load for Dixie that had to get in that night. The captain, as luck would have it, was patrolling the immediate waters, and when he heard my engine he cut his and let us enter the narrow passage from the sea. Then out he came, searchlight blazing, about a hundred yards astern.

I could see the silhouette of the two-inch breech loader, I could see the Guardsman behind it sighting down the barrel. I swung the boat hard over and a loose case of Silver Wedding went over the side.

There was a loud report and a shell whistled over our heads. Right then a lesser man would have given up. Not me. I zigged and zagged waiting for him to reload, trying to get water between us. The searchlight stayed on us like a shadow. Minnie and I were hunched down in the stern trying not to think about the gas tanks just behind us and full, for we had topped them off that evening.

I was inland, in a narrow river, and had no room to move. All I could think of was the open sea. But following us through the entrance was the cutter, blocking our way like a cork in a bottle of rye. I took a chance.

Another shell raised a column of water just to port. I shoved the tiller to starboard, spun the skiff on its side and rushed back toward the cutter at full speed while swerving from side to side. I could see the cannon leading us. He had one shot to do us in, and he could not afford to waste it.

At the last moment I cut hard and went for the left bank of the river. The cutter's bow was hit by my wake, shoving them over slightly to one side. The cannon swung and the lanyard was pulled while we were at point-blank range.

But something got in the way. Something came between us, and it was the superstructure of the cutter. The cannon tore off half the cabin and started a fire which took them more than an hour to quell. The Coast Guard had nearly sunk itself while all we lost was a case of booze and a little time. I could hear the captain cursing the stars while I waited a little way off to see if he was all right. When I saw them getting the better of the fire I ran back up the inlet and delivered the load.

They were waiting for us once on the bay side of the Ocean City Bridge. I was running the hooch to a speakeasy in Somers Point for the third night in a row, a mistake, I will admit. Captain Frye had been tipped by some local that we would be coming in sometime after midnight, and he was tied up to the bridge just where we would pass. I never saw him until the last minute. When I did it was too late to do anything other than keep going. There was a tremendous explosion, and when I looked the cannon was no longer on the bow. It had blown up and fallen overboard. I heard the next day that the ensign had failed to remove the muzzle block. He had gone over the side with the cannon, but was all right. They never quite lived that one down.

When Captain Frye got his Pierce-Arrow I got my second engine. Minnie and Ebby installed it the night it arrived, and the next night we were out at the Row just waiting to have the laugh on Captain Frye. He did not appear, but we had troubles from another quarter. On the way up the bay behind Long-port the new engine cut out. We were fully loaded, two hundred cases of Chickencock, and the tide was coming in hard. I swung the boat over to head back to the open sea, where Minnie could have a look at the engine. But the tide had us, and in a second or so we were pinned broadside to the pilings of the bridge. I had not the power to get us off. The boat was at a wicked angle, threatening to over-turn. I killed the other engine to give myself a moment to think. Just then a voice hailed me.

"You all right down there?"

It was Pegleg! He was up there fishing for stripers all alone. I yelled up to him, telling him who we were. He said he would call the Coast Guard to come and pull us off.

I grabbed a bottle of Chickencock and climbed up onto the bridge.

"It's okay, Pegleg," I said. "We can save the Coast Guard the trouble. Have a drink."

He took a large gulp and handed me the bottle. I put it in the pocket of his old over-coat. Below, Minnie had lit a lantern and was getting the engine cover out of the way. A few cars passed us on the bridge, but I kept my back to them. Pegleg looked down at my boat with wide eyes.

"That sure is a lot of booze, Garvey," he said.

The cases were packed so tightly there was barely room for Minnie to move. But I could see she had her screwdriver out and knew she would not be long.

"That is not booze, Pegleg, no sir. That is camphorated oil!"

"Do tell?"

Minnie got both engines going and we were off and away in half an hour. But the next day I heard a drunk in Muldoon's ask for a bottle of camphorated oil and everyone laughed.

Another time, coming through Corson Inlet a big wave washed right over us, nearly filling the boat. The engines died, and for a moment I thought we were going down. When I looked over the side I saw no more than three inches of freeboard; we were barely afloat.

Though I hated to do it, I gave orders to jettison cargo. Moving slowly, Minnie and I cut away the ropes and began easing cases over the side. We dumped a thousand dollars' worth of Beefeater before I felt safe. Minnie and I took turns on the bilge and soon we had her empty. But the tide had carried us back out through the inlet, and we were by then at sea with no power. I was beginning to worry about drinking water when I heard the sound of an engine.

"Coast Guard," yelled Minnie.

"How do you know?"

"Listen," she said. "Pierce-Arrow."

I couldn't tell one engine from another in the dark, but I took her word for it. We threw the last of the cases overboard and waved a lantern.

Up came the cutter with the searchlight. They must have been very disappointed to find us riding so high in the water. But nothing was said. A seaman threw me a line and Minnie ran it forward to the bow. I left her at the tiller and came aboard the cutter at the captain's request.

"Evening, Garvey."

"Evening, Captain Frye," I said. "Rough night."

"Deep waters for clammin'," he said.

"Well, you get the big ones out here."

"Sure do," he said.

He towed us all the way back to Gardner's Basin, and when I got there I thanked him.

"Don't mention it, Garv," said he. "I know you'd do the same for me."

I told him darn right I would and marched

him over to Dutchy's for a morning of boiler-makers. All the laughs were on me that day. I sat there sipping a Coca-Cola while the word went around that Captain Frye had come as close as he had ever come, that he could have let me founder but preferred to keep the game alive. It was all I could do to keep my mind off that Beefeater rolling across the bottom of the silent sea.

That fall the U.S. Government began to work in earnest. Coast Guard stations were beefed up at every inlet and more boats were purchased. The Atlantic City cutter got a second Pierce-Arrow. Ebby pulled both of mine out and put in a hundred-horsepower Scripps Marine, model F-6. We stayed ahead.

A three-man auxiliary Coast Guard station was set up in Longport, and the Great Egg Harbor Inlet was patrolled nightly by them and the Ocean City boys, who were now intent on catching smugglers. This was not good for me, as that inlet led to most of the pickup spots I had established with Dixie. I was cut off from Somers Point, which had become notorious for its saloons and ware-houses.

There was a speakeasy in Somers Point by the name of the Cat Club. They had a stage there with many acts, all of a lascivious nature. I happened to be there once with Minnie when an announcer, a dwarf, came out in front of the curtain to tell the crowd we were in for a special treat. He asked us to throw pennies on the stage, and about two hundred people emptied their pockets of copper. The dwarf ducked into the wings and the curtain came up.

The stage was bare except for the pennies, which lay everywhere. Then from the other side came running a dozen girls, stark naked. They scrambled all over each other picking up the pennies. Then they ran off. The dwarf came back to stay that not one of the girls was past the age of fourteen! I left and never returned.

Job Point, just behind Somers Point at the entrance to the Great Egg Harbor River, was the safest pickup point on the coast. We would run in there about twice a week and anchor in a small man-made harbor. Minnie would stand up in the bow and give a whistle. Then we would wait. Job Point was a fishing village of no more than ten shacks set in a row along the bank. Soon doors would open and fishermen would appear in long rubber boots.

I would hold the bow to the bank while

they unloaded the cases, walked them through the mud and up to a waiting truck. The driver would sign a note and off we would go, back to our berth at Gardner's Basin. Then I would go by Dixie's casino and get paid.

But when they closed the Great Egg Harbor River to us and our kind it meant a longer run down to Wildwood or up to Little Beach or Long Beach Island, where things were not quite as smooth. Little Beach was a haven for black flies in the winter, greenheads in the summer. Long Beach Island had bad roads and only one bridge, which the police often kept under surveillance. This put a dint into the business which took some time to correct.

It was the senator who came up with the solution. He bribed one of the three Coast Guard Auxiliary men in Longport.

"How did you do it?" I asked him the night he gave me the news. We were at Dixie's and he was winning at craps. The place was jammed and a floor show was going on, so it was easy to speak privately.

"Son," he said, "the government's paying those poor devils less than two thousand a year. Well, I just doubled one of their salaries. Our man stands watch at the Point between two and four a.m. all this month. When he's on, a red lantern will hang from the Longport Bridge. When that lantern's lit anything can go under it."

The lantern worked perfectly except for one small flaw. I could not see it until I had rounded the point. I needed more warning. There were two cutters which might be in there at any time, and by the time I could see the light they might be on to me. I had a long thought about this and ended up by presenting my sister Pumpkin with a large telescope.

She would wake up at two in the morning, go up on the howdah and train the telescope on the Longport Bridge. If the lantern was lit she would hang another, a green hurricane lamp, in the right eye of the elephant, just as she had done at my birth. From the sea I could spot the green light easily and make for the inlet in no time. For her efforts I paid Pumpkin a dollar a night, well worth the expense.

Once through the Longport Bridge I could scoot up Risley's Channel past Hospitality Creek and Whirlpool Channel, cruise by Somers Point and make my connection at Job Point.

I could not see that we were getting any closer to the monopoly that Senator Stone had talked about. The waters were getting crowded with Coast Guard and smugglers, and many arrests were made. I did all I could to keep on top of the pile while waiting for shrewd John Stone to further organize the traffic. I put in a second Scripps Marine, glad to be the fastest, but worried about the increasing amount of close calls. A fast boat can still be pinned down in a channel by two slower ones.

It was also getting darned uncomfortable. Minnie and I, bundled and oilskinned to the teeth, would return in the early mornings stiff with cold. We had an open boat, and a wet ride was all she was. Especially on the nights we had to put out in. The Coast Guard would not go to sea on a bad night, this everybody knew. They would keep a stiff lookout from the shore and alert the police if they saw a landing, but that was all. By Christmas the bad nights were the only safe ones. But the Atlantic in December is a cold graveyard, and I could feel it in my bones. The only nice thing about it was that Minnie piped down. Sometimes she never said a word, just stood there pumping, one ear cocked to the twin Scrippses.

It was she who talked me into a cabin. She designed it and Ebby built it of pine, up in the bow so that I could see where I was going. They put in wheel steering and Minnie ran pipes to the watercooling system to feed a small radiator in the cabin. There was a thick windshield with a wiper, a built-in compass and a hard oak bench for the pilot. They built up the superstructure aft and put in watertight hatch covers so that Minnie wouldn't have to bail so much. She could sit up in the cabin with me and argue. There was exactly enough room for two people: a large one, me, and a small one, Minnie. Things got a little better, though I had to run full speed more often to drown her out.

We went out on some awful nights that winter. Once, when the waves were seven feet in the inlet and it was snowing, we set out for two hundred cases of Canadian Club that Dixie just had to have for a special customer from Chicago. I would make plenty of money on the deal, and that was what I was after. I would not have been near a boat until that spring if I had not committed myself to a life of adventure and great wealth. Big Frenchy was out there on the schooner waiting for me. A truck was waiting at Job Point. Minnie came aboard with a thermos of hot coffee and I cast off the lines.

The Row was covered with snow! I could see by the light of the quarter-moon the spars and lines, the funnels and deckhouses of the boats as they lay pitching in an angry sea. I had brought with me several boxes of salt-water taffy, an Atlantic City speciality that was much in vogue, and had determined to present a box to each skipper on the line. But for all my hailing there was no answer. Finally I headed up to the top of the Row, to Big Frenchy's schooner, and blew my bridge whistle full blast. A door opened on the fifth blast and Alphonse staggered out on deck completely drunk. I told him to get his captain, but he said Frenchy was too drunk to move. He said everybody on the Row was aboard keeping warm together and had been that way for several days. I said I needed two hundred cases of Canadian Club. He staggered below.

In that sea I had no idea how we were going to transfer the stuff. I could not tie up alongside without risking serious injury to my boat. Pretty soon I had my answer. Heavily clad men, not a sober one among them, soon appeared at the top of the companionway, each with a case of rye. Minnie was in the hold and had opened the hatches. One of the drunks tossed a case at her, and she let it smash on the flooring. The man laughed, then fell down.

I made a close pass so that two of them could jump aboard. The men on deck began to throw the cases to the men in my boat, who passed them to Minnie. Pass after pass I made until the last case was aboard. Not one had been dropped. I lost four bottles on the one thrown to Minnie but did not even suggest taking them out of her pay. She was in a wild mood when we headed back.

"I'm a damned ape, is what I am," said she.

"Now don't go on about it."

"And you're a damned fool. What the hell do those guys want with saltwater taffy? You ought to bring 'em some women! They ain't gonna last the winter, ya big squid."

"Ha!" I said. "Imagine a woman on Rum Row!"

"Well, what the hell do you think I am, Floyd?"

"I meant . . . with them."

"You're as bad as any of the poor bastards.

246

First woman they see in a week they throw a case of booze at! And you let 'em throw it!"

"Minnie, you are getting a foul tongue!"

Then she let me have it. I rode out a gale of words I would never repeat. It lasted until we came to the shoals.

We were running in through Townsend's Inlet, a bad place on any given day. I thought I had a good idea of the bottom under me, but the sands had shifted. Suddenly a wall of white water rushed at us.

This comber had come a long way to hit us. It had been born a hundred miles at sea in a northeaster to the south of us. It had rolled through a lot of cold water before hitting the bar. When it hit it went straight for the sky. We happened to be in front of it at that moment.

It was too late to turn. Minnie saw it, screamed and threw her arms around my neck. I had time to hit the throttle. We tore right into the wave head-on.

The glass before us was blown out, the cabin flooded in an instant. We were underwater momentarily before surging to the surface. When I looked, another wave at least as large as the first was bearing down on us from astern. I tried vainly to stay out in front of it but could not go fast enough. It caught us in a steel grip and bore us with it over the shoals.

Lucky for us the tide was high and we had clearance. The engines and cargo were still dry. Minnie and I were wet and shivering wrecks. She was sobbing, still hanging from my neck. I pried her off and told her to check the cargo. When she came back she was quiet again.

I did not want to lecture her, but to keep warm on the long run up behind Ocean City I let her know what was on my mind. I told her I would not stand for foul language, I would not stand for chewing gum—a habit she had recently acquired. I said I was determined to make a decent woman out of her. I said someday she would get married and have children and that it is terribly important for a mother to be a good influence on her babies.

Minnie said nothing. She was squeezed up next to the radiator shivering and pretending to look through the open windscreen. She was covered with snow. I let up after a while when my teeth began to chatter, but was glad I had spoken my mind.

It was all for nothing. Minnie was in a state of shock, half frozen, and I had to take her to the Atlantic City hospital when we got in. She was half dead from exposure.

I felt like a low-down heel. I went around to the hospital the next day when she was better and I brought flowers. I told her how sorry I was that I had not noticed her condition until it was time to unload. I said we had made the delivery right on time, and had been paid. I gave her her seven dollars in an envelope and put in an extra five-dollar bill. I said I would pay the medical bills. And I gave her a packet of chewing gum, saying she could chew it in private all she liked.

Minnie sat up and sighed. She took my hands in hers and looked into my eyes.

"I love ya, Garvey," she said, "but it's hard."

I was in the middle of telling her that I had a similar turn of affection when she burst out laughing and lit a cigarette.

"Minnie!"

"If ya don't like it, clown, get outa my hospital."

When I left she was blowing smoke rings and talking about cutting her hair.

Rumrunning was changing. It was getting very risky, and the money was not coming in as it should. Prices were climbing, but not in accordance with the chances we were taking. I resolved to get a bigger, faster, more seaworthy boat. The senator, at his end, finally put his plans to work.

While Ebby was building me a forty-footer, Minnie, the senator and I drove up to Nova Scotia. Meeting with us were five Canadians, a family by the name of LeBanque who had been distilling rye whiskey for four generations. We held our meeting in the back room of a ship's chandlery in Lunenburg. Big Frenchy, with whom I had an exclusive business arrangement by this time, was there. At the wharf was his old schooner, which looked like it could not make another trip down the coast.

The senator made a deal with the Canadians. He said he wanted ten-year-old-rye, the best they had in their storage sheds. He wanted one-hundred-proof whiskey, their highest grade, and he wanted all of it. His last request came as a complete surprise to us all: He wanted a special label made, ATLANTIC CITY. It was sheer genius. We would have exclusive rights to the whiskey off Rum Row. Big Frenchy would be the sole exporter. I would import. Dixie would distribute for the senator. It all fit perfectly.

The label would identify to a thirsty nation the best booze to be had. And we were the only ones who would have it. It would be a seller's market, right in my backyard!

On the ride home I was happily thinking about the future. Driving the big black Cadillac along I dreamed of the money that would soon come pouring in, lifting me to new levels of prosperity. Minnie sat beside me looking out the window, and the senator sat in the back celebrating the birth of his grand plan.

A gas line let go in Connecticut and Minnie got out to fix it. It was cold out, snow on the ground, ice in the ditches, just as I had always thought Connecticut would be. I could see my breath inside the Cadillac five minutes after I had shut down the motor. When Minnie climbed back in she was too cold to talk. The senator asked if she would like a drink and offered her his flask. Before I could bat her hand away she had grabbed it and was slugging down a swallow. She handed back the flask and patted her chest. I was just about to say something when she climbed over the front seat and into the back with the senator.

Old John Stone clicked his false teeth, something he had the habit of doing when he was at a loss for words, which was rare. Minnie pulled his big plaid driving blanket over her and sat back.

"Minnie," I said over my shoulder, "will you get back here in the front?"

"Warmer back here."

"I'll make it pretty darn warm for you if you don't!"

"Go stuff a turkey," she said.

When I looked in the rear-view mirror she was having another drink from the flask. In her other hand was a lit cigarette. And her legs were crossed. There was nothing I could do but go on driving.

The senator had the inclination to drink while driving; that is to say, he drank while doing everything, and as driving to and from his various contacts filled a certain part of his life he often found himself behind the wheel in an intoxicated state. True, he seemed to be able to perform well while ingesting huge quantities of gin, but driving a car is like driving a boat; it requires a certain degree of concentration. Working the pedals and turning the wheel is simple enough, but negotiating muddy roads with cars coming the other way is pure navigation. I had taught myself to drive after a trip we once made up to Dixie's when he had inadvertently rammed into a line of trashcans on Texas Avenue and had to pay off the police. I found that I liked driving as long as there was nothing to distract me, as long as I could concentrate on the road immediately ahead.

But that night in Connecticut it was all I could do to keep my eyes off the rear-view mirror. Minnie and the senator were cutting up, drinking toasts to Atlantic City hooch, laughing and slapping each other's knees. Snuggled up they were, to keep warm, though I had the heater on high. I wondered when Minnie would become ill. When she did not I wondered where she had learned to drink so much and still talk.

It finally grew very quiet back there. When I looked I found the senator sound asleep, his head leaning on Minnie's shoulder, his arm around her. Minnie was sipping alone from the flask.

"You had better come up here now," I said.

"I'm okay."

"It's not nice, Minnie."

"Come on, Garvey," she said. "He's just a big old daddy."

"He is not your father."

Minnie crawled over the seat and sat next to me. She was quite steady and looked serious, like she had been thinking.

"Garvey, we got to have an understanding. I'm seventeen now and you're nineteen. You're not my father either. I can't even remember my father or what it's like to have one. I feel like I've been on my own all my life. You're the first person who's ever tried to tell me what to do, and I only take it because I know you mean well. You mean everything well. But I'm not going to take it anymore. When we're at sea I have to do what you say; you're the captain. But you can't tell me how to live. I am what I am, and I've been me almost as long as you've been you."

I started to say something, but she held her fingers to my lips.

"You better let me finish, Grover," said she. "What you don't understand is that you don't know a damn thing about women. The only time you make sense to me is when you talk to me like a man. But then you confuse everything when you start talking to me like I'm a girl. You gotta make up your mind what I am."

"You're a girl," I said. I got that in.

"Okay, but that don't mean I don't know right from wrong. I got a good idea of what's good for me, and nothin' you've ever said has had anything to do with that. I'm a girl and I like to have fun."

"We have fun."

"Not always, Garvey. Sometimes it's very rough. I don't have to tell you that. It's been one hell of a winter. Can I tell you something? I hate the ocean. I don't mind the bay, but I hate the ocean. I hate it and I'm afraid of it. If I happen to talk a lot when we're bashin' through the waves it's because I get nervous and you're always there lookin' like some goddam Christian soldier to give me somethin' to holler about, see? It don't mean nothin'. It's just the way I let off steam. When I'm wonderin' if the next wave will do us in. But if you think I don't appreciate what you do, you're wrong. There ain't nobody else in Atlantic City I'd get in a boat with."

"Well, thank you. I don't know of anyone else I'd have with me. And I'll tell you something too. I'm not afraid of motors, but I just don't understand them. I don't know what I would do if I had to worry about them while I'm steering. You give me a lot of confidence, Minnie."

"I want a raise."

"What?"

"Said I want a raise. I want ten dollars a run."

I could not understand how the conversation had gone around to this topic, but figured it was the gin.

"I'll tell you what," I said. "I'll pay you ten dollars a run if you promise not to take another drink."

"While I'm on the boat," she qualified.

"Anytime."

"There you go again, blowhard! I just finished tellin' ya I don't want no more guff about my private life! Keep your goddam ten dollars and find yourself a new engineer!"

Then she crawled into the back seat and fell asleep under the senator's wool blanket. I wondered whether I was losing the best friend I ever had.

11

EBBY built me a forty-foot skiff with a single hundred-and-ninety-horsepower Mianus engine that could push her to twenty-two knots with a load of five hundred cases of liquor. It was launched that spring, just when the market became glutted with cheap booze homemade in the States or trucked in over the Canadian border. The great rush to Rum Row turned to a trickle, and many smugglers were inactive or pursued other lines of work. Not me and Minnie.

In May we received our first load of Atlantic City twelve-year-old, one-hundred-proof, high-grade rye, and it was an overnight success in the speakeasies of my town. The crowd at Muldoon's dubbed it "Atlantic City Proof," the best whiskey around, and the name stuck. Pretty soon we had orders from Philadelphia, then New York. While warehouses in South Jersey stood packed with unsold hooch, our turnover was better than ever. As the senator had prophesied, we had regulated the market, created our own demand. Things became much easier for Minnie and me. Because our boat could hold so much, we only had to make a run or two a week. While Captain Frye and the rest of the Coast Guard waited for their monster Mianus engines, a breakthrough for big-bores, we had no rivals for speed.

Prohibition was in full effect, and more power and money had been granted the agencies whose job it was to enforce it. But we still had our man on the Longport station, the red light still glowed from the bridge. The lantern was the best-kept secret on the island, perhaps the only secret that was ever kept for any length of time.

We did not see much of the senator that summer. He was busy campaigning for re-election, a job he loved. He was on the "dry" ticket now and composed long speeches and written works on the subject of sobriety and respect for the law. In the meantime his mansion was being built over a subterranean warehouse that could store two thousand cases of his private blend. The strange thing was that everybody in Pennsylvania seemed to know about it. He won the election by a landslide.

Minnie took an adventuresome job on Steel

Pier to supplement the money I was paying her, ten dollars a run, and I admired her for her courage. She was back in show business, and the act was called the Diving Horse. A tall ramp had been built at the end of the pier and a horse was trained to plunge from its top, forty feet into a huge tank of seawater. Minnie, wearing a bathing suit and a crash helmet, rode the horse.

Many was the evening that I drove uptown in my brand-new Briscoe, entered the pier from a secret doorway beneath it and walked out to the end to watch the Sea Circus, of which Minnie and the diving horse were the star attractions. Her boss was a tall thin man who wore a soiled raincoat and made a speech to the crowd that was meant to build suspense. Minnie would appear leading the horse, bow to the crowd in the bleachers, then walk the horse up the steep ramp. At the top she would wave, then squat down on the horse's back and give him a hard kick in the stomach. The horse would dive into the water with a great splash. Then it climbed out by a small ramp and received the thunderous applause. Many eyes were on Minnie, whose figure had filled out some and was not that well concealed by her bathing costume. Her hair was bobbed and she wore lipstick. Nothing I could say would change this. She said it was show business. I was ashamed. I was sorely afraid she would be branded a hussy before reaching the age of twenty.

One night I took a solo cruise out to the Row to deliver mail. I had taken this responsibility out of gratitude for what those daring and patient men had done for the trade. I also brought them books and magazines to read, saltwater taffy, which they had developed a craving for, and other necessities to carry them over on their long trips away from Canada. That night I noticed a new ship on the line, a small tanker built of iron. When her captain hailed me I tied up and went aboard.

His ship, he told me, had been built for the government during the Great War and was designed to transport drinking water in its huge tanks below. He had had a brilliant inspiration one night in Quebec and had put it to work. He bought five thousand gallons of gin from a man who was making it in Montreal, shipped it by tank car to the coast and pumped it into his new boat, the tanker. His idea was to transport it down the coast to Boston and bring it into Boston Harbor, where a friend of his owned a waterfront warehouse and had a certain understanding with the port customs. There it would be pumped from his tanks directly into barrels in the warehouse, then bottled at a later date after he was paid and gone. The essence of the plan was the low price of the gin, fifty cents a gallon. A huge profit was offered to his friend, who assured him that all was ready at his end.

But someone had talked. On the long trek from Montreal to the Coast, someone had discovered the nature of the cargo and had spread the word. When he left the dock everyone in the area knew about the big run. Word preceded him to Boston, where federal agents staked out the warehouse, ready to intercept the delivery. By a stroke of good luck his friend found out about the imminent ambush and signaled to the tanker with an Aldis lamp that the deal was, by necessity, off. The captain, whose name was William Patrick Conlin, headed farther down the coast to New York.

But things went no better for him at the Ambrose Bight, and after a week of waiting he continued south. Now here he was, on Atlantic City's Rum Row, with five thousand gallons of good-quality gin and no way to offload. Could I help him?

I told him I would think about it and look around for some way to bring it ashore. I knew I could get a dollar a gallon for the stuff and the money could not be ignored.

I was afraid to say very much about the load to any of my friends in town. News like that gets around very quickly, and there was little time to bring it off. I tried every dock I knew, but none was equipped to receive such a shipment. Then I had an idea.

I arranged with a certain friend of mine to have a hundred empty fifty-gallon barrels trucked to the base of Steel Pier. I made a deal with the pier manager, who asked no questions, to store the barrels at the end of the pier under the bleachers that faced the Sea Circus. Telling no one, not even Minnie, I waited for a calm night. It came the following Saturday.

I ran out to Rum Row and found Conlin, who was in a fit of despair. His crew had jumped ship, leaving him alone and lonely. He had been considering dumping his cargo into the sea and heading back in failure. I told him my plan and he jumped for joy.

At three in the morning we ran his boat and

mine over the three-mile limit and right up to the end of Steel Pier. Captain Frye, I knew, was patrolling the entrance to Great Bay, where there had been a great amount of illegal activities all that week. He was sure to make a final check of the coastline under his jurisdiction, but that would not be for several hours, or not at all if he happened to catch some poor devil. I figured we had two hours, just enough time.

It took nearly an hour to drain the Diving Horse tank of seawater and a few minutes to rinse it out with fresh. Then we pumped in the gin.

My plan was to fill the tank and get our boats out of the vicinity by sunup. I would return as soon as I could to transfer the booze to the barrels and refill the tank in time for the evening show. Everything went smoothly. I paid off Conlin and shook his hand. I cautioned him, however, that something like this works only once and to bring along a more portable commodity in the future. He assured me he would.

I raced back to Gardner's Basin as fast as the Mianus would move me and drove over to Dixie's. She arranged for a truck and several men to pick up the barrels that night after the pier had closed. All I had to do now was get the gin out of the tank and into the barrels, an easy job, as the tank was equipped with valve and hose. As I had been up all that night I decided to take a little nap and took it on top of one of her roulette tables. When I woke up it was noon. I drove over to the pier to carry out the final stage of the job.

I had made one mistake. The Sea Circus had a matinee on Sunday! When I got out to the end, Minnie was leading the horse up the ramp. There was absolutely nothing I could do.

Swallowing hard, I watched her prepare for the leap. The surface of the tank was still and clear. The crowd was hushed. After a long drumroll, Minnie kicked the horse and together they plunged in a long smooth dive that, to me, seemed to last forever.

I watched a hundred gallons or so of high-grade gin splash over the side when they hit. After a moment the horse climbed out. Then Minnie climbed out. Bowing, she looked back at the tank. Then she jumped back in. And then the horse jumped back in.

Several summer revelers sitting near the base of the tank licked their lips. Then up the ramp they ran, diving headlong into my reservoir of pure profit. The word spread. In a few moments the edge of the tank was lined with tourists splashing gin with their feet, cupping it to their thirsty mouths. It made no difference to them that a horse and half a dozen fully clothed people were up to their noses in the tank.

I was worried about Minnie and ran up to find her. She was doing a backstroke across the surface, happily blowing up a fountain of gin from her cheeks, laughing with the rest of the swimmers, who were, by now, quite intoxicated. When she swam near I reached for her hand, but she pulled it away.

Some quick thinker signaled to the lifeguards on States Avenue, and in a few minutes they were out there with life rings and ropes, lassoing the drunks and pulling them in. But in a short time they too were in the tank. The old man in the raincoat, a "dry" as it turned out, decided the only solution was to drain the tank, which he did. I could have cried.

I found Minnie in the bottom of the empty tank, unable to move. The horse lay on its back with all four legs in the air. The lifeguards and the drunks were in a great pile trying to lap up the puddles. My five thousand gallons were below, diluted by the waters of the North Atlantic. I carried poor Minnie to the dressing room.

When she awoke she put her arms around me, kissed me and told me she was in love with me. She reeked of gin and I could not take her seriously. Still, I thought there might be a grain of truth in what she said and determined to broach the subject again when her brain had cleared.

On the way home I realized what a shameful thing I had done. I had no business mixing my trade with an innocent circus act, and by my thoughtlessness I had endangered the health of many people. Thankfully, I was the only one to suffer.

Minnie, in fact, was suffering with an extreme hangover the next morning when I picked her up. I explained to her what had happened, but she had already figured it out. She told me, and I was shocked, that it was one of the best surprises I had ever pulled and that no one connected with the Sea Circus would ever forget it. I knew she was rubbing it in.

"Minnie," I said, "do you remember your words last night in the dressing room?"

"Nope."

"You said your love for me was true."

"Said that?"

"Yes."

"So what?"

"Well, I was wondering if you meant it."

"Do you love me, Garvey?"

"Yes, I do. I want . . . I want to ask you . . ."

"Hold on, cummerbund!" she said. "Don't start askin' me anything this morning. I ain't responsible. You sure pick a bad time to get lovey-dovey."

"You know what I want. You must."

"You wanna take me to a hotel."

"Minnie!"

"You don't wanna take me to a hotel?"

"I certainly do not. I want to . . . propose."

"Lemme outa here!" she yelled, and jumped into light Monday-morning traffic on Atlantic Avenue. I stopped the Briscoe, causing an orchestra of horns and whistles.

"Get a hold on yourself, Garvey Leek!" she screamed. At that moment her headache returned and I had to help her back into the car.

Quietly and calmly I outlined my desires on the way back to Margate. I told her that the idea had come to me in a flash, when she had spoken those words in the dressing room. I said I realized that my love too was true and that I would be the happiest of men if she would consent to be my wife. But I explained that this could not come about for a little while, as she was not yet old enough, I thought, and I had not the money. I wanted to start things off well, to buy a house big enough for a large family. That would take time, perhaps a year or two. Minnie groaned the whole time.

We drove over to Somers Point to have some steamed shrimp and deviled crabs, her favorite food. I thought this might bring an end to her moaning. I could not see her face, as her arms were wrapped tightly around her head. At the clam bar she dropped them and looked at me, shaking her head.

"Garvey," she said, "let's have this conversation when you think I'm old enough and you're rich enough, huh? I told you I loved you and I do. But them's just words. My feelings are more mixed. Right now I don't want to think about no house and family. Right now I don't want no promises and plans. Just be old Garvey and I'll tune your engines and manhandle your booze. We got all the time in the world, honey."

"Will you do me one favor, Minnie?"

"What's that?"

"Call me 'honey' more often?"

"Oh sweet Jesus," she said. "This is goin' from bad to worse."

I gave up. I just knew no way to handle it. I was totally lacking in experience and did not know anyone to advise me. I thought that she would have leaped at the chance. I thought that this was every woman's dream. I did not reckon on Minnie Creek and the generation of girls growing up in the Twenties. Especially around Atlantic City.

We kept far from the subject on our adventures together that summer, and soon it was as if our words had never been spoken. Soon it was just me and Minnie again, doing the short hard haul from Rum Row to the shore, dark nights and high seas.

I moved into the Union Hotel that summer, a nice suite on the eighth floor with large windows that fronted on the Atlantic. I could see Rum Row from there and knew instantly when Big Frenchy was back from Lunenburg with another hold of the now famous Atlantic City Proof, which was making my fortune while other smugglers plodded along. The Frenchman had been approached by others but had kept religiously to our original agreement, selling to me and only to me the special brand the senator had christened. Pumpkin came often to visit with me there, and on my birthday brought me a large banana cake, which we shared with Minnie and Razmataz, who was now in my employ. Razmataz did not like the Atlantic Ocean any more than Minnie, but the money I paid him made the work irresistible. Pumpkin, finishing her third or fourth slice of cake, posed a question.

"Do you think it's wise," she asked, "that the whiskey you bring in is so identifiable with you? Doesn't it make it easier for the authorities to keep tabs on you?"

"The authorities know all about me and always have. There's no way to cover up what I'm doing. It's the people we worry about. We want them to know they can trust what is in the bottle and know that for the extra expense they are getting the best. Every bottle sold creates more demand. Sound American business sense. Anyway, if I'm caught it will not be on the land. I don't do anything illegal ashore. If I'm caught . . ."

"It's Allah's will," said Pumpkin.

Allah very nearly willed our capture a few nights later. We had to bring in a load of some four hundred cases to a place behind Atlantic City called Pleasantville. Dixie had found a new spot there, an old house by a creek that ran directly to the bay. I had tested its depth and found that at high tide I could easily slip in there. Job Point had been recently raided by the FBI and the new spot looked perfect.

We picked up the load and headed in by way of the Absecon Inlet without running lights on the first stormy night that came along. It was rough on the ocean and in the channel, but things quieted down when we entered the bay. I knew the way by heart and slowly eased us through the various thoroughfares that led to Pleasantville. I found the entrance to the creek and crept the hundred yards or so with the engine just ticking over. The way was narrow, the banks almost touching the sides of my big forty-footer.

Suddenly a light was on us and a voice barked out of the night, "FBI. Surrender or we will shoot you down!"

The dreaded letters were barely out of his mouth when I threw the engine in reverse. Then all was noise and confusion. The motor roared, throwing mud and marsh grass and bay water high in the air and over us as we charged backward out of the creek. Bullets from automatic weapons tore through the hull and smashed hundreds of bottles. Minnie and Razmataz were in the stern crouching in a narrow space left aft of the stacked cases. I was, by necessity, in the bow at the controls. I had to steer by instinct as I dared not raise my head. The windshield was shot out, and I could see the searchlight through the gaping holes in the bow. Cedar splinters when it is hit by a bullet, and the lethal shards were flying everywhere. I kept my hand on the wheel, waiting only for the moment when we would reach open water. Miraculously we did so without running aground.

But there in the bay waiting for us was a boat I had not seen before. It was a Coast Guard launch from the Barnegat station, brand-new and very fast. On her deck stood three men with machine guns blasting in our direction. I shoved the engine into forward, threw the wheel over and missed them by only a few feet. More noise and more confusion. The air I breathed reeked of whiskey, a smell I could never abide.

I was out ahead of them and still afloat,

running for a channel I knew from clamming days. I yelled back to see if my crew were all right.

Minnie came running forward, cool as can be, to say that she was fine and that Razmataz was bailing. We had to yell at each other, but we communicated. I told her to sit up on the bow and direct me. I told her the route I wanted to take, a complicated one with many switchbacks that I hoped would elude my pursuers. It was difficult to see anything, but Minnie signaled when she saw banks and I followed her directions. The boat behind us ran aground after a few minutes.

We tore through Beach Thorofare only to find another Coast Guard boat waiting. The ambush had been carefully laid, and I wondered what else they had in store for us. The way was narrow and the boat blocked the passage to the inlet. I headed south down to Ventnor, passing under the Dorset Avenue Bridge with only a few inches' clearance. The Coast Guard were hard on me, firing when there was no danger of hitting anything on the shore.

On the north side of the Margate Bridge was a large can buoy, anchored there to mark the deepwater channel. I thought I might use it to effect my escape. I told Minnie my plan and headed directly for the buoy. At the last moment I swerved around it, then resumed my course. The Coast Guard ran smack into it and stove in their hull.

Razmataz came forward to report that we were sinking. A small-bore cannon shell passed through the transom at the waterline, just missing the engine, and had gone out one side, below the waterline. I told him to get back on the pump and get ready to swim.

The last thing I wanted was to sink in the bay where recovery of my boat and its incriminating cargo would be relatively easy. I wanted to get to sea or as close to it as possible. I felt a little better as the silhouette of the Longport Bridge came into view.

There was no red lantern. That meant the Great Egg was patrolled, possibly with boats alerted to my presence. I thought fast.

The tide was high and at the turn. The bay was now beginning to drain through the bridge to the sea. As the engine began to splutter, I knew what I had to do. I yelled to Raz and Minnie to jump, which they did without hesitation. A few dozen yards before the bridge I threw the wheel hard over and jumped from the gunwale.

Dog-paddling, I watched my nearly new forty-footer smash side-on to the bridge and blow up. She sank instantly and in many pieces, which, I knew, would be taken with the tide to and through the inlet. Unfortunately the bridge, old and rickety, was now burning. I struck out for shore.

Minnie, Razmataz and I regrouped on the marshes, slogged along through the black mud and weeds to the causeway. Sadly I watched as a thirty-foot section of the bridge collapsed into the dark waters. Some tourists, on their way back to the island from a wicked night in Somer's Point, were parked and watching the destruction. They gave us a ride back to Atlantic City, the long way on Route 9 that ran parallel to the bay. I had to go up the fire escape to my suite in the Union for fear that my muddy and sodden clothes would cause a stir. Minnie came with me.

I showered under the hot seawater tap that the Union had installed in every bath, then got in bed thinking about what I had to do the following day and listened to Minnie busy herself in the bathroom. In a few minutes she came out dressed in my bathrobe and sat on the edge of my bed. She asked if there were anything to drink and I said no. I told her she could sleep on the couch, but she stayed where she was.

Minnie was very quiet and did not move. I wondered and asked her if she was all right.

"I got somethin' to tell ya, Garvey," she said.

I was very drowsy but listening.

"I got a little tipsy the other night in Muldoon's."

This was no surprise to me, as I had seen her there on several occasions drinking highballs at the bar. But what she said next certainly startled me.

"I was braggin', I guess, to a friend of mine, and I think I let it out where it was we were supposed to make the drop in Pleasantville."

"What friend?" I asked, sitting up and wide awake.

"Just a guy."

"Who?"

"Some swell from New York," she said. "I can't remember his name. But he must have told somebody somethin'. That's the only way it could have happened."

I looked at her, saying nothing. She hung her pretty little head and played with the bedspread.

Well, there was nothing to be done about it. Minnie had a weakness for booze, and maybe it was my fault. But she was not stupid, and I knew that it was only the drink which had loosed her tongue. It was as much a shock to me to find that she had been having intimate conversations with strangers in a saloon.

Finally, I asked her what she was doing hanging around Dutchy's so much in the first place.

"I don't dive the horse no more," she said. "I got fired after the boss found out it was you who put the gin in the tank. I've been workin' for Dutchy Muldoon. He's got a card game upstairs and I run the drinks."

"Minnie, let's get married!"

"Uh-uh."

"Why in blazes not?"

"I'm just not ready," she said. "Don't know if I ever will be. But I'll sleep with you ... if you want."

"We'll sleep together when we're man and wife," I said.

"Yeah." She went over to the couch and soon was asleep.

The first thing I did on the following morning was drive down to Longport, to the house of a very old and prominent resident there that I had known for some time. I gave him five thousand dollars in cash to repair the bridge. I did not have to tell him it was I who had caused the damage. Everyone knew. That five thousand was the best money I ever spent.

Then I went up to Eberding's and ordered a new boat, fifty-two feet on the waterline. He told me he had some good news.

"I got a new engine for ya, Garv," he said. "She's left over from the war! *Aircraft* engine."

These motors, he explained, were being converted to marine use by the Vimalert Company of Jersey City. The one he showed me in his loft was a four-hundred-fifty-horsepower liberty, called a Vimalert-Liberty, and she was vastly more powerful, cheaper and lighter than anything else known.

"Does Captain Frye know about this?"

"It's his engine," said Ebby. "Goes in as soon as I get a clutch made for her."

"Get me two," I said, laying down hard cash. Ebby said he would have them by the end of the week, that the boat would be ready in a few weeks' time. He promised me an honest thirty-five knots under a full load of one thousand cases.

At the thought of driving a fifty-two-foot Sea Bright skiff at thirty-five knots and more, the depression I had been feeling all morning suddenly left me. I had one more idea.

"Ebby, could you put some steel in her? Some kind of protection?"

"Armor?"

"That is what it is called, yes."

"Well, yeah! Where, all over?"

"Just up in the bow. By the wheel."

He agreed, shaking his head, that it might be a good idea. I thought it was the best one I'd had in some time.

Minnie was gone from the Union when I returned. Asking around, I tracked her down to the beach. She had been swimming, and looked very beautiful in her wet bathing suit. The beach was crowded, and we walked up to the cool shade beneath the boardwalk. I told her what I had done that day. I saved the news about the aircraft engines until last.

I thought she would be excited, but this was not the case. She listened and drew lines in the sand, saying nothing. She looked so lovely in the light which came in zebra stripes through the planking of the boardwalk. I tried to hold her hand, but she shook it away.

"I'm not goin' with ya no more. I made up

my mind. I'm no good for ya, Garvey. I'm goin' my own way."

"You can't mean that, Minnie."

"Yeah, I do. I been thinkin' about it all day. If you'd got hurt last night I swear I woulda killed myself. I coulda jumped off the Union."

"It doesn't matter, Minnie. I must have you aboard!"

"To look after them engines."

"That and for all the reasons I ever had."

"Ya can't trust me no more."

"Sure I can! You learned your lesson. You'll never do it again, I'm sure. I have faith in you, Minnie. I need you." I was pleading. Minnie meant more to me at that moment than I had ever known. I tried to envision myself at sea without her and could not.

"Look," I said. "Quit working for Dutchy. I'll double your salary. Twenty dollars a run."

"I like workin' for Dutchy."

"You do?"

"Sure I do! I like the crowd. Dutchy's ain't a dive no more. He's fixed the place up and he gets a good clientele."

I could imagine. Politicians and racketeers.

"I like to dance, Garvey. I like makin' whoopee."

"What do you mean, 'makin' whoopee'?" I asked.

"You know, Garve. Havin' fun. You're such a stodgy old prude, you know."

"Old?"

"Okay, a stodgy, stuffed-shirt, fuddy-duddy."

This was more like her. And I had to agree with her in many ways. I certainly had no notions of making whoopee. She had begun to smile.

"I'll learn to dance," I said.

"You gotta learn to wear shoes first."

"I'll buy a suit and shoes and you will teach me to dance."

"I can just see ya."

"Come on, Minnie. What do you say?"

"You're such a sucker, Garvey."

"That I may be. But I speak from my heart."

She smiled and kissed me on the lips. I blushed, got up and suggested we go for a swim. The crowd on the beach watched as we crossed the sands and entered the water.

"Who's that?" I heard a child ask its mother.

"That's Garvey Leek and Minnie Creek," she replied. "They're the pair that brings your daddy *booze*!"

12

IN order to make a fifty-two-foot boat invisible she has to go pretty fast. I may not have been invisible, but I knew I was getting fuzzy around the edges. Ebby's new aircraft engines kept me on top, the first and foremost of the Brotherhood of the Coast, as the newspapers liked to call us. My new boat held so much booze I needed to make only one run a week. She handled beautifully, like a boat half her size, except in extremely rough water. In the fall I ordered another one built, but modified for winter tempests. It was somewhat smaller, forty-five feet, and all bow. A heated cabin forward would protect me from the cold. Watertight hatches kept the sea from the cargo and engines, two modified Liberties that Minnie had made perfect in a machine shop in Gardner's Basin. We called the first the summer boat and the second the winter boat. Side by side they rested at a dock not thirty feet from the Coast Guard station, the envy of every powerboat enthusiast on the island.

Beginning the following winter I stopped bringing in anything but Atlantic City Proof, my greatest profit lying there. My name, in some circles, became one with the highline blend. People I met on the streets began speaking to me with a twinkle to the eye, a nodding of the head to show we shared a common secret. I gave cases of it at Christmas to the town's leading businessmen and politicians. I even had a case sneaked over to Captain Frye's cottage one night when he was out at sea looking for me. A few nights later I found a new government-issue flare gun in a wooden case on the end of my dock. It was a distress signal in case I was ever going down in the dark. I took it with me on every run, knowing if the captain ever saw its red glow in the sky he would be there to save us.

Captain Frye became a great hero the following winter. One night in March, far at sea, he came upon a disabled freighter bearing a Panamanian flag. Her engines were burned out and the sea was rising with the wind. The captain took her in tow and headed for Absecon Inlet. About eight miles off the beach the freighter collided with the cutter and stove her in. Captain Frye had to jump for it. The water was very cold. With him were his first lieutenant, an ensign and a seaman first class. Captain Frye was thirty years older than the oldest of them, but he kept the coolest head.

"Boys," he said while pulling off his clothes and dog-paddling, "the last one to the beach is a dead man." Whereupon he started stroking.

The first lieutenant, a local waterman named Fogel, was a strong swimmer, having spent his youth as a member of the Beach Patrol. Taking a bearing on the Atlantic City skyline, he set out behind his captain, stroking mightily through the swells now breaking in the sudden storm.

The ensign, whose name was Doughty, had been drinking all the night before and was too weak for the marathon swim. Removing his trousers and knotting the legs, he trapped air in them and created his own life preserver. In the breast pocket of his peacoat he discovered a pint of gin. He clung to his inflated pants, sipped the gin and eyed the seaman first class.

The seaman first class, a dirty little coward whose name has never been spoken since, had a cork lifering and would not share it. It was easily large enough to support two men, or three, but he defended his exclusive right to it with hard, frantic thrusts from his legs and arms. There was no use swimming with it either, as it acted like a sea anchor in the billows. Thus he drifted a few yards from Doughty and watched him sip the heart-warming alcohol in silence.

Eight miles swam the captain and the first lieutenant, pausing only to take a new bearing on the shore. They should have stayed together. But Fogel, a sprinter, took up a faster stroke. He feared death from freezing if he lingered near the slower Captain Frye. Frye was slower, but steady. Soon he found himself a quarter of a mile behind Fogel, glimpsing him momentarily just before the break of dawn. Fogel was on his own, a pity, because Frye had something to tell him, something vital.

What the captain knew and the lieutenant had forgotten was that no man could make it safely through the surf. For nearly half a mile the huge swells dashed themselves on a series of sandbars built up by a winter of storms and strong currents. Reaching the surf in a semi-exhausted condition, a man was sure to drown in the clutches of the enormous hollowbacks that could suck a lifeboat under when they liked. Yet just beyond the breakers was the beach and relief. Frye had a plan.

The current, he knew, had been steadily sweeping them southward. They were now off States Avenue, on the north end of Atlantic City. Frye judged they would arrive at the surf line off Virginia Avenue. Looming there, above and beyond the breakers, was the monstrous Steel Pier.

No one in my town doubted the fate of a swimmer trapped beneath the pier. Barnacle-encrusted pilings, hundreds of them, waited for helpless victims like a school of blood-mad sharks. It was worse than keel-hauling, more feared than a rock jetty to the lee of a foundering craft.

Fogel, far ahead, decided to try his luck in the surf. On other, warmer days he had tamed the waves and ridden shoreward upon them, using only his body as a planing surface. But now it was a gray, angry dawn and Fogel had stroked eight miles in icy waters. Still, he reasoned, the surf was his only chance.

Frye knew better. He knew every inch of his shoreline and he remembered that at the very end of Steel Pier, just beyond the first breaking waves, was a ladder of sturdy oak used by the divers in the Sea Circus. If he could find the ladder among the treacherous pilings he would not have to deal with the surf!

Fogel entered the first break as a weak yellow sun appeared on the horizon behind him. The waves were fifteen feet from cap to trough. He stopped swimming and waited for the largest to come along. On it he planned to ride directly to the beach, its surge bearing him swiftly over the somewhat smaller breaks to come. The wave he chose would mean the difference between life and death. He had barely the strength to buoy himself up in the water which now began to numb his aching limbs.

A monster comber appeared on the horizon, and Fogel made his decision. He began to swim once more, his salt-blinded eyes hard on the boardwalk some distance away. He maintained a forward motion, fighting the suck of the hollowback piling up behind him. At the last moment he windmilled his arms, slashing the water before him. Then, feeling the thrust of the water around him, he folded back his arms and surfed down the sheer face of the wave.

The swell was too big, and it buried him, forcing the air from his lungs. Struggling to the surface, he was borne along, gasping for air and swallowing foam, until he arrived at the second break, where the waves rose again, not as high, but with terrific strength. Fogel's head popped from the water, his lungs filling with air, just as he crashed over the white water and into the blue. Again he was buried in the soupy froth, again his lungs were crushed under the immense weight of water. Nearly unconscious, he was swept to the most treacherous line of all, the vertical shore break which fell from ten foot to a shallow bottom of hardpacked sand. He literally flew from the face of the boomer and was half drowned when it landed on him.

His body was smashed to the sand, washed like a rag doll back into the break, drawn up again and cast headlong to the beach. His skin was blue and he had not a thread of clothing left on him. Salt water drained from his open mouth. His eyes stared vacantly at the mud on which he lay.

Captain Frye neared the end of Steel Pier, looking for someone on deck who might throw him a line. There was no one. His numbed mind fought desperately to remember the exact location of the ladder. In the end he had to guess.

The pilings produced strange currents which bore him this way and that, reaching for him with their poisoned parasites. The swells rose and fell, nearly trapping him beneath the deck, which, at times, was only a few feet from his head. In the gloom he spotted the ladder and made for it. Using the last of his strength, he fended himself off a concrete piling, lacerating his left hand in an instant. But in the next, his right hand found a rung. Slowly, his body beginning to grow rigid, he climbed. He reached the boards in time to fall exhausted upon them. A watchman found him a few minutes later and revived him with several gulps of Atlantic City Proof.

Fogel's form appeared lifeless when spotted by an off-duty lifeguard, who set about pumping quarts of water from his stomach and lungs. There was no reaction. As a last resort he breathed air into him, and Fogel coughed. He was rushed to the hospital, where he remained in a coma for three days. Though he was soon back at work, he was not himself again for some time.

Meanwhile Ensign Doughty and the seaman first class drifted south, Doughty treading water and swilling gin while the sailor clung to his precious cork ring. The coward begged for a sip of the liquor, but Doughty would agree only in exchange for a handhold on the preserver. In his piteous state the seaman first class refused. When the bottle was empty, Doughty struck him with it and gained a hold. Fortunately, in another pocket, the ensign found still another pint and was able to revive the frozen boy.

They were quite drunk two hours later when picked up off Wildwood by the Corson Inlet Coast Guard. Doughty they said, bore a light-hearted grin throughout his rescue and did not officially report the seaman's actions. The boy, a Burlington County landlubber, was transferred from his post and forgotten by all.

Captain Frye was the hero of the day. His praises were sung in every saloon and speakeasy on the island, and never did he pay for a drink the rest of that winter. In the spring he came to me with a warning.

Minnie and I were having lunch on the end of Captain Starn's dock, a basket of steamed crabs at our feet. Razmataz was bailing out the summer boat in preparation for our first run of the spring. The winter boat was being overhauled at Ebby's, both engines to be replaced with larger ones called Gar Wood Liberties. The engines in the summer boat were spanking new. Captain Frye appeared behind us and, wishing us a good morning, sat down and had a long look at my boat.

"Well, Garvey, I've got some bad news—not that it'll affect you any. Times are changin'. It's the government again. They're doin' away with the three-mile limit."

I told him I had heard rumors to that effect but had not believed them.

"They passed a law in Washington that'll shove international waters out to twelve miles! You know what that means, boy?"

"It means your job will be four times more difficult." He knew I meant my job as well. Already I was thinking about the size of my gas tanks.

"Yup. They know that. And they think it's too much for the Guard. They're throwin' in the Navy! It's a power struggle, is what it is."

"The U.S. Navy?"

"Destroyers! Escorts! Chasers! It's the big guns, Garvey boy."

I wondered what the range of those big guns was, but did not bother to ask. I knew they could hit anything they could see. Then again, I was invisible. But the prospect of an encounter with a real warship awed me.

"Darned federal meddling," I said.

"Yup," said the captain. "I just wanted you to know." Then he changed the subject. "How you doin', Minnie Creek?"

"Damn good, captain," she replied. "Have a crab."

The captain refused politely, drawing from a pocket a silver flask and sipping from it. "I got a problem. My port engine's got a knock and she don't rev like the starboard."

"Is it a knock or a kind of a bung?"

"More like a bung, bung, bung. Half-speed."

"Bearings. She's shot, captain. Ya only get a year or two out of 'em."

Raz had the bilges dry and we cast off, waving to Captain Frye, who waved back with the silver flask. It was a bright clear morning and I decided to run out to the Row and give Big Frenchy the news. When we got there the line was jammed with smugglers. I tied up next to Dutchy Muldoon's old scow. I wondered what he was doing aboard the schooner that held the only available supply of Atlantic City Proof in the world. I found him drinking with the captain. Everyone, it seemed, had heard the news.

"Garvey, lad," said Muldoon, "it's been a cold winter. Now things is ten times worse."

"Bigger gas tanks," I said.

"Me, I don't like being out of sight of land," said Big Frenchy. "I'm a coaster, you know."

"You need a new boat," I said.

"You bet. I can pick up a trawler," he said.

"That'd be a lot more booze, Frenchy," said Dutchy. "A lot more Proof."

"*Oui.*"

"What we're gonna need, Garvey," said Muldoon, "is more cooperation between us. They're ganging up on us, we gotta gang up on them!"

"I'm independent," I said. "They can do their worst. I'll do mine. Alone."

Big Frenchy winked at me. Muldoon scowled.

All over the Row men sat talking and drinking, realizing an era was about to end. In ten days the ships would weigh anchor and head for the horizon. Why, they said, the government could do as it pleased out there and no one would be the wiser. I took Big

Frenchy aside, took him up to the bow and had a private talk.

"Get that trawler," I said. "Load her to the decks with A.C. Proof. I'll take all you've got. Thousand cases a run and I'll pay ten percent more. Just keep it coming."

I told him to have everything he had left ready by the following evening. Empty, he could return to Canada and buy his new boat. The distillers would lend him the money if necessary. The Frenchman agreed.

We started our engines in the late afternoon, which prompted the other crews to start theirs. Thus it was, a short while later, that the entire Atlantic City fleet of rumrunners steamed through the inlet in ordered file, quite a sight to see. Seventeen boats of all descriptions made a show of strength to assure the island populace and the rest of the country, for that matter, that supply would continue to meet demand. At a price increase, of course.

The next night, a cloudy one, we were loaded down with booze and headed up a narrow river to a place called Port Republic. Dixie was waiting for us with eight darkly clad men. I knew some of them from previous pickups; some were new. Beside her Buick, parked in a ditch, stood a long low Oldsmobile. Shadowed figures smoked cigars in the back seat.

"Chicago crowd," she said, pointing to the Oldsmobile with her thumb.

"The mob?" I asked.

"The big boys."

"Who?"

"Louie the Gimp and Three Fingers Frank. They're lieutenants for Fat Al Buddha."

I had read about them in the papers. Two of their band had been gunned down by a rival mob and the streets of Chicago turned into a battlefield. Three Fingers Frank was wanted in New York for murder in the first degree. Louie the Gimp ran the booze to Chicago's North Side. The supply must be getting pretty low, I thought, for them to come all the way to Atlantic City, where they would have to pay top dollar for the good stuff from Dixie. Now here they were, climbing from the Oldsmobile, walking toward Dixie and me. Louie the Gimp, a short man, tried to conceal his stiff right leg as he walked. A henchman handed a bottle of Atlantic City Proof to the other man, who uncorked it and took a swallow. Two of his fingers, index and middle, were missing.

"Evening, Frank," I said as he stood before me.

"Who you?" he asked.

"He's the captain," said Dixie. "That's his boat."

"You got a nice boat, kid," said Louie the Gimp.

"Thanks," I said, trying to hide my nervousness. The truth is I would rather have faced a hurricane a hundred miles at sea than these two men on the land. Evil reeked from them. Evil and vice and corruption and greed.

Minnie came up whistling, her hands in her pockets, her eyebrows fluttering.

"Hi ya, kiddo," said Louie. He obviously liked what he saw. Minnie lit a cigarette and tried to look as tough as she could.

"Hey, ya got grease on yer face," said Frank.

Minnie wiped the grease from her cheeks with the back of her hand, which only smeared more on them. The mobsters laughed. Minnie strutted away.

"So you work for Dixie, huh?" said Louie, shifting his little pig's eyes to me. I saw no point in explaining that I worked only for myself. I nodded.

"Well, pretty soon you's gonna be workin' for Fat Al. Everybody's gonna work for the Fat Man, right?"

Dixie and I exchanged glances.

"Fat Al," exclaimed Three Fingers Frank, "is very interested in Atlantic City. He thinks you got a little gold mine here. All's it needs is a little organization, huh?"

"I'm not in the position to say," I said. My voice stammered, sounded hollow.

"Yeah," said the Gimp, turning away. Frank paid Dixie for the load with an enormous wad of hundreds. Truckdrivers started their motors, and soon we were left alone. Dixie shook her head.

"It's a mess," she said. "People like them have been pouring into town all winter. It's been quiet so far, but I wonder."

"How do you mean?" I asked.

"Well, it's always been a sort of unwritten rule that the mob keeps its activities out of town. They come here to relax, to talk business, to see who's still alive. And they leave their gangs at home. It's changing."

"What's the senator say?"

"He told me to treat them like any other

298

customers. I wouldn't have brought them here, but they insisted."

"What did they want to see?"

"You."

"I was afraid of that. Do you think they'll try to muscle in?"

"It depends upon whether or not they think it's worth it. They'd like to buy directly from the Row, but it's a new line for them. They're feeling things out."

We said goodbye and Minnie cast off. On the way back to the basin she stood before me in the bow.

"Scared, weren't you?" she asked.

"Yes, I was."

"They could see it."

"I've no doubt of that."

"It was a mistake, Mumford."

"I couldn't help it, Minnie. I'm repelled by everything they stand for. What can I do?"

"Garvey," she said, "if you can't play with the big boys, don't play with the big boys."

Minnie left for Muldoon's as soon as we were docked. Razmataz helped me clean the boat. I asked him what he thought about the turn Minnie's life seemed to be taking.

"Nothin' you can do about it, Garvey. That girl's got her own mind. She don't know a mistake till it's too late. I hardly ever see her anymore except on this boat."

"Well," I said, "the city's filling up with gangsters and they have some sort of attraction for her."

"Just don't forget who was the first gangster she ever met."

"Which one was that?"

"You."

"I'm no gangster!"

"You so sure?"

"I'm a rumrunner."

"Well, that's a crime. And you sure do have it organized."

"I don't have a gun or a gang. I am not violent, nor do I aggress my enemies—"

"Maybe that's what she misses," said Razmataz.

I drove back to the Union feeling low, realizing the truth in what Razmataz had said. But I could think of no way to change the state of affairs. All I could do was hope that someday I would change my ways and that Minnie would change hers. I saw myself in her eyes backing down to those mugs, shaking and scared like a darned idiot. Perhaps the next time would be different.

Pumpkin had a surprise for me the next

day. She made me drive her downbeach to Margate, to a shop on the new parkway that the town had built. The store, a small one, was called Pearl's Pastry. Pumpkin then announced that I was half owner. We went inside to meet Pearl.

Pearl was half Pumpkin's age, but somewhat fatter. My sister, as I have pointed out, was exceedingly stout but carried her weight well, in a matronly fashion. Pearl was just plain fat. But she had a pretty, young and intelligent face and seemed to know everything about baking French pastry. I sampled her wares, liking especially her almond croissants, the first I had ever tasted.

I could tell that Pumpkin and Pearl were fast friends. They punched each other playfully on their arms, munched doughnuts and laughed the whole time they talked. Pearl, however, was nervous when she spoke to me.

"I'm sure the business will be a great success," I said. She nodded.

"In fact," I went on, "I have an idea which might help you. I have connections with several of the large hotels in Atlantic City and I'm sure they would like to order pastry in quantity."

Again Pearl nodded. Pumpkin took her arm.

"I imagine you could sell a thousand doughnuts a day in Atlantic City."

"A thousand a day," said Pearl looking at her feet.

"That's a little out of Pearl's line," said my sister.

"Oh?"

"She likes variety, you know. Doughnuts are so simple. When would she have the time to make her *pâté de marrons,* her *flans* her *pêches à l'eau-de-vie?* A thousand doughnuts indeed!" They both laughed and began to wrestle on the counter.

"Simplicity is the essence of American business," I corrected her. "Simplify, expand, dominate."

Pearl and Pumpkin tittered together. This made me laugh too, a little louder than the ladies. They stopped abruptly.

"Pearl's interest is not in money," said Pumpkin, looking at her watch.

"No?"

"No. It's in pastry. An *artiste,* you see. She's half French."

Pumpkin nodded to Pearl and they excused themselves momentarily. Walking behind a

302

display case, they knelt on a small Turkey carpet facing east. It was noon.

So, I thought, Margate now has two Moslems. One of them is my sister and the other my partner.

"What half of the business do I own?" I asked on the way back to the Union.

"The property," said Pumpkin. "You own the whole block. It'll double in value every five years. Meanwhile, you get a third of the profit. It should be lucrative, brother dear."

I patted my sister's knee and she squeezed the bulging bag of pastry beside her.

Pumpkin had not consulted me on this acquisition. I had given her free rein to invest the capital I had lying about. I could not bank it for fear of interference by the authorities. We were building toward the future, more respectable days ahead. I had only told her to give priority to real estate on the island, preferably in Margate where the land was still relatively cheap. I owned lots now, large ones on the beach and bayfront, and I intended to build on them.

Atlantic City, a wasteland all that winter, was blooming now with spring. The boardinghouses were full, and hundreds of couples strolled the boardwalk. Prohibition, it seemed, had done more for the town than any other single event. Bars and brothels openly sold their wares to the curious tourists eager to have some summer fun. Whiskey was selling for a higher price than ever before. On every bottle of the best I made a profit. As the money poured in I wondered how long it would last. I wondered how hard I would have to fight to stay on top, or if I would fight at all.

13

IN the summer of 1925, four men walked into the Union Hotel and took the elevator to the eighth floor, where a party raged in Room 888. Their leader, a short man who limped, knocked on the door, saying, "Room service." The others stood back, guns drawn.

When the door was opened by a pretty blond girl she was pushed aside. The gunmen sprayed the room with bullets, then fled. They left behind them three wounded men, one of them near death. The guests staying in Room 888 had given as their address the Grosvenor Hotel in Chicago.

The four gunmen used the elevator to descend to the lobby, which was empty at this very early hour of the morning, four a.m. But by the time they reached the street and a waiting Oldsmobile, the police had arrived. The gunmen directed sustained automatic fire toward the police. One of the mobsters fell on the way to the sedan.

The man with the limp jumped in the back seat, firing through the rear window. His cohorts mounted the running boards, Thompsons spattering the street. They drove in a mad rush toward Pacific Avenue.

I was driving my new Cadillac slowly down Illinois Avenue on my way home to the Union after a night at sea. The getaway car came surging toward me, bullets flying in all directions, the rear wheels spinning, grasping for traction. My windshield shattered before my eyes.

I skidded the Cadillac sideways, threw on the brakes and dove for the street, looking for cover. My car blocked their path; they had to stop. In the blue glare of a streetlight I saw a line of trashcans and raced for them. I jumped into the largest of them, finding it empty. Though the thin tin walls of the container offered no resistance to flying lead, at least I was hidden. I waited to see what the mobsters would do.

"Where's Frank?" I heard the man in the rear seat yell.

"Back on the street!" said a man on the running board.

"Go get him."

The Oldsmobile spun around and drove at high speed back toward the boardwalk and the waiting police. Machine guns thumping, they cleared their way to the wounded man. He was gathered up, tossed in the back seat under a barrage of gunfire. Lights went on in the neighborhood, people peered from windows. A baby cried and someone yelled, "Oh Jesus, Mary and Joseph, the world's gone mad!"

Back came the Oldsmobile, bearing directly for my car. At that moment another car, black and full of policemen with drawn revolvers, arrived at the scene. Their car stopped behind mine and the law-enforcement officers took up positions behind the Cadillac. The getaway car stopped, spun around once more, headed for the boardwalk. I jumped from the trashcan waving my car keys. The police waited the moment or two I took to move my vehicle, then sped past.

Realizing there was no exit from Illinois Avenue, the gangsters drove up the wooden ramp to the boardwalk, where they turned south. The police, at some distance, followed. In a wide segment of the boardwalk just in front of the partially completed Convention Hall, the getaway car spun in a classic boot-legger's turn, reversing its direction. Back they roared toward the oncoming police, who fired wildly as the car passed by. In the darkness and confusion the driver of the Olds-mobile lost his sense of direction and took a right turn at the entrance to Heinz Pier. Thinking they had gained access to Pacific Avenue, the hoodlums raced out along the pier, an old one of great width.

But Heinz Pier was short, and at the end stood the largest roller coaster in the city, a ride called the Loop the Loop. Through its seasoned pine supports crashed the car at great speed, throwing long dartlike splinters in all directions. A fifty-foot section of the coaster collapsed—just as the car passed under it and tore through the railing, flying forty feet through the air and into the sea. Four felt hats bobbed to the surface. The next day when the car was raised, no trace of its occupants was found save for a half-empty bottle of Atlantic City Proof.

The day after the shooting, business in Atlantic City was normal; a crazed rush from beach to bar, twenty-four-hour stage shows and open gambling. But a pact had been broken. Mob violence had erupted in the city, guns had been drawn and fired in anger. The town was no longer safe for racketeers or any-one else.

My suite at the Union was numbered 889,

the room next door to that which had come under attack. The men from Chicago were identified as minor thugs of the South Side Gun Club, a rackets organization which rivaled the notorious group headed by Fat Al Buddha, who was in Canada at the time undergoing a rest cure for nervous stomach. It was coincidence which had brought the gunplay so close to me, coincidence or destiny. I resolved to move from the Union.

I bought a brick house on the parkway in Margate and moved in the day the bed was delivered. I bought a Rolls-Royce, a white one, to replace the Cadillac, which was riddled by bullet holes. Razmataz took the small apartment over the garage. There was a nice room for Minnie on the first floor, but she declined my offer of accommodation. She preferred her place, the back room of a fun house on the boardwalk at New York Avenue. She said she liked her privacy.

Minnie spent her days in greasy jeans and washed-out flannel shirts. Her room was filled with fishing rods, crab traps, wooden cases stuffed with tools, kewpie dolls, stuffed animals, pillows with sewn-up mottoes, sea-shell ashtrays, fish nets, fashion magazines, a disassembled marine engine, driftwood, an old harpoon, orange crates and a Victrola with dozens of swing records that played whenever she was home.

Most of her time was passed in tuning my engines over at Ebby's. She installed new ones, repaired old ones, devised new systems for cooling and lubrication. She gave advice to all the baymen who came to her with mechanical problems and often kept some of my closest competitors on the high seas.

When the day was done she changed. Her work clothes were dropped in a corner and replaced by tight silk dresses and rolled dark stockings. She scrubbed the black grease from her face and applied dark-hued rouge to her lips, mascara to her eyes. She dusted tiny silver stars into her hair and pasted them to her cheeks. She smoked Lucky Strike cigarettes in a long rhinestone holder. She tottered into the wildest speakeasies on high heels and kicked them off when somebody asked her to dance. Minnie could dance like three girls and was never afraid of attention. She was known by every bartender in Atlantic City, and they all loved her.

Minnie loved the big hotel bars, the corner clubs on Pacific Avenue, the cabarets and casinos tucked away in boardinghouse basements or under arcades. She liked to hang on the arm of a high roller and help him win or lose his money at every game in town. As long as a man was nice to her, bought her dinner and drinks, danced with her and helped her home if she was drunk, he was a friend. I know she had many offers of marriage, but she turned them all down. "I'm a butterfly," she would say, and anyone who knew her had to admit it. But they would always add that she was about the prettiest butterfly they had ever seen.

Minnie drank too much, and I used to tell her so. But after a while I learned to keep my admonitions to myself. While I worried about her liver, her pancreas and her stomach, she danced, drank and ate as she pleased. She drove herself until there was no energy left in her body, and in the early mornings she would fall asleep at a table, her curly-haired head resting on crossed arms.

I asked my dad once if he knew a solution to the problem. I asked him, in all innocence, how you make a woman stop drinking. He told me you hit her with the bottle and finish it before she gets up off the floor.

But then he cautioned me seriously. "When a man drinks," he said, "he needs an excuse. When a woman drinks she has a reason."

The only reason I could see was that she was unable to decide which part of her was the real Minnie Creek, the flapper or the engineer. I know that often while working on engines she would talk about the goings on of the night before. At night she would usually make everyone gasp with her stories of rum-running, or bore them with details about carburetors and connecting rods. On the dark nights we spent together at sea she was the way I loved her best. She was cool, deliberate and drawn completely into the adventure of the moment.

Our biweekly runs to the Row grew more intense. The risks were raised, the seas crowded with traffic. We moved quickly, wasting not a moment nor an action. A thousand cases of liquor are not transferred at sea easily; a twelve-mile journey at full speed and often under pursuit is no simple exercise. Control and maintenance of a boat such as mine required all our concentration and efforts, leaving room for no mistakes.

Minnie and I worked off all our nervous anxieties through constant squabbling, words that meant nothing and were forgotten a few moments later.

"Give her more spark, chowderhead," she would yell.

"Don't tell me how to run this boat, shrimp!" I would reply.

At times we made more noise than the engines.

One day in the spring of 1926, Dixie drove to my Margate home at three in the morning, pounded on my door and woke me up. She had news of serious implications. There had been a shootout at Dutchy Muldoon's and a man had been killed. Dutchy had been taken to police headquarters and released. But his statement to them implicated the dark forces of the mob which was gaining strength in Atlantic City. Dutchy, she said, wanted to see me. I followed her uptown in the Rolls.

Dutchy was sitting across the bar from Bullets, who was drunk and playing the radio loud enough to wake the neighborhood. I asked Dutchy what had happened.

"Ah, but it's the old story, lad. We were havin' a game. I was losin'. I've been losin' all the winter to these new boys, these rogues you might call them. Then, just as my little doggy jumped into my lap, I caught one of 'em cheatin', puttin' the big ones where the little ones should be. Funny I'd missed it before. I think, Garvey, they work as a team."

"You always held good cards, Dutchy," I said. It was true; Dutchy's luck was renowned.

"Aye, but until this winter, Christmas last, when these boys showed up. Anyway, as I stand from the table, the one pulls a gun. A big one it was; a cut-down shotgun such as are used by the police."

"Good God, Muldoon, what did you do?"

"Well, I took it away from him, naturally. I threw it from my window there. But the other was ready for me. He fired, the bullet just missin' my head."

"The dirty skunks!" I said.

"There's more! I'm lyin' on the floor pretendin' I'm scared see? The one who was cheatin' kickin' me now in the ribs here. The other one tells me I'm finished. He tells me I'm a stubborn man.

"Ya see, Garvey boy, these boys have been after my business. They wanted my bar and offered me money, which I refused, naturally. So, this boy is tellin' me how they'd tried to buy me out and, in failin' that, had tried to

314

cheat me out. But it had come to this. They said there was nothin' left to do but pull the trigger, as I'd given 'em little choice. I could hear the hammer cock on the boy's forty-five.

"Well, Bullets here came through the door with a tray of beers. Up into the air they went, and before they hit the deck I was up and on the boys. The first went through the window and he's gone. The second I plugged with his own gun. They've just taken him out. But I'm in trouble now, I am."

"From the other one?"

"Garvey, these boys is small fry! I know who's behind 'em and that's what I told the police. I told 'em as it was Fat Al Buddha who sent 'em, for he's everywhere now. He owns the two saloons down the block and is buildin' a casino up on North Carolina Avenue. You know what the coppers said? They said they never heard of him. Then they got real nice and let me go, writin' it off to common self-defense. They know, Garvey, and the fix is in!"

"What can I do?"

"I dunno, lad, but I'm tellin' ya this. It's not just the bars they're after. It's the business, the whole business, and that means Atlantic City Proof. And they know all about you and Dixie. They know about the senator, though they show a bit more caution with him. The senator is not such an easy man to reach as you or me."

"Thanks, Dutchy," I said getting to my feet.

"What will ya do, then?"

"Talk to the senator. Think of something."

"Good lad."

Greed. Greed was on the land, in the air. Greed would go to sea if I could not stop it. I had an enemy now, and that enemy was greed. Dixie telephoned the senator to tell him I was on my way.

I drove alone in the Rolls, speeding through the dark pine barrens that kept Atlantic City the island it was. More than the narrow bay which divided it from the mainland, the scrub pines with their unpaved roads, their gloom, cut us off from Philadelphia and the rest of the world, made us think we were invulnerable to outside interests, pressures, greed.

I got lost in a place called English Creek, stopped at a filling station to ask my way. The attendant informed me of my mistake, taking ample time to wash all the windows of my car, to check the pressure in the tires. On impulse I asked him where a man could buy a drink in English Creek. He said to go down the road a mile and look for a sign announcing the residence of the stove cleaner.

I found it, a hand-painted sign in the gravel yard of an unpainted house. It read, "Stove Cleaning—Done to Perfection." I knocked on a pinewood door and was admitted by an elderly gentleman, the stove cleaner himself. We passed through his living room, where an old woman was listening to the radio and waving away flies. We stopped in the kitchen, a bare room furnished with a large table, a chair and a sideboard. He asked me what I wanted.

"A quart of the best rye you have."

"That would be Atlantic City Proof," he said, and produced a bottle with a familiar label. The price was five dollars. While paying I mentally broke down the cost. Big Frenchy had paid fifty cents for that bottle in Lunenburg. I had paid a dollar for it on Rum Row. The senator, through Dixie, who worked on salary and commission had paid me two dollars. The stove cleaner had paid three, I imagined, passing it on to the customer at a two-dollar profit. It seemed to me that through my endeavors many people were

317

making money, money they could spend on the good things in life. The nice thing was that I was making as much, or more, than anyone. A dollar a bottle! Just for risking my life and liberty once or twice a week, every week of the year, every dark night, every storm. Nobody could begrudge me that. But it looked like they were going to try. Fat Al Buddha had his greedy eye on the dollar I was making.

I passed through Philadelphia in the darkest hour of the morning, found my way up to Scranton, which was just waking. The senator's servant, taking my hat, escorted me to a side porch, where old John Stone was having breakfast with a beautiful girl. His wife had passed on and he was spending his dollar a bottle on what he wanted. The girl, after being introduced to me, excused herself politely and left the porch. Birds twittered on the cut lawn. Beyond it I heard voices from the tennis courts.

"Any blues biting?" asked the old man.

"Just little weakies."

"Nothing in the world like a panful of fried weakfish."

"Hard to clean," I said.

"Why Garvey," he said with a droll smile,

"you haven't cleaned a fish in years. In your own way you're one of the laziest men I know. Outside of myself, that is."

"I never liked work," I said.

"Nope. You've that in common with every criminal I've ever met. And you share one more trait with that bunch."

"What's that?"

"You fancy yourself just a little bit smarter than the rest of the world."

I grinned.

"Fortunately the resemblance ends there."

"I'm not greedy."

"Nope. Nor dishonest."

"Thank you," I said.

"How's Minnie Creek?"

"I guess she's happy. You know Minnie, senator. Either she tells you how she's feeling, which is bad, or she doesn't tell you, which is worse."

"When are you going to marry that girl?"

"We don't talk about it anymore."

"Your problem is that you're both so incredibly romantic. If one of you were rational you'd be raising children by now. If just one of you had his feet on the ground you'd be settled. But your feet are flying over water and hers are kicking over a dance floor and you never get the time to really see each other."

I felt sad and fell quiet. I brought up the reason for my visit and told him about the shootout in Dutchy Muldoon's. He knew all about it.

"The Buddha wants in, boy. When he gets inside a ring, the ring vanishes and there's just him left. That's what he did in Chicago, and that's what he wants to do to Atlantic City. We'll all wind up working for him if he has his way."

"I'd sink my boat first," I said.

"He'd make sure you were tied to it."

"I see."

"Fat Al Buddha has never been to Atlantic City; he doesn't know what a boardwalk or a bathhouse looks like. To him the town's a pin on the map, but the pin is green. His main line is booze. He has it brought in over the border or made in the backwoods of Kentucky. He deals in enormous quantities of cheap liquor, and he always makes a profit. He buys low, sells high. Sometimes he doesn't bother to buy it; he steals it. Did you ever steal anything, Garvey?"

"A bayonet."

"A bayonet?"

"French. I took it from an outhouse when I was a little boy. I had to return it."

"You learned a cheap lesson, boy. Balance, the scales. When you take something from somebody you tip the scales. You *have* to give something back to restore the balance. You know what it is you give back? Power!"

"Power?"

"You give him some of your power. You give a part of your personal power to someone you have already made an enemy. Then he has more power than you and he will use it to take all that you have."

"That is romantic, senator."

"That's just why it applies to me and to you. We believe it. It does not apply to Fat Al Buddha. He's a rationalist. He just takes and forgets about it. We're not names and faces to him; we're numbers in his little book. Right now we're in the wrong column. The way he sees it, we're costing him money. What goes in our pockets should be going in his."

"What can we do?"

The senator sighed and drank a few inches of Atlantic City Proof.

"I don't know, son," he said. "Come up with an answer and I'll help you in any way I can. But I'm getting too old to think. I've won all my battles in back rooms with men I respected but didn't fear. The Fat Man plays by different rules, and I'm scared. I'm scared for me and I'm scared for you. It's you that has to come up with something. You're strong; you're young."

"Age doesn't matter, sir."

"Oh, Garvey, but it does. You know what I hate about it all? The way time passes. Garvey, it's unfair: you're young for such a short time. You're old for so goddam long..."

And when he said that his face fell, his eyes watered. I was looking at an old, old man who was finally admitting that he had somehow lost a precious gift that was supposed to be his forever. It was the same look that crossed Dad's face when he gazed at the expanse of water which covered Point Farm. It was the look of final and inevitable defeat.

I lowered my head, toyed with my gold watch chain, tapped the shiny toes of my wingtips, sipped my orange juice. What he said sank in. It was up to me.

"When is he coming?"

"In two weeks he wants to see me at the Bayswater Hotel. He says he's having a party. You're invited too."

The Bayswater was the newest, grandest

hotel in Atlantic City. Mobsters and politicians had suites there, and we were supplying its huge basement saloon and gambling room with Atlantic City Proof.

"Two weeks from today Fat Al will tell me to move aside. He won't offer money, he won't make threats. It's understood that if I don't do what he wants I'll be eliminated. All we can hope for is a compromise."

"You don't just eliminate a state senator, sir."

"You do when he's a booze king, when he's made a fortune breaking the laws of the land."

I stood and paced the room, my heels clicking on his marble floors. Outside the birds sang, the squirrels chattered. I could not think. Something was missing that had to be there. At once I realized that I was too far from the sea. I needed the slap and crunch of those hollowbacks, the surge and rush of the tide over hard sand. I had to get back to my island home where the sun went up and came down over a changing sea, where people weighed their problems on long walks on deserted strands.

"Senator," I said, "I'm going to think of something."

He slapped his knee and smiled, looking younger again.

"Yup," he said, "you will, Garvey. I know you will."

When we said goodbye I felt like a soldier being sent on a dangerous mission by his general. I felt alone.

The awful weight upon my shoulders began to lift as I reached the Jersey Pines. Through them I sped until the land cleared before me and I was on the marshland causeway, my new Rolls humming along, the tule weeds waving in the onshore wind. By the time I crossed the Margate Bridge I was whistling a popular tune.

I picked up Razmataz at my house and drove him up to Ebby's. Ebby and Minnie had my new rumrunner waiting for me, and I put my mind off business and onto boats.

She was huge. Her bottom planks were three-inch-thick Jersey pine; solid enough to take anything I could give her. Amidships were mounted a Wright Cyclone engine, flanked by two matched Sterling Vikings. She had armor up by the bow and a miniscule cuddy cabin with two bunks. Oil gleamed on her exposed motors, and fresh paint brightened her lapstraked sides.

Ebby, with a gallon jug of home-brewed beer, looked proud. Minnie, smoking one cigarette after another, looked tired but happy. A crowd collected around the boat, and in that crowd were smugglers and Coast Guard, fishermen and harbor bums, joined as one in their love for sea craft. She was the biggest and fastest boat ever built in the area. She represented the dreams of many, the labors of a few. We broke champagne on her bow and slid her to the water. I invited every man on the dock for a ride, and most accepted. The others were content to watch and shake their heads.

That night I went to see Pumpkin. I had told no one about the menace I was now dreading, and I had to share the weight with the strongest person I knew, my sister. She was living with Pearl in a frame house on the beach at Margate. We had chosen the house together, partly for its solidity and partly for the tall tower at one corner which afforded a clear view of the Great Egg Harbor Inlet and the Longport Bridge. Mounted in the tower now was a long and shiny brass telescope that could, at night, distinguish signals from stars.

Finding her alone in her herbarium, I told her my true feelings about the state of affairs and the events which were to come. I told her that I was determined to keep what I had, to help my friend and patron, the senator, to keep Fat Al Buddha and all those like him far from the gay innocence of Absecon Island. She listened while watering her plants. Then, handing me the watering can, she led me to her kitchen, where she made tea, mint tea.

"Very scary, brother dear," is what she said.

I nibbled at a marzipan, waiting for her to expand.

"In the first place you really don't know who you're dealing with."

"And he does not know me either," I said.

"In the second place maybe it's getting out of hand."

"I am at my best when things are out of hand. I have been out of hand all my life."

Just beyond her window broke the waves of Margate, and as they fell, one by one upon my consciousness, I sipped my tea and listened to my sister's sweet silence.

Pumpkin's serenity always had this effect upon me. I became calm, my mind stopped racing from cause to effect, from one bad alternative to another. The feeling was as if I lay floating upon the surface of still water. As

I sighed I began to sink and the water slowly numbed my body and brain. At last I lay comfortably on the bottom, in the soft black mud, and above me were fathoms of green sea which shielded me from the sun, the sky, the land and all my petty problems. When she spoke her voice seemed close, seemed inside my head.

"Big Al is having a party?" she asked.

"That's what the senator said."

"Can I come?"

I snapped out of my trance, floated to the surface and found myself back in her kitchen.

"You cannot. What possible good would that do?"

"I don't know, Garvey. Maybe I could help somehow."

"Absolutely not. The only thing I can think of doing is somehow showing him that I'm tough, that I'm not easily pushed aside. How can I show up with my big sister?"

She paused for some time, the same smile never leaving her lips. Then she looked down at the table and whispered, "I've never been to a party."

"Come on, Pumpkin!" I said. "I come to you for help and now I feel like a heel. How about Allah? What can he do for me?"

"I already asked him that. He gave me the same answer he always gives me, the best answer there is."

"What did he say?"

"He said, 'Help yourself.'"

Just then Pearl walked into the kitchen, stark naked, and drank her cup of tea while we changed the subject.

14

IT looked like Fat Al and the slammer bluefish were going to arrive at about the same time, midsummer, when Atlantic City goes half crazy from the sun. I put him out of my mind and ran booze for the thirsty thousands at the shore. Often we had to spend days at sea, bunked on Big Frenchy's trawler, waiting for bad weather or moonless nights when the long run in would be a safe bet. But my new boat carried so much hooch that each run paid for her twice over, and Pumpkin had her hands full finding new investments. The Rum Row watermen often came aboard to chat with Minnie and me, asking us to spin yarns of our adventures. I never liked to talk about them then, but Minnie did.

"Boys," she would say, "did you hear about the time we broke down off Peck Beach with three cutters comin' at us outa the moonbeams? Had to give five hundred cases the deep six in half the time we loaded 'em out here. We did it and wrote the load off to bad luck. Only, Razmataz here had other ideas, and he was on the beach every morning for a week. The seventh day the cases started showin' up, one or two, but that was enough to let him know where they was. He came back that night, drivin' a wagon. Tide's dead low that night and the mud was covered with cases!

"He gets half of them in the wagon when the Ocean County Sheriff's Department shows up in two Model T Fords. Raz takes off down the beach beatin' hell outa the horses. The Fords are bearin' down on him, racin' across the mud. Raz heads for the southern inlet where the low tide leaves a bar you could build a house on. Tide's comin' in by the time he gets to the end of the bar. The boys in the Fords think they got him, 'cause he's got nowhere else to go. Raz just whips them horses into the water. The horses swim and the wagon floats! He's headin' for them dunes down there where the truck's parked. The sheriff's men double back, but there's five feet of water comin' in the gully! They run back to the middle of the bar, only now it's half its size. Raz sits in the wagon up on the beach drinkin' a bottle of A. C. Proof, wavin' at 'em and laughin' like a madman.

330

Hell, he's only a hundred yards away. They yell over that there's not a man of 'em that can swim. Raz hollers back that he'll come get 'em if they promise to help him load the truck. What could they do? Raz got 'em, all right, but the cars were gone for salt water. True to their word, they swung the load to the truck and asked for a ride back to town. Raz gave 'em the wagon and half a case, the generous boy, and delivered the load that night to the swankest speak in Linwood. I was there with a friend of mine, the dude who owns the place, and you shoulda seen his face when he looked at his order all covered with mud and seaweed! But a bottle's a bottle and a cork's a cork; Linwood was wet that night, and nobody needed a label to know the stuff was Atlantic City Proof!"

And the sailors would hang their mouths open and dream about doing some real smuggling where the profit goes to the man who takes the real risks, and the devil may take a coward to a saltwater grave.

Other runners were out there too, and on the starry nights they had their stories to tell. We passed the hours like a band of rogues, brothers of the coast, laughing at the law, at the landlubbers, at ourselves. It is odd that

331

the funniest stories are always the ones that ended in disaster. But it was all so incredibly romantic! We were contrabanders and our lives were led day by day. And if they ended on some dark cold night at sea, then that was part of it all. A sad story made us cry no less than a happy one, and no more. Irony and deceit played their parts along with heroics and guile. Every incident provided a stirring tale, though the man who told it was more often drunk than not.

Once a deepwater Canadian asked Minnie how much she made out of the business.

"Two and a half a day," said Minnie Creek.

"Only two and a half dollars?"

"Hell no! Two meals and half a bunk."

Then everyone had the laugh on me. Those boys liked to have a laugh on Garvey Leek. I had a bigger boat and more money than any of them. I let them laugh and I laughed with them. Pumpkin had always told me that the biggest mistake a man can make in life was to take himself too seriously. You do that, she said, and Allah starts to giggle. She said not even the Prophet thought very much of himself. She told me that she had a dream once that Mohammed came back to earth and found himself inside the biggest mosque in Cairo. He looked around and turned red.

"It's nice," he said to the muezzins, "but you can't roll it up and put it on the back of a camel. We never know when we might have to ride for our lives!"

Old John Stone drove down to the shore the day before the big meeting at the Bayswater. He looked older than ever, like the fun had gone out of him. I tried to cheer him up, but he was hard on the silver flask and morose. We both went to bed dreading the next day. In the morning Minnie and I kept busy cleaning up the boats, tuning engines and arguing.

"I'm going with ya," said Minnie.

"No you are not!"

"Look here, Leyland, there ain't no hotel room in Atlantic City I can't go to if I want."

"Minnie, you just better do exactly as I say or you go back to the beach with a box full of dry ice and popsicles."

"You ever been slammed upside the head with a two-inch open-end wrench?"

"Have you ever been paddled publicly with a nine-foot oak oar?"

Well, it kept us busy and relieved the tension. But that evening I was frantic. The senator and I were alone in my dining room, dressed for dinner and the evening ahead. John Stone smoked cigars and wore black. I wore a white suit with a white silk tie. He asked me if I had come up with an idea, and I outlined my plan.

"The only way to handle it, sir, is by prevarication. All he really knows about Atlantic City is that you can get anything you want here. We are going to tell him that, even though it's a lie. We are going to tell him that our operation is part of the legal system down here, and has been since the beginning of Prohibition. To fight us he has to fight the United States Coast Guard, the Navy, the FBI, the Internal Revenue Service, Immigration, the Atlantic City Police Force, the Postmaster, the county sheriff, and the mayor. We are only telling him what he knows to be true, even though we know just the opposite."

"It won't work."

"It is all I can think of."

The telephone rang, and it was Dixie telling me that Big Al was in town. He had asked her to cater the party, which was in our honor. He had requested flowers, many flowers.

"Flowers?"

"Roses, daffodils and lilies."

"Oh my God, Dixie . . ."

"Don't go, Garvey."

"I have to."

"You could leave town."

"I will leave this town when you do."

"Okay. I'm sending a case of champagne."

"Send two."

"Right. Well, good luck, Garvey, and take care of yourself. Stay jolly and maybe he'll fancy you."

"I do not want that man's friendship."

"I can think of a worse relationship."

"Don't."

I did not tell the senator about the flowers. We drove up to the Bayswater in the Rolls. The hotel was on Florida Avenue, which was paved all the way to the boardwalk. I looked at the vacationers on their front porches, each rooming house more gay than the one before. I envied their innocence as they sat fanning themselves and talking about sunburn, beach fleas and new amusement rides. And I guess they envied me for my car. If only they had known the sickening dread building inside me, the thought that this night might very well be my last. Was it a trap? Was he as ruthless as the newspapers painted him?

The doorman, a local lush, welcomed us to the Bayswater and winked at me as I entered the hotel. Built the winter before, the huge building was decorated in red velvet and gold leaf. If there were any society people in Atlantic City that summer they were all checked into the Bayswater. The style was eighteenth-century French, and there was not a straight line built in any piece of furniture. Golden cherubs drifted across the ceiling of the lobby, while a burgundy carpet stretched into every corner of the immense room. Empire-waisted ladies strolled through ornate arches, chatted behind the potted palms, looked my way with interest. Their husbands, in evening dress, puffed cigar smoke into the seashore air and spoke loudly of the stock market. Senator Stone and I walked purposefully to the elevator and took it to the top floor.

Pausing in the long hallway, the senator took a drink, then held the flask in the air.

"Atlantic City Proof, boy! The sweetest baby in the baby parade," he whispered.

"Sir?"

"I've kissed a lot of babies, Garvey. This one's the sweetest of all. We made her so sweet that everybody wants her. Everybody wants a kiss."

"Yes, sir."

"Whatever you do, Garvey, don't let him know you're scared."

"I am not scared."

"Well, don't let him know I am."

I looked at the louvered door at the end of the hallway and knew that through it could come nothing as fearful as some of the waves I had faced the winter before. When one has fought nature—fought and won—people do not seem so threatening. Yet I understood that once that door opened my life might change forever. A thousand things raced through my mind as I walked the gloomy corridor, distorted images of people I loved fled my imagination as I knocked. The door swung open instantly, and standing there was someone who could only be Fat Al Buddha himself.

Fat, fat like Pumpkin's Pearl, he was. Short, short like some ice-cream happy boy on the boardwalk. Beneath a set and thick-lipped mouth his jaw extended out and up toward me.

"Yeah?"

"Mr. Buddha?"

"Yeah?"

"I am Garvey Leek. This is Senator John Stone."

"Where?"

I stepped aside. The senator waved to the Fat Man.

"Hi ya, senator," he said. "Come on in, pal."

The suite was enormous and far more elegant than any I had ever seen. The furniture was white wicker, the carpeting white straw. White silk curtains were pulled aside, revealing a long row of windows that fronted the dark ocean. Fat Al led us to a white wicker bar. We were the only people in the room. There must have been fifty dollars' worth of arranged flowers standing along the walls. The effect was funereal, but that may have been my imagination. I felt trapped, confined.

Fat Al reached behind the bar and produced an unopened bottle of Atlantic City Proof. For the first time he smiled.

"Class," is what he said. "Real classy booze."

The senator nodded and looked at me. I smiled at Fat Al, who was tapping his thick fingers on the bar. He was young, no more than forty, and in his white tuxedo looked like a little dictator. His chin never left that upward-tilting angle. His eyes were steady, small, but protruding like a ghost crab's. Fat Al was ugly.

"Class, boys! Quality. It's all I drink."

"I'll send you a case, sir," I said.

"Don't call me sir, kid. Only cops call me that."

"I'll send you a case, Alfred," I replied.

There was a long silence. I nudged the senator, who finally spoke.

"Let's have a drink," said Senator Stone.

Fat Al pulled the cork out of the bottle with his teeth and tossed it over his shoulder. His eyes never left us.

"When friends come to see me I throw away the cork, huh?" Then he laughed with his whole body, like an ape.

He filled three glasses halfway with a steady hand. I turned my back to him and walked to the row of windows, through which came warm and salty air. My eyes fastened on the line of twinkling lights far out on the horizon. Rum Row, twelve miles away, winked at me.

"Hey, big boy," said Al from behind. "What you say your name was?"

"Garvey," I said without turning around. "We're gonna have a toast."

"Garvey doesn't drink," I heard the senator softly say.

"You wanna glass a water, Garvey?"

I nodded. In a few seconds I felt his hand on the small of my back. I turned, and he handed me a glass of water. He raised his glass, looked from me to the senator, and said, "To the future, huh?"

We drank to the future. I returned my gaze to the dark sea with the little red lights. Fat Al punched my arm with a meaty fist. Pain shot up to my shoulder.

"So you're the boy who brings it in, huh?"

"I bring it in, Al."

"Which one of them little lights has got the A. C. Proof?" he asked. His crab eyes squinted.

"It's different every night. Tonight it's the third boat down, looking south."

"How can ya tell?"

"I can tell."

"Boy, I wish I had a smart cookie like you workin' for me. You know what I got? Idiots. Hey, take a look. Lemme show you my idiots."

He led me to a closed door, opened it. The

340

senator and I looked in. Sitting on two double beds were four men in black tuxedos. Spread around them on the white bedspreads were small black pieces of machinery. Big Al's men were cleaning their guns for something to do.

"Idiots, right?" he yelled into the room.

The four men looked up and spoke in unison.

"Right, Al!"

Fat Al closed the door with a look of disgust.

"Idiots. You know why I keep 'em around? Because they do what I tell 'em." His eyes shifted back to me.

"Boy, I wish I had a smart cookie like you," he said.

We faced each other, Fat Al's chin pointing at me like a boxer's glove. I sipped my glass of water.

"What do you want, Al?" I asked. My expression was blank. I was tired of games and felt like leaving. I dislike being looked at like a dead fish on a dock. Fat Al shook his head and returned to the bar. The senator sat in a big wicker chair nearby. I waited.

"I want booze," said Fat Al Buddha.

"Booze we got," said the senator. His voice trembled.

"Yeah. You got it. You got the pipeline. I wanna be on the end of the pipe, huh? I want to distribute."

"You already do," I said.

"Yeah. I ran a couple loads of Proof. Ya know what happened? I didn't make no profit. That is not the way to do business, right?"

"Everybody profits on Atlantic City Proof," said the senator.

"I'm not talkin' nickels and dimes, Senator," he said. "I'm talkin' profit. It's a long way from A. C. to Chicago. The way you boys got things set up, it ain't worth it to me. We gotta make some changes. You follow me?"

"I am way ahead of you," I said.

"Good. Then you know what I'm talkin' about. I can only see one way to work this out —my way. The way I work is quantity."

"We can handle any quantity you want," I said.

"Yeah?"

"Yeah."

"I get a discount for quantity?"

"Naturally," I said.

"Okay," said Fat Al, "okay." He perched himself atop a barstool, studied his folded hands. He was pretending to be deep in thought, yet I knew that this entire business had been thought out before. If he would stick to business, I thought, we might actually be able to work something out. As much as I disliked dealing with an arch-criminal, I knew I had little choice if he presented a legitimate offer. Business is business.

"So, what's the discount?" he asked.

"What kind of quantity?"

"All."

"All?"

"Everything you bring in. How much?"

I turned back to the window to compose myself. This was the catch. Fat Al wanted sole distributorship; he wanted control. Nothing else mattered to him. Once he had control, Atlantic City Proof became his and I became his lackey. Dixie would be eased out and Senator Stone would be pushed out. It was simple extortion set in business language. I gathered my courage.

"Nope," I said.

"Nope? What do ya mean?"

"You do not get all, Al. Nobody gets all.

Anybody can get as much as he wants, but nobody can get all."

"If I want all I get all!" he screamed.

"Nope."

I turned to face him, my arms crossed, my legs spread as if on the deck of my boat. Al jumped from the barstool, knocking it over. His arms flashed violently in the air, his face distorted in rage. I backed away.

I had never witnessed rage in a grown man, and it was unnerving. It was as if the animal instincts of a fat and spoiled child were suddenly released in an adult who had never been crossed.

"*Nope?* Why ya big hick, who the hell do ya think you are? Nobody nopes *me!* You hear me, ya dumb damn idiot? *Nobody* nopes me! J. Edgar Hoover don't nope Al Buddha! God almighty don't nope the boss! Ya hear me, punk? *Nobody nopes me!*" He slammed both fists on the bar. He jumped into the air and crashed both feet onto the floor. He picked up a glass and smashed it against the wall. He went to the bedroom door, opened it and yelled in, "Nobody nopes me, right?"

The gunmen looked up. Most of their weapons were assembled. "Right, Al!" they said.

He slammed the door. "Idiots!" he yelled at me. "You think I left Chicago to come to this here honky-tonk for a nope? You're in my back pocket, boy!"

Again I faced the windows. I heard the senator excuse himself and me. He said we were leaving. I heard Fat Al Buddha say nobody was leaving except on a stretcher.

He screamed at the ceiling. "Nobody's leaving, right?"

From the bedroom came the four voices: "Right, Al!"

He stood before me, his limbs and face quivering. He jabbed his finger into my chest.

"No nopes!"

Again his finger caught me, hard, in the stomach. I silently resolved to stop him if he did it again. I knew that a word from him would bring his mugs into the room, their machine guns ready to cut me down. There would be nothing I could do to stop them. But I could stop Fat Al's finger, and this I would do regardless of the consequences. I would stop him and neither of us would ever forget it. I held my breath.

I think he read my mind. He was aiming another poke at my chest when he stopped, ran to the bar, grabbed the bottle of Atlantic City Proof and smashed it on the bar. He came back and held the jagged end in my face, turning it slowly. My back was to the wall, my arms ready to spring. But the sharp glass was close to my eyes and I doubted if I could fend off a sudden jab. The bottle shook in his hand.

"You are gonna *beg,*" he whispered.

There was a sharp rap on the door. The senator stood quickly and opened it. Fat Al lowered the bottle and laughed.

"You're a lucky cookie," he said, then turned toward the door. I could not believe my eyes. Standing there in a hotel uniform, and pushing a large metal table on wheels was Razmataz.

"Party time!" he said, and wheeled his table into the room. Behind him, in line, were Dixie, Pumpkin, Pearl and Minnie Creek.

I sat down.

The ladies were dressed in the most modern and immodest manner. Feather boas and sequined short dresses. Rolled stockings and bobbed hair. Dixie, looking like a board-walk queen, stood aside as Pumpkin, Pearl and Minnie came strutting by, each with her finger in the air. They were singing a song, one I had never heard.

"Atlantic City! Atlantic City Proof . . .
  We're telling the truth,
  It's the bump in the bottle that's a little
    uncouth!
Atlantic City! Atlantic City pie . . .
It's the . . . one-hundred-proof . . . twelve-
    year-old . . .
High-grade . . . Canadian rye!"

They danced in a circle around Fat Al, who stood there dumbly holding the broken bottle. Pumpkin reached out and pinched his cheek. She shook her hips, and soloed,

"Hey, take me down to the beach, high roller,
  And leave your roll behind,
  Don't pay it no mind,
  You got to get some sunshine!"

Then Pearl chimed in,

"Oh, won't ya walk me down on the boardwalk,
  Where all the cards are wild?
  You silly child,
  We're gonna make some moonshine!"

Minnie and Raz joined the chorus. Hands waving, feet prancing, they finished the ditty and one by one kissed Fat Al Buddha on his flabby cheeks.

"Party time!" said Razmataz, and launched a champagne cork across the room. Minnie held a bottle between her knees and aimed the cork at me. I ducked and the cork flew by my ear. I shook my finger at her and pointed to the door with my thumb. She laughed and raised the bottle to her lips.

Raz pulled a white cloth from an object on the lower shelf of his table. It was a Victrola in shining walnut. He wound it up and placed the needle in the groove. The song was "Carbarn Lil," a great favorite that summer in the bawdy houses. Pumpkin and Pearl danced for Fat Al, who seemed spellbound. Razmataz gently took the broken bottle from him, found a cigar and passed it to the open-mouthed mobster. Dixie put her arm around him and said, "So how do you like the girls, Al?"

Fat Al clapped his hands, sat down and pulled Pumpkin onto his lap.

"Boy," he said, "for a big girl you sure can dance! I'll bet you're a show girl."

"I am," said Pumpkin.

"Where do you dance?"

"On the beach, honey," she said. "Between the tides."

15

IT was Minnie who opened the bedroom door. Just inside it, listening to the music, were Fat Al's four thugs. Minnie grabbed the closest one and pulled him into the room. The rest followed, leaving their guns behind. They looked at Fat Al, but their boss was engaged in tickling Pumpkin, always a very ticklish person. Between fits of laughter she tickled the racketeer, tousled his thinning hair and tweaked his nose. Pearl and Dixie danced with the gunmen and the party was on.

I cut in on Minnie and a man with a missing ear. Raz had put on a fast number called "How Do You Don't," and I faked the Black Bottom as best I could. I danced Minnie into a corner behind the bar.

"What the heck's going on?" I asked her.

"It was Pumpkin's idea, Maxwell. She said you wouldn't get shot if we were around."

"What do we do now?"

"Well," said Minnie, "a party's a party. Let's make whoopee!"

"Minnie, a minute ago my problem was getting the senator and myself out of here as quickly as possible. Now I have to get us all out of here. Fat Al is crazy. He's insane."

Minnie glanced at the public enemy, who was on his feet learning a new dance. Pumpkin's hands were on his hips, pushing him this way and that, bouncing him off the wall, spinning him around. She called for a tango and Raz said that would be next.

"He don't look so bad to me," said Minnie.

"This was not meant to be a party, Minnie. It was a setup."

"What's he want?"

"Everything. And he won't let me out of here until I hand it over to him."

"I'll dance you to the door."

"Then what? How do all of you escape? And what will it matter anyway? He'll just be laying for me. If I run now I can't stop until I get to Miami, Minnie."

"Maybe if we show him a real good time . . ."

The thug with one ear cut back in on me and I was left alone. Over his shoulder

Minnie winked at me and said, "Relax, Roland."

I drifted over to Raz, who was quietly high-stepping to the tune. He grinned at me and raised a silver dish cover an inch or so. Beneath it was an automatic pistol. I slammed down the cover.

"Have some champagne, Garv," he said. He loosed two corks with his thumbs. They ricocheted from the ceiling, and one of them bounced off my head.

"Since when do you take orders from Pumpkin?" I asked him.

"It was more like a favor. You think I wanted to come to this party?"

It was a party, an Atlantic City summer party, and the excitement grew. Everyone was dancing except me and the senator. I stood around with a forced smile on my face while Senator Stone snoozed in a wing chair. The hoodlums danced with the girls, Razmataz kept the champagne gushing and Fat Al would not let my sister out of his sight.

Pumpkin tangoed him over to me, dipped him nearly to the ground, raised him off his feet. Fat Al landed hard and laughed.

"What a kid!" he said.

"How do you like my Latin lover,

Garvey?" she asked me. Before I could comment, Fat Al stopped dancing. The crazed look returned to his eyes momentarily.

"You know this guy?" he asked Pumpkin.

"Who doesn't? He's the biggest, bravest and best rumrunner in Atlantic City. The law can't touch him, Al. And when you get it from Garvey, you get the best."

"He's a smart cookie. But where I come from he's a little cookie."

"You're not in Chicago, Al. You're in Atlantic City, and Garvey's no cookie. He's a ten-ton wedding cake. You be nice to him, silly boy, or I'll be blue."

"He's a nice kiddo," said Al. I knew this meant that he'd let me live a little longer. Maybe until the champagne ran out.

"Great party, Al," I said.

"Yeah." He tangoed Pumpkin clear across the room, barging directly into Dixie, who was trying to sober up the senator with a two-step. They both landed on the floor. Pumpkin squealed with joy. Senator Stone moaned.

One of the gunmen had set Pearl on the bar and was showing her how to dismantle a Thompson submachine gun. She was having difficulty winding up the drum. Her shoes were off and much of her body was flowing from her dress. She never stopped giggling.

Minnie had a bottle of champagne in either hand. She stood with her legs spread over a hoodlum who lay on the floor with his mouth open. Minnie was attempting to empty one of the bottles in a steady stream into his mouth. She soaked his tuxedo while stealing a sip for herself and the hood came up swinging. Minnie caught his arm and threw him over the bar. Raz hit him with a bottle and he was out for the time being. Minnie looked for another partner and found me.

"I don't know about you, Yusif, but I'm havin' a ball!" she shouted.

I had to dance to talk with her. I could not dance, and trying made me feel ridiculous. Yet I had to tell her my plan. I was concerned with getting us all out the door and into the elevator before the Chicago crowd knew what was happening. Minnie would not hear of it.

"You didn't come here to run away, did you, Garvey?"

"I did not come to be threatened with a broken bottle and four armed killers!" I said. "Minnie, this is real. We are in a terrible danger—"

"Aw, stow it, ya old maid. He's forgotten

all about ya. Come on, Garvey, gimmie a kiss."

Before I knew it Minnie was bending me backward, her lips on mine. It was no time for romance.

Raz was changing the record when Fat Al pounded on the bar for silence. His arm was around Pumpkin and he was smiling.

"I like Atlantic City," he said. "I'm gonna buy me a summer place here and get some fun."

Pumpkin said she had some property on North Carolina Avenue that was a bargain. Fat Al said they would go and see it together, the next day. I knew the lot she was talking about. I owned it. Maybe he would let me give it to him. Over my dead body.

Fat Al pointed to me.

"Let's drink to the captain," he said. "You havin' fun, Mr. Nope?"

"Yup," I said.

"Hey! That's more like it. That's what the Buddha likes to hear. Hear that, boys? He said yup! Yup is the magic word, right, boys?"

"Right, Al!"

Even the girls yelled, "Right, Al!" I almost

said it myself. But I did not. I smiled and sipped my glass of water.

"The captain is the cookie! He's the key to the Proof! I'm the king and he's the key, right?"

"Right!"

"Yup!" yelled Al.

"Yup!" yelled everybody but me.

"The captain here says Fat Al can't have it all."

"Boo!" screamed the girls.

"He says I can get all I want, but not all there is."

"Nope," I said.

"He's a Democrat, right?"

"Right!"

"But he comes across; he delivers. He takes the boat out, and he brings the booze in. It's a big deal?"

"You're damn right it is," said Pumpkin. "He's made a fool of every Coast Guard from Toms River to Cape May. Chase Garvey Leek and you're up Sugar Creek!"

"Yeah?" asked Al.

"Yeah!" responded the girls. I looked modest.

Fat Al walked to the window, directed

everyone's gaze to the red lights of Rum Row.

"See them lights? See the third from the left? That's a boat full of A. C. Proof. Right, Garvey boy?"

"Yup."

"Full to the brim?"

"It was a week ago. But I have been a little busy . . ."

"Har, har, har! You been a little busy. How come you ain't busy tonight?"

"Because of you."

"Because of the moon, right? It's a full moon. I know a little about your operation. You don't go out in no full moon."

"I do if I have a big order."

"What's big?"

"Five hundred cases."

"I want a thousand."

"When?"

"Tonight."

Fat Al spread his arms, and Pumpkin ran to them.

"Come on, Alfy," she said. "It's a party."

"Well, look at him. He ain't havin' no fun. He's a fish outa water. He ain't drinkin', he ain't dancin' . . ."

"I'll go tonight," I said.

"Like hell you will," said Minnie Creek. She knew that if I made the run she would have to be there, and Minnie was into her second bottle of champagne and at a party with the Chicago big boys. "Like the man says, Garvey, it's a full moon."

"A technicality," I said. I was ready to go, and Fat Al was ready to let me go. Besides, it was a challenge I had to accept.

Fat Al clapped me on the shoulder. "What do you say, kiddo? You goin'?"

"Yup."

"How long will it take?"

"I'll be at the Causeway Boat Works by five a.m. Dixie knows where that is."

"And I'll be there to meet ya. Right, boys? Right, everybody?"

"Right, Al!"

"Somebody has to go with me," I said.

"What for?"

"To bail."

"Har har! You got a leaky boat?"

"At fifty-plus she leaks, yes."

"Take one of my boys."

"No. I need someone who knows about boats."

"Me," said Minnie.

358

Fat Al looked at her. "You? You're just a dolly!"

"I know how to bail. I'm goin'."

It was settled. Dixie said she would lead the trucks to the boat works. Fat Al's boys would drive the load north. I would be paid cash on the barrelhead, twelve thousand dollars profit for a night's work. If the Buddha wanted to pay me. If he would let me exist.

I drove to Gardner's Basin in silence. I cannot say the same for Minnie. As the champagne wore off her anger mounted. She began to say things she did not mean. I stopped the Rolls in front of Dutchy's, which was packed with a summer crowd. Inside, the band was playing "Golden Slippers" and the audience was up and strutting.

"Get out, Minnie," I said. I reached over her and opened the car door. She slammed it shut.

"I ain't goin' in no Dutchy Muldoon's."

"I'll drive you home."

"I ain't goin' home."

"I've had a hard night, Minnie, and you are making it harder. I'd rather go alone."

"You couldn't get those motors goin' without me. You wouldn't get five feet from the dock."

"I'll try."

"Why are you doin' this, Garv?"

"Money, Minnie. Money . . . and the chance to go on making money."

"What's money if you can't have fun?"

"A party with Fat Al Buddha is not my idea of fun. Bringing a load in tonight is. Don't ever forget this, Minnie—I love what I am doing. For the money and for its own sake. I love it and that's why I do it. I'm a rumrunner, and so are you."

"But what does this prove? If he's gonna nail you, he's gonna nail you. Garvey, you can't play with the big boys . . ."

"All I can do is what I'm good at! I can't talk sense to him, I can't bluff him. All I can hope to do is show him how good I am, that I'm the best! Then maybe he'll have some respect for me . . . just enough to let me go on doing my job, taking my buck a bottle."

"And go right on runnin'," said Minnie.

"Yup. I'm good at running. I'm chased a whole lot more than your average man. I've forgotten how to give up; I don't recall how to surrender. But I don't fight, Minnie. I run away. And I'm fast, right?"

"You're a fast man, Garvey. I admit it."

"I need you, honey," I said.

"Okay, Quincy, let's go. I won't say no more about it. But I just want you to know right now that I ain't about to ruin this here dress." Minnie patted her sequins, tried to pull the hem down to her knees.

We left Muldoon's gaiety behind and drove quietly over to Gardner's Basin. The moss-bunker fleet was in and the commercial docks were crowded with big dark hulls. At my end of the basin, boats were built for another kind of commerce. There was the Coast Guard cutter, clean as a whistle, at her dock. To the left were my rumrunners, gray and sleek and awesome. To the right was Ebby's boatyard, the place where they all were built. I have often wondered why we all stuck so close together. Things would have been a lot simpler that night if I had moored somewhere else.

Because hardly was I aboard when Captain Frye strolled out on his dock, looked at the moon and spoke to me.

"Evenin', Garvey," said the captain.

"Evening, Captain Frye. Nice night."

"Sure is. Just look at the moon."

"Boy, what a moon."

"Full moon, Garvey Leek," he said.

"Yes, sir. You sure wouldn't want it to be much fuller."

"It's like daylight, Garvey. You can see for miles."

"Yup."

Minnie cranked over the engines, which I throttled up to a roar, then settled when they were smooth. The big thumping throbs spread out across the water and filled the air below the docks of Gardner's Basin. Captain Frye held up a finger.

"Wind's changin', Garvey."

I licked my finger and held it up. "Yes, sir."

"Wind's hauled, boy. That ain't good this time a' year."

"Squalls," I said.

"That's it, squalls. Just ran right through Cape May."

"Sir?"

"Workin' it's way up the coast, Garvey. Squall line. Took down every power line in Cape May County."

"When's it supposed to hit here?"

"Your guess is as good as mine, Garvey. You know squalls."

"I got time for a boat ride."

"Maybe."

I told Minnie to cast us off. As she passed by I noticed she was wearing a slip. A very small silk slip.

"Cover yourself!" I whispered.

"Aw, shut up, Garvey," she said. She tossed the bowline on the dock. I began to ease my boat away.

Captain Frye pulled a bosun's whistle from his pocket and blew one high note. Lights in the boathouse went on and two of his men appeared. Captain Frye climbed aboard the cutter and they followed.

"I can't talk you outa this, can I?" he asked.

"No, sir."

"Then may God help you."

I throttled up and moved out of the basin. The cutter was moving too.

We shot out of Absecon Inlet at top speed. The farther we got from land, the higher ran the sea swell. The wind was freshening, blowing August-warm and full-moon-steady. Pretty soon Minnie was working full-time on the bilge pump.

We made the Row in under twenty minutes. Big Frenchy was surprised to see us.

"Business or pleasure?" he asked.

"Business.'"

"Business is business. How much?"

"One thousand cases, Frenchy. Soon as you can get them aboard."

"D'accord!"

Alphonse and the Frenchman loaded the cargo nets and swung them over. Minnie and I stowed the cases. The swell was up now, and the transfer was dangerous. But we had done it so many times before that we knew the rhythm and worked with it. Not a bottle broke.

I climbed aboard the trawler to pay up. When I had peeled off the last thousand-dollar bill I gave my old friend a warning.

"I'm fighting the mob, Frenchy, and I don't know who's winning. If the Chicago crowd gets in and I'm out of the way, things will change out here. If you want to fight too, it's your decision."

"I don't sell Proof to anybody but you, my friend."

"What if I'm dead?"

"Then the first person who tells me he's taken your place will get a full load . . . right through his hull."

We shook on it.

Back aboard my runner I found Minnie stripped to her step-ins. Her little dress was carefully rolled up and tucked in a shelf in the cockpit, her slip and her high-heeled shoes swinging on a nail. She sat back on the stern with her arms around her breasts. Before I could speak she held up her hand.

"I got grease on my hem, Harvey, so don't give me no hard time. I'm in a mean mood."

I flung my silk jacket at her, swore at the stars and started my engines. Their sweet throbbing drove the tension from me, and soon I was concentrating on steering. The wind was up to thirty knots and the tops of the swells were spilling over themselves. I gave the squall half an hour to hit. By then I'd be in the bay.

The shortest way in was the way I'd come out, Absecon Inlet. Somewhere in the middle was the man I'd have to dodge. Fully loaded I could do fifty knots. The cutter could do forty-five; I had the edge.

I thought I would pound the three-inch pine bottom right out of my boat on that ride in. I could hear every nail, rivet, bolt and plank complain. Joined with these sounds was the tinkling of twelve thousand bottles of booze, the noise of the wind, the thud of every wave. It was the worst run I ever had to make; and it was the best.

To dodge the captain I ran a little north; north because the swells were running north and the following sea was less dangerous to my cargo. Seas lashed over us and Minnie pumped them out. Then it began to rain.

A cold rain fell in sheets, and I knew the squall was on. The full moon was affecting everything, raising the seas ever higher, casting a weird glow over the boiling ocean. When I neared the Brigantine breakers I saw a light to port. It was a red light, a flare. Someone was in trouble.

I could not ignore a distress signal. Spinning the wheel, I headed in the direction of the light I had seen. Another flare went up and I moved in. After a minute I saw the cutter. She was hove to, her side to the waves that were breaking over her. Captain Frye had lost his power.

Between strokes on the pump, Minnie had been tending our engines, keeping connections dry, adjusting the carburetors. Nobody, not even the U.S. Coast Guard, had an engineer like Minnie Creek.

I ran up alongside the cutter and one of her sailors threw me a line. Standing off, I pulled and steered at the same time. The current off the inlet was terrific, and I could see us bearing down on the long Brigantine rockpile, a hundred yards to starboard. The line was joined to another, thicker line—the towline used to save ships in trouble. Minnie crept forward over the stacked cases, took it and lashed it hard to the sternpost. I gave the throttle a nudge and we moved off.

The towline grew taut and I felt the strain of the cutter as I swung her around hard on to the seas. She was riding low on the water, and I could see men bailing hard. The wind was up to fifty and steering was poor. I could move but slowly for fear of snapping the line.

But we made headway. I ran for the lights from Captain Starn's dock, the lights of the tall hotels beyond. Somewhere up there a party was raging, but I knew my friends were as concerned as I. Everything would be all right if I could just make it to the bay.

Absecon Inlet developed a ground swell as high as any I had ever seen. At times my boat seemed to stand on her transom; at times she seemed ready to jackknife into the trough before me. But her high bows had been built by the best, built to take the worst, and we took everything that came along. I could not see for the rain. I could not hear for the wind. The boat, at times, had to find her way alone.

Midway up the channel the wind went down, blocked by the buildings to port. I could tell by the tug that the cutter was still behind, but how well she was floating I could not say. I drove hard for the basin, throttling up as far as I could. The brute aircraft engines surged and never missed a stroke.

Suddenly we were pooped by a rogue wave and the stern was buried under a white mountain of foam. Hundreds of gallons of salt water crashed into the hold as the wave got under us. I shoved the throttles full open and rode down the crest, dragging the cutter behind me. The wash came forward and ran up to my knees. The engines never quit.

"Minnie!" I yelled. "Minnie!"

No answer came from the stern. I lashed the wheel and jumped up on the cases, trying to shield my eyes from the rain.

"Minnie, for the love of God . . ."

"Shut up and steer, Sterling!" came a voice from the darkness. I heard the bilge pump begin to scrape its leather washer on galvanized tin. I jumped back to the wheel.

That wave had been the ocean's last try. The channel began to calm as we worked our way inland. Soon we were off Rum Point near the entrance to Gardner's Basin. I towed the helpless cutter to her dock, and Minnie cast off the hawser. The squall had blown over us and was beating the hell out of lonely Brigantine, where there was not much to damage. I eased my boat alongside the cutter.

"You okay, captain?"

"I am, Garvey." Captain Frye was soaked to the skin, his white hair streaming down his weathered face. He looked both happy and sad. The moonlight shone on my cargo, a thousand wooden cases all bearing the black stamp, Atlantic City Proof.

"I got to go, sir."

"I guess you do."

I put her in gear.

"Garvey?"

"Yes, sir."

"I thank you."

"It's my fault, captain. I'm a damned fool."

Minnie laughed, but she never stopped pumping.

16

THE back bay was eerie under the moon. I was alone, the only boat on the water, and as gray as the marshes around me. The tide was high and the meadowlands alive with mud creatures, furry, feathered and shelled. Muskrats raised their heads and chattered, heron and egret slept on single legs. Morning was not far from the marshes, and the booze was coming to Atlantic City! All the old thrills returned to me, and I vowed I would be a smuggler as long as Prohibition held out. After that I would find something else to do; but whatever it was I would have a hull below me and engines behind. I was a fool and I'd always be one.

The old Causeway Boat Works loomed into view, standing there like a ruined fortress dying in the mud, her gray sides rotting and her roof about to fall. We were early, and there was no sign of the trucks. I wondered if the party at the Bayswater had broken up and if my sister were in her bed. Fat Al had looked upon her with his crab eyes . . .

I reversed my boat into the building and cut the engines, lit a kerosene lantern with a damp match. Minnie closed the engine hatches and walked forward, my jacket covering her breasts. I looked at my ruined silk suit, stiff with salt and stained with perspiration. I'd never liked fancy clothes, anyway. She sat down on the cockpit coaming and lit a Lucky Strike from the lantern.

"What time you got?" she whispered.

"Three-thirty."

"Well, the old pump's suckin air, Garvey. The bilge is dry. Port engine needs a rebore. We'll get Ebby to pull her today."

"This run is not over."

"Just about."

"What are you worried about?"

"Fat Al."

"You think he might try to pull a fast one?"

"I'm not sure. This would be a perfect place for him to do me in. The police would think it was the FBI, and the FBI would let them think it."

"But he don't wanna rub you out, Garvey. He needs you."

"I'm not sure he knows that. I stood up to him, Minnie. Not all the way, just a little bit.

But I think I went further than anybody else has in a long while. I went a little way, but I may have gone too far."

"What can you do about it?"

"What can I do? If his boys come in with those guns I'm a dead man, Minnie. There's nothing I can do."

"Then quit worryin', Wilbur. Let's get some sleep."

She jumped down into the cockpit and sat beside me on the steering platform. She snuggled into my arms, kissed me on the cheek and fell asleep. I tucked the lapels of my jacket around her and tried to think.

I could run. I could get the devil out of there, drop off the load somewhere else and cruise down to Florida. I could run rum from Jamaica to the Keys. I could buy a plantation. I could change my name and never come back.

Never come back to Jersey? Never see my friends again? Never look out over Point Farm at the hellhole of Great Egg Harbor Inlet? Sell my mansion in Margate? Trade it for a frame house full of insects? Look at palms instead of pines? The heck with Florida! I would take my chances with Fat Al

Buddha and be shot down in a boondock boathouse if it came to that.

I threw a tarp over the load, then went back beside Minnie and fell asleep.

I awoke at the sound of tires stopping on gravel. The sky outside had turned to light-gray, the stars were gone. I heard several car doors slam, footsteps. I woke up Minnie, who wanted to tell me about a dream she had had, but I hushed her. I blew out the lantern and let my eyes adjust to the semi-darkness. People were moving onto the dock.

I recognized Fat Al and Pumpkin in the lead. Behind them trooped the four gunmen, Pearl and Dixie. Razmataz came last. Under one arm he carried two ice buckets with champagne, and with the other arm he supported Senator Stone, who was walking with difficulty. Fat Al stopped beside the cockpit and looked at Minnie and me.

"This is some boat, kiddo," he said.

"Thanks."

"Where's the booze?"

Minnie and I climbed from the cockpit and pulled off the tarpaulin. The tightly packed cases came nearly flush with the deck. There was barely room left for another bottle. Fat Al's eyes widened.

"What you got?"

I tore the top off a case, pulled out a bottle and tossed it to him. "Atlantic City Proof. One thousand cases, twelve thousand bottles."

Fat Al uncorked the bottle, sniffed it and passed it to one of his thugs, who drank and nodded. Everyone seemed relieved.

"Load it up," said Al.

Two trucks were backed to the huge doors and the transfer began. I asked the mobster for my money.

"You'll get it, kid," he said. Over his head I saw Pumpkin waving her finger back and forth, a worried expression on her face. She looked tired, as if she had danced all night, which was probably true. Pearl was still shifting her feet in a two-step, and Dixie was humming. I wanted to talk privately with my sister, but Fat Al held her hand. When she could she shot me warnings with her eyes.

Half the load was in the trucks when Al pointed a gun at me. It was a little gun, half-hidden in his fat fist; just a small black hole pointing my way. He told Minnie to get out of the boat and me to stay. He told me to put my hands up, which I did.

"You ever been to Chicago, kid?" he asked me.

I shook my head.

"Too bad. You mighta learned something. Chicago's a city of one-way streets, two-way men and three-way women. They all get along because they know how to take orders. The cops take orders and the mayor takes orders and even the kids take orders. And all the orders come from me. My brother has a restaurant. He's got a breakfast special: two eggs any style, pancakes, fried potatoes, two strips of bacon, two slices of toast, half a honeydew, coffee, milk and orange juice . . . twenty-five cents! Everybody asks, 'How does he *do* it?' He does it 'cause I tell him to. He ain't made a profit in years, but he's alive. But you? You don't take no orders, do you?"

"He can take orders, Al," said Pumpkin.

"He sure can," said Dixie.

Pearl, the senator and Razmataz joined in.

"He just took an order, Al," said Minnie. "Thousand cases."

Fat Al spat on the dock. "You know what I'm talkin' about, don't you, kid?"

Fat Al's pistol was directed at me, and four submachine guns were aiming in. My arms ached from holding them up, and I dropped them to my side and sat on the cockpit coaming.

"Al," I said, "you are just a little fat crab, a scavenger, a bottom creature. You live in a world of waste and darkness. People do as you say because they fear you; you can pinch their toes. I made this run because I wanted to get to sea and forget I ever laid eyes on you and your kind. No, Al, I am not afraid of you."

I said this because it was true. I was not afraid of Fat Al; not at that moment. Because at that moment Razmataz was holding his pistol in Fat Al's ear.

"Put your gun in the water, boss," said Raz, "and tell the goons to put their guns in the water."

Al dropped his pistol and nodded to his boys. One by one the lethal machines splashed into the bay. Al's hands were up, but he did not look concerned.

"Okay, kiddo. You got the luck. Now what are ya gonna do?"

"Get his money, Minnie," I said. I knew I would need all the cash I could get for a new life in Florida. Would Florida be far enough? "Get all his money."

Minnie produced a thick roll of bills from

Fat Al's pocket. Minnie started counting thousand-dollar bills and gave up. She tossed me the roll.

"Everybody who is not from Chicago," I said, "get in the boat."

Dixie helped Senator Stone into the cockpit. Minnie and Pearl helped Pumpkin, who had a tear in her eye.

"So long, honey," she said to Al. Then she forgave him in Arabic. "Remember, there is only one boss . . . and Mohammed is his Prophet," she added.

Suddenly, a voice barked through a megaphone.

"FBI! You're surrounded. Throw out your guns and come out with your hands up!"

"Minnie!" I said, "start the engines!"

Minnie jumped into the engine compartment. Al's gangsters ran to the windows. I saw automatics in their hands.

"They're in the bushes, boss! Everywhere . . ."

Fat Al still had Raz's pistol in his ear. He pushed it aside and ran to the window.

"Hey," he yelled. "Can we settle this outa court?"

"You have thirty seconds," boomed the voice. "Then we're coming in."

My engines roared, then settled to a throb. Fat Al ran back to me. Raz had cast off the lines and was safely aboard.

"Get me outa this, kid," said Al. "If they get me they'll wanna know who you are. Get me outa this and you'll never see me again."

I wanted to leave him there and take my chances. But I knew there would be a shoot-out. If a federal agent was killed I knew I would be directly involved. I had no choice.

"Get in the hold. Tell your men to get rid of those guns. If I see one gun we go nowhere."

Razamataz threw four more guns in the water, patted the hoods down, then helped them into the boat. The cockpit was crowded, but there was room to steer. I raced the engines and looked ahead.

No boats. The agents were on three sides, but not on the water. If the cutters were out there somewhere waiting for me, at least I would have a chance to run, to dash, to die at sea. If they were not, I would escape and nothing could connect me with the contraband on shore. I swung the transmission lever to forward and shoved over all three throttles.

Bullets burst through the doors behind us, but they were aimed high and whizzed over our heads. My rumrunner shot out of the boathouse like a cannonball. In the predawn light I saw a man stand up from the marshes, a machine gun to his shoulder. I swung the wheel hard over, the boat canted and took the burst in its half-inch thick armor. The noise was terrific. I saw men running across the meadows, stumbling in the mud. I saw water spouts race toward the hull, heard bullets slam through wood and into steel. I kept my head down and swung the wheel.

I knew the way out of that death trap by heart. But the bay, even at high tide, was shallow there, the channel narrow, and I had to look to see where I was going.

A triangle marks the channel, a red triangle of wood, nailed to the top of a cedar pole stuck in the mud. In a peek to port I spotted the marker and turned for it. But, in turning, I exposed my cargo and crew to the murderous blast from the shore. We listed in the direction of fire just as they got their cannon working.

It was a small cannon, but its single report drowned out all other noise. It was well-aimed, because the three-inch shell smacked dead center on my cargo of Atlantic City Proof. Through hundreds of bottles the projectile passed, then tore violently through my three-inch pine bottom, just missing the keel.

They only had time for the one shot. I completed the turn, rounded the marker and leveled off for the winding trip to Beach Thorofare.

Booze and baywater filled the bilge. Minnie ran up to say we were sinking. I told her to get back on the pump. She said it was useless, we were holed.

"Open the sea cocks!" I yelled. "Maybe the water will flow through!"

"There isn't any sea cocks, stupid! They're on the other boat, for the love of God."

"Buckets! Get everybody bailing!"

"No buckets!"

"Dump the cargo!"

"Dump the cargo!"

Cases of Proof began to fly. Everyone in the boat was knee deep in a saltwater cocktail, heaving cases to save his life. Fat Al was so weak that he struggled with the same case in a dozen attempts to get it over the gunwale, then gave up. Pumpkin and Pearl were on the top of the pile, the only dry spot on the skiff. But there were too many cases; we were going down.

My only thought was the channel, Absecon

Inlet, where the bottom was forty feet down and my rumrunner could rest forever. We were only minutes away, but slowing down. We were resting more deeply in the water now.

Pumpkin climbed down from the stacked cases to tell me something.

"We're sinking, aren't we? We haven't a chance?"

"No chance. One minute, maybe two," I said. I could not look her in the eyes.

"Where? Where will we sink?"

"In the channel, I hope. If we go down in here we all go to jail."

"We can't sink in the channel," she said.

"Why not?"

"Alfred can't swim! None of his friends can swim a stroke. They'll drown!"

"Good! Great! Our problems are over."

"Garvey."

"Pumpkin."

"Don't be ridiculous."

Letting six men drown, taking them to their deaths, was a ridiculous notion. Pumpkin realized that before I did because she was not driving a fifty-foot boat at fifty knots, and Fat Al did not remind her of a little crab. Her words woke me.

I had to decide at Sandy Beach, a neck of land that separates Gardner's Basin from the channel. It was left, to the inlet and the dark swells racing seaward now with the tide, or right, to the little lagoon and only eight feet of water—all of it in full view of the Coast Guard. Half the load was still on board. The police would have a clambake while arresting us.

But nobody would drown.

In a turn that sent the cases crashing, I entered the basin. My dock was only a hundred yards away. We were settling, but we could make it. Maybe we could simply run away. Florida was beginning to sound good again.

Pumpkin nudged me. "Stop the boat."

"I can make it to the dock."

"Do as I say, Garvey."

I stopped the boat.

"They may be waiting for us in here," I said. "We must get away."

"No one's waiting for us. All they know is what I told them."

"You?"

"I phoned from the Bayswater, just before we left for the boat works. That's all they know; that there was a load at the Causeway

Boat Works. They don't know who you are. I had to do it. I knew what he planned to do. I thought you'd stand a better chance with the law than with Alfred."

"Pumpkin, why did you call the FBI? Why didn't you call the Coast Guard? Captain Frye might have figured out something."

"I called him. He was intoxicated."

"We're going down, Pumpkin."

First the engines went dead. The water rose to my waist, then my shoulders. Then it came in over the sides. I felt the keel touch bottom.

"Watch, Garvey. Watch what's going to happen," whispered Pumpkin. She began to tread water beside me and Minnie.

We treaded water. Pearl, Dixie, Razmataz and the senator treaded water. Fat Al and his boys climbed up on the cases.

All my friends could swim; all my enemies could not. It stood to reason: good people *should* float.

At once, we struck out for the dock.

"Hey," whispered Fat Al. "We can't swim."

"Try," I said, demonstrating the backstroke.

We had a little trouble with Senator Stone. He could swim, but not in the right direction.

Pumpkin and Pearl herded him like pilot whales.

At that moment the local Gardner's Basin fishing fleet, men who had been out all night and had just finished culling the catch, were paid off. Out onto Commercial Dock they strode, blinking in the morning light, lighting pipes and passing bottles of home-brewed beer, bathtub gin and Vineland wine. Commercial Dock was right next to mine.

We had to hide under my dock. The tide was nearly to the dock, so that we had to duck under a plank to get in. Inside we treaded water and clung to pilings, waiting for something to happen.

The fishermen were very interested in the activity at the center of the basin. Six suited men seemed to be marooned on an island of wooden crates. The men were waving their arms, but not yelling. The fishermen sat on the pilings, squinted in the sun and waited for something to happen.

Nothing happened. Captain Frye must have been out cold. Perhaps he had thought the city would never let him forget being rescued at sea by a rumrunner full of whiskey, and had drowned his regrets in the bottle. The prize catch of all time was only a hundred yards from his dock, and he did not know it.

I explained the problem to Minnie. She swam over to the Coast Guard dock, climbed up the ladder. On the end of the dock was a bucket of cherrystone clams, set there to purge. Minnie drew a few clams from the bucket and gauged their weight. The fishermen widened their eyes.

Minnie was in her step-ins, white silk step-ins that seemed to disappear when wet. She didn't know which side of herself to keep to the crowd, and didn't care. She was aiming in on the big windows of the observation tower, where the captain slept.

Side-arm, she winged a clam in a perfect arc that crashed through plate glass at its apex. She stopped to listen and Gardner's Basin stopped to listen.

"Captain Frye?"

No answer. She threw another clam and called again.

"Captain Frye? Goddammit, stick your head out the window."

A hand, clutching a half-empty bottle of Atlantic City Proof, rose above the sill. Captain Frye's face followed it. His hat was cock-eyed on his head, his eyes were nearly closed.

"Mornin', Minnie," he said.

"Mornin', captain," said Minnie.

"You don't have no clothes on, Minnie."

"Just havin' a little swim, is all, sir."

"That's nice."

"Some boys out there in the water, captain." Minnie pointed behind her to the wooden island. "They can't get in. Would you come down and get 'em?"

"Sure thing, Minnie."

Minnie turned to dive, stopped, turned back.

"You better bring your old gun, sir, and some of your boys."

"That so?"

"Bring your big boys," she said. Then she dove back into the bay and disappeared.

Captain Frye was on duty alone, it was plain to see. While he was slowly coming downstairs, we climbed a ladder and hid in the bushes. In a minute he was outside in the sun. His khaki uniform was wrinkled and damp, his feet bare. Over his shoulder he carried a long twelve-gauge shotgun. He took off his cap and he scratched his head. The whole crowd on Commercial Dock waited in silence.

The captain climbed into the rescue boat,

the same boat I had borrowed so long ago. He pulled out his knife and cut the rope that held the boat up the ways. The boat ran down the ramp, hit the bay and glided toward the middle, the captain at the tiller.

The boat came to the island with a bump. The mobsters climbed in while Captain Frye peered over the side at the sunken boat full of contraband. He looked from face to face until he recognized Al from his photograph in the newspapers.

"Mornin', Al," he said with a little smile.

"Who're you?" Fat Al's voice rang out over the water.

"Name's Frye. Captain Frye, United States Coast Guard. What's the trouble?"

"No trouble! One of my men's coming to pick us up."

"I'll take you in."

"Thanks, but we'll wait. Nice out here."

"What's that you're standing on?"

"What?"

"Them cases. Looks like orange crates."

"Yeah. Oranges. Put too many of them in the boat, ha."

"What's that they say on them?" The captain slowly read the stamps. "'Atlantic City Rye. One Hundred Proof Canadian Whiskey.

Twelve Years Old.' Hey, would that be booze?"

"No."

"Not booze?"

"No."

"I don't know, Al. Better put 'em in the boat so's I can have a look."

"It's okay, captain," said Al. "My boys'll be here any minute."

"Put 'em in the boat, Al." Captain Frye rested the twelve-gauge on the gunwale, changed his tone. "Nice and slow."

The gangsters began loading the whiskey into the rescue boat. Soon their island was underwater and sinking. When they were up to their necks, Captain Frye let them come aboard.

The police, the mayor, the town council and the entire force of the Ventnor Ladies' Patrol for a Dry America were waiting on the dock.

We made our getaway during the applause.

17

I RAN into Captain Frye on a Hog Island trolley car at the loop in Longport. I had walked there along the beach to have a look at Point Farm, or where Point Farm would be if the tide ever went out far enough. It was a clear crisp day in the fall, the sea gleaming with what we call "September sparkle." I was alone, my mind filled with thoughts of the past, dreams of the future. When I climbed aboard the waiting car I saw the captain in the rear seat with a bottle of Atlantic City Proof between his knees. I sat next to him on the wicker seat, put my legs in the aisle.

"Mornin', Captain Frye."

"Mornin', Garvey. First ride on the new line?"

"Yes, sir. Sure is."

The conductor rang his bell and the doors cranked shut. We were off in an electrical whirr, headed along the bay in the direction of Margate, a few stops away.

"Nice time of the year, fall," he said.

"Summer people all gone, things back to normal."

"Stripers are biting."

"That so?"

"That's what they say. Biting in the Mudhole, biting off the bridge."

"Time to get out the old bucktailed lure."

"Yup. That's what they say, sir."

"They say it'll be a mild winter."

"I hope so."

"Heard you bought that there rumrunner that went down in the basin," he said.

"I bought it at the auction."

"The booze didn't come with it, did it?" he chuckled.

"No, sir. That was evidence."

"Yup! Put those Chicago boys away for five years."

"That's all?"

"Well, when they have a chance to get around to Mr. Buddha's taxes they'll never let him out. Now, what are you plannin' to do with his boat? Fast boat, they say."

"I'm making her over into a pleasure boat."

"That so?"

"Captain, I've gone legitimate. You don't have to worry about me anymore."

"Oh, yeah?"

"I figure Prohibition will be over soon. So what we did, the senator and I, we bought a distillery."

"Which distillery?"

"The one that makes that booze you're drinking, Atlantic City Proof."

"You bought it?"

"Yes, sir. Picked it up for a song. Got to think of the future, sir. I've been running around so fast I've never had time to think. But now I know what I want. Security, responsibility, respectability. What's money for?"

"I think Pumpkin's been talkin' to you, boy. How's she doing?"

"She's well. She and Pearl are studying the occult."

"That so?"

"Yup. Talking to the spirits of old French poets."

"What do they talk about?"

"Soon as Pumpkin learns French I'll tell you."

"And your dad? How's he doin'?"

"He and Mamma May redid the inside of the elephant. Modern."

"Modern?"

"That's what they call it. Lots of plastic."

"I never liked it."

"Well, like Dad says, the bugs don't eat it."

"You can't hammer a nail in it."

"Nope. That's true."

"And Minnie? What's she up to?"

"Still working for me. She just got a room up on the boardwalk, behind a bicycle shop. I'm heading there now."

"I hardly ever see her at Dutchy's these days," he said.

"She hangs out at Dixie's. Likes the band."

"I don't like the crowd."

"New York," I said.

"Well, at least we don't have to worry about Chicago any more, Garvey."

"Thanks to you, captain."

Captain Frye raised the bottle, read the label for the thousandth time. "Thanks to you, Garvey. I may have got the credit . . ."

"Let's just say it was a concerted effort."

"Someday I want to hear the whole story, boy."

"Someday I'll tell it, sir."

Margate had whizzed by, and Ventnor was almost gone. The trolley rumbled along at a good clip, the conductor ringing his bell just for the heck of it. No one was on the windy streets; no one wanted to go to Atlantic City, closed down since the week after Labor Day. New hotels were going up, and Pacific Avenue was paved the whole way. The captain and I rode in silence, each thinking his own thoughts, but glad for the company.

He was a famous man now, the captain, and his photograph was everywhere. He had singlehandedly snagged the biggest, meanest, most low-down mobster in the country, had caught him red-handed with a load of illegal liquor, and the government was grateful. Upon retirement he would be offered the post of chief, a high rank of the Atlantic City Beach Patrol, where he could spend summers on the beach and winters in the boathouse seeing that the lifeboats were kept in good shape. But I was sure that between now and then he would scour the salt sea where the law's the law, and a smuggler's life a long and lonely one . . . as long as he was not around. I was certain that never again would he bring that cutter close to me and Minnie.

Minnie Creek. I was on my way to see her, to spell out a few of the things on my mind. Above all else, I had Minnie on my mind, and I wanted . . .

"Gettin' off, Garvey," said the captain, rising. "Gonna have a few words with Muldoon. He wants to put in another shuffleboard and I aim to talk him out of it. Can't stand the sound of all those quoits. No more clammin', eh? I hope that don't mean no more Proof."

"I've learned my lesson, sir. But I'm sure there's some other fool around." I held out my hand and we shook.

The captain got off at Mississippi Avenue, and I got off at Tennessee. Walking toward me, a banjo on his back, was Razmataz.

"Where you goin', Garv?" he asked, as if he didn't know.

"Going to visit with Minnie."

"How come you're ridin' the trolley?"

"The Bugatti broke down."

"Again?"

"Again. Where are you going?"

"I don't know. I'm going down to the corner and see which way the wind blows me."

"South," I said.

"Well, I believe I'll go south. We runnin' tonight?"

"Nope. Not tonight, not tomorrow night, Raz."

"When we runnin'?"

"Friday. When Ebby and Minnie get the new engine in the winter boat."

"How many engines we got in that skiff?"

"Well, this one will make it four."

"We flyin'."

"Yup. Invisible."

"See you Friday, then."

"Midnight. Gardner's Basin."

Minnie was sitting on the boardwalk, a bottle of beer beside her, straightening the bent fork of a tandem bicycle. I sat down and helped her, pulled until the fork was true. The sun was setting, the day over. I asked her to go for a walk. She wheeled the bicycle inside, washed her hands and face, came out and locked up the shop.

"Where we goin', Grimsby?"

"South."

We walked down the boardwalk, Minnie and I, walked toward the setting sun. In the summer the sun sets back on the bay, but at this time of the year it swings around and sets over Longport. The last beams came right up the boardwalk, blinding us to the beauty of the beach to our left. Winter-brown seagulls wheeled above our heads, pigeons shivered in locked shop doorways. Arm in arm we were, and as calm as the sea lapping the shore. The chill north wind blew at our backs, blew summer south, down to Florida where it's always spring and you have to be crazy to believe it.

We stopped to rest by the roller coaster, found a wind shadow in the lee of some rusting cars. Suddenly my heart pounded with the excitement of the moment's promise; at last the time had come when I would make Minnie mine. We gazed over the wide beach, its silver sands unmarked by footprints, level, bare and cold. We looked beyond the beach, at the ocean as flat as glass, as smooth as high-grade rye aging in a hickory barrel. I held her hand.

"Minnie," said I, "my affection for you is no secret."

"Likewise," she said.

"Our love is tried and true."

"Both."

"Our stars are crossed, Minnie. Our destinies intertwine."

"Like an anchor rope."

"That's not bad, but I would say more like the inseparable mated lobsters of the quiet ocean depths," I suggested.

"Yeah."

"Mated and inseparable," I repeated.

"But fiercely independent."

"The summer's gone, Minnie. It makes me want to cry. The only thing that stops me is knowing you will be with me yet another winter. And when winter's done, why we will be together, right here, watching rolling chairs filled with lovers."

"Smooching by the sea," she said.

"Yes. And the saloons will be filled with . . ."

"Atlantic City Proof."

"That, and the harmonies of happy songsters, decent, God-loving tourists; whiskey-drinking, working-class souls who consume all that we supply."

"At a dime a shot," she reminded me.

"Or more. Dixie's Silver Slipper has three wheels."

"Dutchy's put in a dart board."

"Captain Starn has a new net, purse seine."

"Captain Frye has a new cutter."

"Bigger, but slower."

"Ebby is building a yacht."

"A yacht?"

"A yacht, my darling, for us."

"Power?"

"A pair of Grey Marines."

"Overhead valves," she said. "Slow but steady."

"She will be big, Minnie. Big enough for us and others besides."

"Razmataz . . ."

"Of course. And others. Little ones."

"Little friends."

"Yes. Children of the sea."

"Like us."

"Well, they will look like us."

"Yeah, I guess they will."

"Minnie, I've waited long enough. Tell me true: do you love me?"

"Yup."

"Will you marry me?"

"Well, what's the deal?"

"Deal? What deal? We get married, that's all. We live together, we start a family, little children of the sea, scurrying from bow to stern, a house on the parkway, a seat on the Board of Education . . ."

"That's all?"

"What else?"

"Can I have a bank account?"

"Sure! I own the bank. Picked it up for a song."

"Money in the account?"

"What else are you going to put in it?"

"*I* don't put it in, Plimpton, *you* do."

"I do?"

"You put it in; I take it out."

"How much?" I asked, my mind racing.

"Make me an offer."

"I'm offering you my life."

"We were speaking cash."

"Twenty dollars a week."

"Ha!"

"Minnie! How can you be so callous?"

"How can you be so cheap? Twenty bucks! That don't cover my bar bill."

"I'll give you a tab at Dixie's."

"You will?"

"Up to ten dollars a week. I'll give you an account at Blatt's department store."

"Garvey, there's nothin' like cash."

"How about a settlement? Tell me how much you have and I will match it!"

"I'm broke."

"Broke? You've been working all winter!"

"Workin' for you all winter, I've been. I've been workin' for you all my life. That's why I'm broke, ya damned, dumb, prissy . . ."

"Watch it, Minnie," I said. She held her tongue. Minnie squeezed a handful of sand, watching the grains fall between her legs, watching until the last grain was gone. This gave me time to think.

"I'm not going to give you a lot of money, Minnie."

"Nope."

"But I will set you up in business."

"What kinda business?"

"I don't know. What would you like? I own two hotels on Pennsylvania Avenue."

"Not me."

"I own a lot of the Reading Seashore Line."

"Not my line."

"An amusement pier?"

"Never."

"Well, what?"

"I want a casino."

"Minnie they're *illegal*."

"I'd call it 'Creek's.'"

"Creek's. That is no name for a casino. A casino means class, it means style." Unwittingly I had warmed to the idea. Why not? Sure they were illegal, but they might not always be. In the meantime their owners were getting rich, like me.

"How about 'Minnie's'?" she asked.

"How about 'Minnie Leek's'?"

"Now that's got a ring to it."

"I will do it. I will put up the property and build it. Pay me back out of the proceeds."

"Naturally."

"No interest."

"Nice one."

"Then your answer is yes? You will marry me, Minnie, and be mine forever?"

"It's a deal," she said, holding out her hand. "But I get the bar tab and thirty a week until things get going."

"Twenty-five."

"Okay."

We embraced, shaking hands all the while.

Miles at sea a coasting schooner wore ship on a rising west wind, turned to the horizon and ran hell for leather to nowhere. And somewhere out there was Big Frenchy waiting for our next run. Ten years he had sat there waiting, dreaming of an inland acre or two in the south of France. His patience alone gave me faith in the future.

I knew that Minnie and I had a few bars yet to cross, a few inlets to leave behind us. I knew that she drank too much and she talked too much. I knew that there would always be grease beneath her fingernails, rouge on her cheeks. But what could I do?

I could take her to sea, back out to sea on the darkest nights when the moon hid over the horizon. I could feed gas to those engines until they sounded like rubber rubbed on rubber. And there among the tinkling of bottles, the smell of booze and oil and salt sea air, I could hold her close to my side and watch that old demon rum run wild across the open sea. I could make us both invisible, ghosts ghosting through the blackness of nights at sea when you can see the stars but not the waves ahead.

For I knew that there is no wave upon the sea, nor wind from any corner of the world, that can stop two souls joined in purpose, that can lessen the longing in the eyes of true lovers, that can flutter the eyelashes of love.

THE END

FICTION TITLES
in the
Ulverscroft Large Print Series

Enquiry	*Dick Francis*
Flying Finish	*Dick Francis*
Forfeit	*Dick Francis*
High Stakes	*Dick Francis*
In The Frame	*Dick Francis*
Knock Down	*Dick Francis*
Risk	*Dick Francis*
Band of Brothers	*Ernest K. Gann*
Twilight For The Gods	*Ernest K. Gann*
Army of Shadows	*John Harris*
The Claws of Mercy	*John Harris*
Getaway	*John Harris*
Winter Quarry	*Paul Henissart*
East of Desolation	*Jack Higgins*
In the Hour Before Midnight	*Jack Higgins*
Night Judgement at Sinos	*Jack Higgins*
Wrath of the Lion	*Jack Higgins*
Air Bridge	*Hammond Innes*
A Cleft of Stars	*Geoffrey Jenkins*
A Grue of Ice	*Geoffrey Jenkins*
Beloved Exiles	*Agnes Newton Keith*
Passport to Peril	*James Leasor*
Goodbye California	*Alistair MacLean*
South By Java Head	*Alistair MacLean*
All Other Perils	*Robert MacLeod*
Dragonship	*Robert MacLeod*
A Killing in Malta	*Robert MacLeod*
A Property in Cyprus	*Robert MacLeod*

NON-FICTION TITLES
in the
Ulverscroft Large Print Series

We hope this Large Print edition gives you the pleasure and enjoyment we ourselves experienced in its publication.

There are now more than 1,400 titles available in this ULVERSCROFT Large Print Series. Ask to see a Selection at your nearest library.

The Publisher will be delighted to send you, free of charge, upon request a complete and up-to-date list of all titles available.

Ulverscroft Large Print Books Ltd.
The Green, Bradgate Road
Anstey
Leicestershire
England